All in the Furry Family

Cat Tales Book 2

Eileen O'Finlan

Print ISBNs
Amazon print 9780228633891
Ingram Spark 9780228633907
Barnes & Noble 9780228633914
BWL Print 9780228633921

BWL Publishing Inc.

Books we love to write ...
Authors around the world.

http://bwlpublishing.ca

Copyright 2023 by Eileen O'Finlan
Editor Nancy M. Bell
Cover art by Michelle Lee

Dedication

For Cindy Kazanovicz

Acknowledgments

Much thanks go to the following people for their assistance in making this book a reality: Jude Pittman and everyone at BWL Publishing, Michelle Lee for her always amazing cover art, Eileen Charbonneau for her superior content editing, Nancy Bell for line editing, the members of my writing group (Lee Baldarelli, Barbara Lamacchia, Cindy Shenette, and Rebecca Southwick), my sister, Cindy Kazanovicz, who read each chapter as it was written and gave valuable feedback, and the many family and friends who allowed me the use of their pets' names and something of their personalities for the Cat Tales series: Cindy Kaznovicz (Greyson, Dusty, and Winthrop), Linette Provost (Rufus), Carol and Dennis Parker (Buster and Sasha), David and Sirisha DiTullio (Bruce Lee and Professor Chewy), Jennifer and Michael Bragg (Shirley and Orange), Chris and Rachel Bergman (Professor Bob, Professor Gromit, Rivet, and Hazzard), Debbie Spears (Platelicker), and Teresa Sanders (Lucy aka Mama Cat).

Table of Contents

Chapter 1
Being Followed

"There they are again." Smokey nods in the direction of two cats loitering across the street as she and her best friend, Jasmine, exit Meowers, their favorite lunch spot in Faunaburg.

"They're still following you?" Jasmine asks.

"I see them everywhere I go. It's creepy."

"Maybe you should tell the Police Dogs."

"Tell them what? That I keep seeing the same two cats, but they never do or say anything to me?"

"Are you sure it's always those same two?"

"Yeah. I'm sure of it because they remind me so much of my parents. The Russian Blue looks just like my dad and the Maine Coon like my mom. Younger, though."

"They do remind me of you and Autumn Amelia," says Jasmine as she and Smokey continue down the street, the cool September breeze making their whiskers twitch. "Except that the Main Coon isn't calico because it's a male."

Smokey glances back over her shoulder. The two cats haven't moved, but they're both looking at her. A shiver runs down her spine. "If they're near the parking lot again after work I'm going to ask a security guard dog to walk me to my car."

"Good idea," says Jasmine. "I still think you should let the Police Dogs know your concern. It wouldn't hurt to have a report on file."

"I'll think about it. Meanwhile, I've got so much to do." Smokey's boss, Abigail Fluffington, has officially made Smokey her partner, announcing it at the same time she shared the news of her engagement to Smokey's cousin, Greyson. The wedding is to be held in the chapel at Oneness Park, the place for all furs and feathers that Smokey had a part in designing.

"I still can't believe Greyson is marrying Abigail Fluffington," says Jasmine.

"Neither can I, though Autumn Amelia claims she's long saw it coming."

"Will Autumn be catering the reception?"

"Need you ask?"

Jasmine giggles. "It will be the wedding of the century."

"That it will." Smokey checks the time on her phone. "And I will be uninvited if I don't get back to work."

"Is Abigail still driving you up the curtains?"

"Like you can't imagine."

Ever since Abigail made Smokey her partner at Fluffington ArCATechture, she's insisted on drilling Smokey in every aspect of the business. She constantly comes up with scenarios, in which something goes wrong, and wants Smokey to explain on the spot what she would do. Smokey appreciates all the knowledge and wisdom Abigail is imparting through this method, knows it will be invaluable as she continues to build her career and, when Abigail retires, takes complete charge of Fluffington's. But Abigail's non-stop barrage of information peppered with questions that feel like an interrogation, is getting to be a bit much.

Jasmine giggles. "Better you than me."

"Thanks a lot," says Smokey.

As they approach the Faunaburg Office Tower, Jasmine says "I have to get back anyway. Louisa and I are meeting with Dash this afternoon."

Louisa, a great blue heron, had been a member of the web design team Jasmine formed when Oneness Park was still in the planning stages. They hit it off so well that after that project ended the two of them decided to start a web design business together. Soon after, they hired a deer named Dash to do their marketing.

"Do you still like working with Louisa?" Smokey asks. Jasmine had been a freelance web designer. Smokey was surprised when she announced that she was dissolving her own company to start a new one with a partner.

"I do," says Jasmine. "It's great being able to bounce ideas off each other. I feel like my creativity has really increased. I'll always be grateful for things working out so that I had to form that team. Otherwise, I might never have met Louisa or known how much better it is to work with a partner."

"That's good," says Smokey. She tries to feel happy for Jasmine, but something about it bothers her. She's had difficulty warming up to Louisa. The few times they'd met, Louisa had been cordial but aloof. Smokey didn't know what to make of her. She reminds herself that Jasmine is the one working with Louisa and as long as they get along, that's what matters. So far, their business venture seems to be doing well. Still, she can't shake the negative feeling.

After saying goodbye to Jasmine, Smokey rides the elevator to the suite of offices occupied by Fluffington's.

"There you are, Smokerina." Abigail, an elegant Persian cat, emerges from her office the moment Smokey steps into the lobby. "Come into my office. I've pulled a stack of old accounts from the files. I want to go over them with you."

Smokey asks, trailing her former boss. "Closed accounts? Finished projects?"

"Yes," says Abigail. "From before you started working here. I want you to know the history of Fluffington's. Also, as we go through them, I can tell you the details of everything that happened while they were in progress. We'll see how you would deal with the issues that came up on each."

Smokey fights a sigh as she eyes the tall pile of folders on Abigail's desk. "Do we have time?"

"That's only the first drawer. It will take days, weeks, even, to get through them all. You did delegate your own projects amongst the staff as I suggested, didn't you?"

"Yes, but–"

"Then we have nothing but time. Make yourself comfortable. Let's get right to it."

They are halfway through the first file when Abigail's cell phone rings.

"It's Buster," she tells Smokey. "He's the printer doing the wedding invitations. I need to take his call. Keep reading through the file."

Smokey sits back in her chair and tries to continue reading.

"Yes, I see it," says Abigail, pulling up her email. Smokey glances at the screen to see an image of an invitation on white paper with two pink roses at the top.

"I don't know," says Abigail. "It's young looking. I want something more mature. I don't think pink works. Please try something else."

Abigail slips the phone back into her pocket. "I hired Buster because he's the best specialty printer in Faunaburg," she tells Smokey. "I do hope he'll come up with the right design. We've tried several."

"The wedding is getting close. I thought the invitations would have been done by now."

"I know, they should have been, but I want everything to be perfect. Buster has told me that at this point it will have to be a rush order. I don't care. As long as they're just right."

"How many samples have you looked at?"

"I think I've seen stationary with every flower under the sun, some with clinking nip-pagne glasses, others with floral borders, and I don't know what all."

"What are you looking for?"

Abigail gets a perplexed look. "That's the problem. I'm not sure. I thought I wanted flowers and a lot of pink, but after seeing some samples that didn't seem right. So, I'm trying out several styles. Nothing fits yet."

Smokey wants to argue that the invitations are not that big a deal, but she knows better. No detail is too small for Abigail Fluffington. "I'm sure you'll find what you're looking for soon."

"I hope so." Abigail sighs. "I never realized how much work it is to prepare for a wedding. There's so much to do. It's overwhelming."

Smokey feels her eyes widen. Abigial Fluffington rarely admits to anything getting the better of her. "At least you don't have to worry about the food. Autumn Amelia —"

"That reminds me. I must go over the menu again. I want to change some things. Would you ask her to call me?"

"Of course." Smokey knows her easy-going sister is starting to get annoyed. This will be the fourth time Abigail has wanted to change the menu. "Autumn will want it finalized soon."

"And that dessert chef that works for her, what's her name?"

"Sukey."

"Yes, Sukey. Why can't I remember that cat's name? I must talk to her again, too. And I want her to make a groom's cake as well as the wedding cake. Greyson's your cousin. What do you think he'd like?"

"Shrimp," Smokey says, laughing. Greyson's love for shrimp is legendary.

Abigail looks puzzled for a moment, then bursts out laughing. "No, really," she says. "What kind of cake?"

"Greyson will eat anything. But seriously, if you can get Sukey to make some kind of shrimp-flavored frosting he'll be in heaven."

"Hmm..." says Abigail. "That's a thought. Enough about wedding preparations. Let's get back to business," she says tapping the files with her paw.

At the end of the day, an exhausted Smokey leaves Faunaburg Office Tower. As soon as she steps out the door, she notices the same two cats she saw earlier loitering near the employee parking lot.

Not again. She retreats back into the building to ask a security guard dog for an escort. All the way home, she keeps asking herself, *who are they, and why do they keep following me?*

Chapter 2
Interruptions

"It's almost time. Is everyone ready?" Autumn Amelia asks this question every evening before the dinner rush. She already knows the answer. Her restaurant staff is top notch. Mama Cat's Kitchen has done so well in the year it's been open she's had to add more cook and wait staff.

"Ready, Chef Autumn," says Sally, her sous chef. The tip of the beagle's black and white tail waves proudly. Autumn is delighted that Sally loves working with her. The poor thing was miserable under her last boss, the great Chef Gustav. He may be one of the best chefs in the world, but he's also one of the worst bosses. Autumn, on the other paw, wants every fur and feather on her staff to thrive. She respects their individual strengths and loves to see them all continuing to grow in expertise. With it comes tremendous pride in their work, from perfectly presented and delicious entrees to dishes and silverware so sparkling clean she can see her reflection.

The door between the kitchen and the main dining room opens far enough for Tanner, the black Labrador maître d' to poke his head in. "Chef Autumn, we're already full, with a waiting list. Patrons are lined up at the door." Having delivered his message, he returns to his station near the entrance.

"Oh, my whiskers! I think we get busier every night," says Autumn, smoothing her apron. "Let's not keep our patrons waiting." She turns to the waitstaff lined up near the door. "Go out and be pawsome!"

The waiters head for the dining room. Within minutes they begin returning to the kitchen with orders. The chefs fly into action. Much has been prepped ahead of time, so now they are ready to cook whatever had to wait and put everything together. Autumn peruses her kitchen, making sure every plate is elegantly presented. She stops to taste test some dishes, sauces in particular, adding something here and there, but satisfied that they have learned her recipes so well. Waitstaff come and go in rapid succession, bringing in orders, bringing out trays of food.

Autumn is finally used to the flurry in the kitchen as bodies move around her like leaves in a whirlwind. For years she worked from home, alone in her own kitchen. Overseeing her own restaurant is a dream come true but more work than she'd ever imagined. She thinks of it as controlled mayhem and thoroughly enjoys herself.

"Where are the rest of the shallots?" asks Jason, the saucier, a hefty racoon.

"There," says Sally, pointing across the room.

"Can we make the coconut and cilantro sauce for the Mast Biryani without the cilantro?" asks a waitress, a charming all white standard poodle, coming in from the dining room.

"So, then just coconut sauce?" asks Sally, rolling her eyes. She's got five plates lined up in front of her making sure everything on them is placed just so.

"Yeah. I guess. The patron says she loves everything in Mast Biryani but she's allergic to cilantro."

Sally sighs and looks over at the saucier. "Jason?" she asks.

"Don't worry," says Autumn, noticing his harried look. "I'll whip up a sauce for one. No cilantro."

"Thanks, Chef Autumn," says Jason.

Autumn moves off to a counter and stove at the back of the kitchen, a space she's reserved for herself. It's where she creates new recipes.

As she works, the noise and bustle of the kitchen disappears. Autumn falls into a trance-like state. This is her bliss. Being head chef is amazing, but she laments that so much of the cooking has been taken out of her paws. Still, she's able to indulge her love for creating new recipes. It's what she's known for and why Mama Cat's Kitchen, named in honor of her own Mama Cat who imbued her with the love of cooking, is in such constant demand.

After pouring the mix from the blender into a frying pan, she is interrupted by a tap on her shoulder. "Yes?" she asks without looking up.

"Might I trouble you for a few moments?" Autumn snaps out of her trance. That voice does not belong to anyone on her staff. That is Abigail Fluffington.

"Abigail, what are you doing here?"

"I need to speak with you about the menu for the reception. I asked Smokerina to have you call me, but I never heard from you."

"When did you ask her?"

"This afternoon at work.

"I haven't seen or spoken to Smokey since we both left the house this morning. She was probably waiting until I got home tonight."

"No matter. I'm here now. May we talk?"

The kitchen noises that had vanished while Autumn was engrossed in making the sauce have returned. As she turns to look at Abigail, she glimpses the flurry of activity in the kitchen. "We're very busy, Abigail. Can't it wait?"

"It will only take a few minutes. The wedding is in less than three months."

Then you should stop changing your mind every five minutes, thinks Autumn, but she says, "Let me finish this sauce first."

Sukey, the pastry chef, appears on the other side of her. "We're running low on moth flour, Autumn. I have enough for tonight and tomorrow, but we'll need to get more soon."

"Sally is placing an order tomorrow. It's on the list."

"Can we get extra? I can't believe how fast I'm going through it."

"Sure. I'll bring some from home to tide us over."

"Thanks."

"Oh, Susie, I need to speak with you, too," says Abigail.

"Susie?" asks Sukey, raising her eyebrow whiskers.

"Her name is Sukey, not Susie," says Autumn. Abigail has been working with Sukey on her wedding cake for months. It's inexcusable that she can't remember her name.

"My apologies. Sukey. I'd like to meet with you as soon as I finish talking to Autumn Amelia."

"I'm busy, Ms. Fluffington," says Sukey.

"It is very important. I've changed my mind about the cake, and I need to discuss a groom's cake for Greyson."

"I can see you tomorrow morning around ten."

"That's not convenient for me. Surely you have a few minutes now."

"I really don't," says Sukey who turns on her heel and stalks back to her station.

"Well, that was rude," says Abigail.

Before Autumn can respond, Sally slides in next to her. "Is that sauce ready yet?"

"Perfect timing." She hands the frying pan to Sally.

"Alright, Abigail. To my office. We need to do this quickly. My help is needed in the kitchen."

"Of course, of course. This won't take but a moment."

Thirty minutes later Autumn's desk is strewn with lists of menu items each of which Abigail has approved then discarded.

"I've never known you to be so indecisive," says Autumn. "You usually know exactly what you want. What on earth is the problem?"

"I wish I knew," says Abigail. Her eyes glisten. Autumn's annoyance vanishes as she watches the grand dame of Faunaburg's business world fight back tears.

"You do want to marry Greyson?" she asks.

Abigail's eyes go wide. "Of course!" She takes a deep breath. "Ever since I was a little girl, I dreamed what my wedding would be like. Then, when I went into business, I worked so hard to make Fluffington's a huge success that I didn't have time for anything else. Oh, I dated now and then, but I was determined that nothing would impede my career."

Autumn nods.

"Don't get me wrong. I'm very proud of what I've accomplished. But now that I'm older, I've found something I had grown to believe I would never have. I am in love. Deeply, hopelessly in love. It's come at an unexpected time in my life. I'm nearing retirement. Greyson has already retired. We aren't kits anymore."

Abigail quickly wipes a tear away with her paw.

"When I first started planning, I thought back to my youthful dreams. Then I realized that everything I'd decided on was too young for a couple our age."

"Abigail, you should have whatever makes you happy," says Autumn.

"Yes, but I realized, a bit late, I'll admit, that all that pink and flowery stuff isn't what will make me happy now. I'm not sure what I do want, and there isn't much time left to plan."

Autumn thinks for a moment, then says, "What comes to mind when you picture the wedding now?"

"I don't know." Abigail balls her paws up into fists and slams them down on her lap.

"Elegant and sophisticated. Am I right?" asks Autumn.

"Yes, exactly. But what is that?"

"You're asking me? Abigail, you are the embodiment of elegance!"

"So, I should be able to figure it out. Why can't I?"

Autumn sighs. "I'll go through the online menus of the most upscale restaurants in the world. Then I'll put together a few menu options and we can meet again. How does that sound?"

"Oh, Autumn, you are a dear. What would I do without you? Now, about the cake. Would you let Su..." Abigail stops abruptly. She's forgotten the pastry chef's name again.

"Sukey," Autumn offers.

"Yes, Sukey. Could we use your office now to discuss the cake?"

"Can't you find a way to meet with her in the morning as she suggested? You own Fluffington's. It's not like you have ask permission to come in late."

"Yes, of course. I suppose she'll be better disposed towards me if I do that. But we can do it here?"

"Yes. I will give her a paws-up on your idea of elegant and sophisticated. She might be able to bring some ideas to the meeting."

"That would be wonderful."

"And Abigail, Sukey is a Siamese. They tend to be a bit high-strung. But you won't get a better, more beautiful wedding cake anywhere."

"You could make a perfect cake, I'm sure–"

Autumn cuts her off. "I've never made a wedding cake in my life. It's a specialty. I wouldn't want to try my paw at it for the first time on yours. Sukey is an expert. You won't be disappointed. Now, I need to get back to the kitchen. Shall I tell Sukey you'll see her here at ten tomorrow?"

"Please."

As they step outside Autumn's office, Abigail grabs her arm. "Oh! I've just thought of another word."

"Another word?"

"Yes, to go with elegant and sophisticated. Include romantic."

"Okay."

"But not too romantic. Don't go overboard. But a hint of the romantic would be lovely."

Autumn nods. "I'll keep that in mind."

"Wonderful. Ta-ta."

Autumn leans against the doorframe as she watches Abigail stride away. She closes her eyes and lets out a long sigh. "I can't wait for this wedding to be over," she says under her breath before heading back to her kitchen.

Chapter 3
A New Neighbor

"I'm going for a walk," says Autumn after she's cleaned up from breakfast. It's Saturday and she doesn't have to be at the restaurant until a little before noon, but Smokey thinks she looks tired.

"Why don't you go back to bed? You got home late last night."

"No," says Autumn. "If I do that, I'm apt to sleep too long and I'll feel miserable going into work. Getting out in the air will wake me up. I just hope we don't have too many nights like last night."

"Aren't you happy that the restaurant is doing so well?"

"Of course, but last night was the busiest it's ever been. I thought my paws were going to fall off from all the running around."

"I thought you said things slowed down once school started."

"They did in Beaks and Whiskers," says Autumn referring to the informal dining room at Mama Cat's Kitchen where the youngsters like to hang out.

Smokey chuckles. "So now it's the adults' turn?"

"I guess so because it's busier than ever in The Meadows. I love it, but it would be nice to get a break once in a while."

"You really need to stop working for Furry's," says Smokey. "I know you feel loyal to Tabby Furry, but Mondays and Tuesdays are supposed to be your days off. You need that time to relax."

Autumn sighs. "You're right. It's just that Tabby has always been so good to me. I hate to leave her without a specialty baker," says Autumn.

"Leave detailed instructions for all the recipes you've created."

Smokey knows that Autumn Amelia's creations are the reason Furry's Confections has done such a booming business. Furs and feathers come not only from Wild Whisker Ridge, but from all the surrounding towns to buy her treats.

"I suppose I could," Autumn agrees, but Smokey hears the reluctance in her sister's voice.

"Autumn," she says, getting up from the kitchen table and putting her paws on Autumn's shoulders, "I think you will have to. Otherwise, you are going to burn yourself out. You need to have a life apart from cooking. I know you love it better than anything, but if you burn out wouldn't that be a growling shame?"

Apprehension flickers in Autumn's eyes, though she says nothing.

"Come on," says Smokey. "Let's go for that walk."

The little cottage in Wild Whisker Ridge that Smokey and Autumn Amelia inherited from their parents sits back from the road. The long driveway is shaded by trees so that they can't see the street until they get to its end. Once on the sidewalk of Zephyr Lane they notice a moving van unloading furniture at a house down the street. The sisters have been speculating about who their new neighbors will be.

"I should make something for them," says Autumn. Maybe dinner. They're not going to have time to cook until they're settled in."

"In your copious spare time?" asks Smokey.

"We should welcome them to the neighborhood."

As they approach the house, they notice a handsome black and white cat directing the two rottweilers from the moving company. "He must be our new neighbor," says Autumn. "Let's introduce ourselves."

"Autumn, he's busy." But Autumn is already heading across the street. Smokey sighs and follows her.

"Hi, I'm Autumn Amelia Koshkyn and this is my sister, Smokey. We live in a cottage over there." She points down the street. "You can't see it from the road, but between those two trees is the dirt driveway."

"Nice to meet you both," he says. "I'm Buster Parker."

"We don't want to hold you up," says Smokey. "Welcome to the neighborhood."

"Thank you. I think I'm going to like it here."

"We hope you will," says Autumn. "I'd like to make dinner for you and your family. How many will I be cooking for?"

Buster's eyes widen. "That's awfully nice of you, but it's just me. I figured I'd grab a bite somewhere."

"Oh," says Autumn. "How about lunch? I can drop it off when I leave for work."

"Don't go to any trouble."

"It's no trouble," she says.

"Autumn is a chef," Smokey interjects. "She runs Mama Cat's Kitchen at Oneness Park in Faunaburg. Have you heard of it?"

Buster's eyes grow wider. "You're *that* Autumn Amelia?"

"That's me," she says.

"Have you been?" asks Smokey.

"Only to On the Side," he says referring to the take-out section of the restaurant. The food was fantastic. I can only imagine what it's like for a sit-down meal."

"Thank you," says Autumn. "Come by anytime you're in Faunaburg. You'll be my guest. Do you get into the city often?"

"I work there," he says. "I own a printing company. I've lived in the city for years, but I've always wanted a home in a rural area. The timing seemed right, so here I am.”

“You own a printing company?” asks Smokey. “And your name is Buster. You must be doing the wedding invitations for my partner, Abigail Fluffington.”

Smokey notices Buster’s whiskers tremble for just a second. “Uh, yes. Ms. Fluffington is your partner?”

“Only recently. She was my boss, but she made me her partner after the completion of Oneness Park.”

“That was quite an accomplishment,” says Buster. “For a while I didn’t think that park would ever happen. Jerome Ratley gave you a hard time, if I remember correctly.”

“He did, but when we changed it from a cat park to a park for all furs and feathers, he finally came around.”

“Well, I’m glad it became a reality. It’s a wonderful place. Weren’t you the lead architect?”

“At first, but when we changed plans, we went with co-leads. It was a great experience. I’m so glad we were able to do it.”

“Hey, Mr. Parker, where do you want this table?” calls one of the rottweilers.

“We should let you get back to moving in,” says Smokey. “It was nice meeting you.”

“Nice meeting you ladies, too,” he says.

“I’ll stop by with a sandwich on my way to the restaurant,” says Autumn.

As they continue their walk, conversation focuses on their new neighbor.

“He’s very handsome,” says Autumn Amelia.

“You think so?” asks Smokey, unable to keep the teasing from her voice.

“Don’t you?”

“I suppose. I think he liked you.”

“What do you mean?”

“I saw how he looked at you. He probably can’t wait for you to drop off that sandwich.”

“It’s the sandwich he’s interested in, not me.”

"Well, you are *that* Autumn Amelia, after all. I still think he's interested in *you*."

Back at home, Smokey sits at the kitchen table, entertained by Autumn's obvious preoccupation with making the perfect lunch for Buster. She's decided on a tuna sandwich but adds celery and coarse-grain mustard to the mix of tuna and mayonnaise. After piling the tuna between two slices of homemade multi-grain bread, she wraps it in a brightly colored cloth sandwich bag. Then she puts some pickles and olives in a small container. She chops some carrot sticks and cuts a few cherry tomatoes into flower shapes. After placing these in another container and adding two salmon cookies for dessert, she packages everything into a food carrier.

Even though Smokey sits at the table the entire time, Autumn seems to have forgotten she's there. As she works, she hums merrily to herself. It appears to Smokey like she's floating around the kitchen.

At first, Smokey is amused, but the more she thinks about it, the more she starts to feel troubled. What if Buster asks Autumn out on a date? Autumn has never been on a date. If he tries to take her to a restaurant it could be a disaster with Autumn's penchant for unconsciously eating whatever food happens to be passing by on a waiter's tray. Or entering the kitchen uninvited to improve their recipes. And, what about this Buster cat? They've only just met him. Yet, Autumn seems to have fallen for him. What if he isn't as nice as he seems? Or what if he was just being polite? Smokey suddenly regrets telling Autumn that she thought he was interested in her. She might have gotten her sister's hopes up for nothing.

"It's all ready," says Autumn, scooping up the carrier. I'll drop this off at Buster's and head to work. See you tonight."

After Autumn leaves, Smokey grabs her cell phone and calls Jasmine.

"Hi Smokey, what's up?" asks Jasmine.

Smokey relates all that has happened. "I don't know what to do," she finishes.

"Why do you have to do anything?"

"I told you, we hardly know anything about him."

"It sounds like Autumn Amelia is going to make a point of finding out," Jasmine says and laughs.

"But she's so naïve. What if he's not such a great guy?"

"Then Autumn will tell him to get lost."

"I don't want her to get hurt."

"Oh, Smokey, you're being overprotective. Let her have some fun."

"I will if it turns out he's okay. And right for her. And is really interested. I need to find out more."

"About him? I think Autumn's the one who should do that. She's not a kit, Smokey. Back off."

Smokey is stung. Why doesn't Jasmine understand?

"I'm not trying to spoil her fun," says Smokey. "I just want to be sure—"

"Sorry, Smokes, I've got to go," Jasmine interrupts. "Louisa just arrived."

"Louisa? Are you at work on a Saturday?" When Jasmine and Louisa went into business together, they decided to rent office space instead of working from home saying it felt more professional, especially for meeting with clients. Smokey thought it was a waste of money but couldn't convince Jasmine of that. Louisa must have been behind it.

"No, we're not working. I'm at home. Louisa and I are going shopping for stuff for the office. I'll talk to you later, okay?"

Smokey stares at her phone after Jasmine hangs up. *What just happened?* "It's that darned Louisa," says Smokey aloud. She doesn't say her next thought out loud, but she can't help thinking it. *She's stealing my best friend.*

* * *

"I hope you like tuna," says Autumn, holding out the food carrier to Buster.

"I love it," says Buster. "But I'm sure I'd love anything you made. Your reputation precedes you."

"Well, I do love cooking. I see the van's gone. Is everything in?"

"Yes. Now to unpack. Fortunately, living in a small Faunaburg apartment means I didn't have much to bring with me, so it shouldn't take too long. I may need to do some shopping, though. The house is going to look a little sparse."

"Need any help? I'd be happy to lend a paw."

"Great! I'm not much at decorating."

"That's really my sister's specialty, but I enjoy it, too. We can always ask her advice if we get stuck."

"I don't want to hold you up. I know you've got to get to work."

"That's okay," says Autumn. "It's my restaurant. There's no one to dock my pay if I'm late."

"Of course. I forgot." Buster laughs. "I own a business, too."

"I don't own Mama Cat's Kitchen," says Autumn. "Miguel Gato owns it, but he's given me carte blanche so for all intents and purposes, it's mine."

"Sounds like a sweet deal. I enjoy printing, and I'm capable of the finance end of it, but it's not the part I like very much. I guess no job is perfect. That's why I like to get away on my boat when I can."

"You have a boat?" asks Autumn, her heart skipping a beat. Ever since she was a kitten and got a colored-glass pirate ship, she's daydreamed about captaining one of her own.

"Sure do. I thought about bringing it here, but I'd only have to haul it back to Niptucket when I want to use it."

"I love Niptucket. We try to get out there at least once every summer."

"I grew up there," says Buster. "I keep the boat at my parents'. They've got room for it and that's where I use it anyway. Do you like boats?"

"Love them, though I don't know much about sailing."

"Well, how about I take you and your sister out sometime?

"We'd love that!"

"Great. I should probably put this sandwich in the fridge. Thanks so much for making it for me."

"Let me know if you'd like any help settling in."

"Will do."

On the drive to Oneness Park, Autumn keeps thinking about Buster. She hopes he'll ask for her help decorating his house. She really hopes she'll get to see his boat and even go for a sail on it. Wait until Smokey finds out he has a boat on Niptucket!

Most of all, she keeps thinking about how handsome he is. His face is white on his mouth and cheeks and in a wide line upwards that narrows the higher it gets. The black fur starts at his eyes and goes back to the top of his head and ears. But there's the most adorable black triangle from his nose to his mouth. His whiskers and all his paws are white. He was wearing jeans and a tee-shirt, but from what she could tell the rest of him was mostly white fur with big black spots. She giggles as she realizes his markings remind her of a miniature cow. So adorable!

Autumn is so lost in her reveries she pulls into her parking spot at Oneness Park without even knowing how she got there. As she strolls to Mama Cat's Kitchen, she wonders at the feeling of floating on air. Autumn has never had this reaction to man-cat before. She can't wait to tell her best friend, Dusty.

After letting herself in through the employee entrance, Autumn heads for her office. Upon opening the door she's caught up short by the sight of Sukey sitting at her desk and Abigail Fluffington across from her.

"Oh! I'm sorry," says Autumn, backing out and closing the door.

"Autumn Amelia, come back in here," calls Abigail. "For catness' sake, it's your office."

Oh, right, thinks Autumn. She opens the door again and goes in. "I forgot you were going to meet in here today. Wait, wasn't that at ten? It's almost noon."

"Yes, well, it went longer than we expected," says Abigail. "But I think we're finally finished."

A glance at Sukey tells Autumn that this has not been an easy process.

"Did you decide on cake?" she asks.

"Yes. Maybe. I think so," Abigail stammers.

"We've got it narrowed down to a few choices," says Sukey. "What do you think of these, Autumn?"

Sukey spreads out some pictures on the desk. One is a multi-tiered cake with white frosting and a cascade of red roses running down the tiers at an angle, another is all white with pearl-like accents, and the third is similar but with gold accents.

"They're all lovely and certainly elegant and sophisticated," she says. "The roses on this one add that touch of romance you're looking for, Abigail. Don't you think?"

"Yes, I agree. Yes, I think that's the one to go with."

"You're sure?" asks Sukey.

"I think so."

"I need you to be sure, Ms. Fluffington."

"I know. Oh dear, I've never been so indecisive in my life. Whatever is wrong with me?"

"You need to relax," says Autumn. "I know you want everything to be perfect, but maybe you're overthinking. All these cakes are gorgeous. There's no wrong choice."

"You're right, Autumn. That's the one," she says tapping her paw on the picture of the cake with the cascading red roses.

"Okay. We're set." Sukey places the picture into her portfolio.

"Thank you," says Abigail, shaking Sukey's paw. "And thank you, Autumn, for helping me decide."

"No problem."

"I'll leave you two to your restaurant work. Ta-ta!"

Just as Abigail reaches the door, she turns back with a gasp.

"What is it?" asks Autumn.

"The groom's cake. We never discussed it."

"I can't do it now," says Sukey. "It's time to prep for today. The restaurant will be opening for lunch soon. You'll need to make another appointment."

"I'll call you once I check my schedule."

"For a head start, are you looking for something sophisticated, elegant, and romantic for the groom's cake, too?"

"Oh, dear. I hadn't really thought about it." Abigail knits her eyebrow whiskers. "I suppose it should hold to the theme. On the other paw, I don't want Greyson to think I'm overly serious, so I think it should be something...Oh, I don't know." She places a paw over her mouth in concentration. "Yes, I do!" she says raising that same paw. "It should be whimsical."

"Whimsical?" asks Sukey.

"Yes. But tasteful, of course. I can't wait to see what ideas you come up with. Ta-ta again, ladies."

Once Abigail has left, Sukey looks up at Autumn with an expression of pure exasperation, then drops her head in a face plant on the desk.

Chapter 4
Changes

Smokey is staring at her phone, too stunned by Jasmine's abrupt end to her call to move. Before she can put the phone down it begins to purr signaling an incoming call. Her cousin, Greyson's name pops up on the screen.

"Greyson, hi!" she says.

"Hi Smokey. How's it going?"

"Okay, I guess."

"Just okay? What's wrong?"

"A little tired," she tells him, assuming he doesn't want to hear all about her problems with Jasmine and Louisa. "There's a lot to learn now that I've become Abigail's partner."

"Abigail's overwhelming you?"

"Well..." she doesn't want to complain to Greyson about his fiancée, but the truth is Abigail is driving her up the curtains.

"That's what I thought," he says.

"It's not that bad, just a lot all at once. I'm sure things will calm down."

"It's not just you, is it?"

"What do you mean?"

"Dusty called, asking when I'd be coming up. Abby has changed her mind several times about the wedding gown and bridesmaids' dresses and Autumn has mentioned to her that she's doing the same with the menu selections and the cake. Dusty was hoping I could calm her down."

"Can you?" asks Smokey unable to keep the pleading tone from her voice. She silently blesses Dusty who, as Abigail's sister, can get away with more than the rest of them.

Greyson laughs. "That's why I'm calling. I've booked a flight. I'll be there on Monday. But don't tell Abby. I thought I'd surprise her."

"Oh, that's wonderful! Would you like to stay with us?"

"I'm going to stay in Faunaburg. That way I can take care of the DJ and talk to Miguel's bartender about working the reception."

"That makes sense. I can't wait to see you. Autumn will be delighted, too."

"I can't wait to see you ladies, too."

After ending the call with Greyson, Smokey's doorbell sounds. She finds Chrissy, her neighbor from a few streets over, on the front step.

"It's such a lovely day, I thought I'd drop this off for Autumn Amelia," she says handing Smokey a folder.

"Thanks. Autumn's at the restaurant, but I'll give it to her when she gets home. Would you like to come in? I'll make us some catnip tea."

The two cats sit at the kitchen table sipping tea and reminiscing about Chrissy's great aunt Holly Berry, affectionately known to all as "the Empress." Holly Berry passed into the Great Oneness shortly after Oneness Park opened.

"It was almost like she was just waiting for that park to be created," Chrissy says. "Ever since Autumn Amelia told her that it was in the works, it was always on her mind, even if not much else was by then."

"I'm so glad she got to go to the park. I remember the day you brought her," says Smokey. "She had tears in her eyes watching all the furs and feathers enjoying themselves together. I'd never seen her so happy."

"She told me afterwards that she felt she was getting a tiny taste of what the Great Oneness would be like, and she couldn't wait to go. I miss her, but I just picture her like she was that day only magnified, and I can't help but smile."

"She was quite a character," says Smokey.

"That she was. Oh, I don't think I told you that the house sold."

"When did that happen?"

"A few days ago. The closing is next month."

Chrissy had inherited her great aunt's house, but now that she was no longer looking after her aunt, she didn't need to work from home anymore. After she returned to the office, she got a fantastic job offer on the other side of the county. She didn't like the commute, so she decided to sell the house and move closer to work.

"Do you know anything about the buyer?" asks Smokey.

"Only that he's a professor at Verdant University. An older gentleman, I think. A dog. His name's Chewy."

"Just him? No wife or family?"

"Nope, he's a widower. If he has pups, they're grown. He's a Maltese and Yorkshire Terrier mix. That's pretty much all I know."

"Are you excited to move?"

"Yes, but I'll miss Aunt Holly's house and this neighborhood. It's a lovely place to live."

"It is. I've always wanted to have a luxury apartment in Faunaburg like Abigail Fluffington's, but I know I'd miss this place."

"Autumn would stay here. If you move, you'll be able to enjoy both places."

"That's true. I love the excitement of the city. It's Autumn who's the country cat. I think it's pretty, but she just revels in it. She adored your great aunt's gardens. I wonder if Professor Chewy will continue to keep them up."

"I don't know, but I think Autumn wants to replicate them here. That's what's in the folder. It's my aunt's listings of everything she planted with care instructions. There are even diagrams of the layout. She made lots of notes over the years. In one of her more lucid moments, she handed me that folder with the instructions that I give it to Autumn Amelia after she was gone. To be honest, I've been so busy that I'd forgotten all about it until I found it last night while I was packing."

"Autmn will be delighted, though I don't know when she'll find time to garden. She's busy these days."

"Well, it's all there when she's ready. I have to continue packing, now. Thanks for the tea."

Smokey sits on the sofa after Chrissy leaves thinking about all the changes that have recently entered their lives – a partnership at Fluffington's for her, the restaurant for Autumn, old neighbors leaving and new ones arriving, a wedding that will bring her partner into her family. And now the possibility of Autumn falling in love. She can barely get used to one thing when something new is added to the mix. *Ah, well, at least they're all good things,* she thinks. Then she remembers her concern about Autumn's interest in Buster, her phone call with Jasmine, and Jasmine's abrupt ending of the call the moment Louisa showed up. Are they all good?

Another call announces itself on her phone. This time it's Abigail Fluffington.

"Hello, Abigail," she says, hoping she's not going to be expected to study old accounts on the weekends.

"Smokey, I've just had an idea that I think will help you tremendously as a partner at Fluffington's."

"What is it?"

"I think you should get a degree in business."

"Go back to school?"

"Yes. You are highly qualified in architecture and design, but as a partner and, eventually, owner, you should have a background in business."

"But –"

"I have an MBA, you know."

"But we have an accountant."

"And he's wonderful, but you need to have good business sense. I've worked too hard to make

Fluffington's a success. I would be heartbroken if it floundered because of poor business management."

Smokey's stomach flips. Maybe Abigail is right.

"Um...okay. I guess it wouldn't hurt to take some courses."

"That's the spirit. And don't worry, Fluffington's will cover the cost. Dusty has just started her second year at Faunaburg Community College. She's done amazingly well. You could get into the same program. Unless you'd prefer to go somewhere else. But I have closely monitored what Dusty is being taught and I completely approve."

"FCC is fine. The semester has already started, though, hasn't it?"

"I checked and you can still get in. You'll have to apply immediately though, so hurry up and get online. Ta-ta!"

"Sheesh!" says Smokey as she heads for her laptop.

* * *

Autumn Amelia stands on her back porch gazing at the yard. In her paws are the papers Chrissy dropped off the day before.

"What are you doing?" asks Smokey, joining her.

"Trying to figure out what I can adapt from Holly Berry's garden. I can't do all of it. I wish I could, but it's too much. The herb wheel I made this year did well. She taught me how to make it," she says indicating the plantings of dill, rosemary, thyme, parsley, and sage between the spokes, and catnip in the hub. "I'd like to try some of her flower plantings. I'll put them beyond the vegetable garden. I wish I could design it like she did with paths winding between them, so they create multiple gardens."

"When would you have time?" asks Smokey. "Not only do you have to plant it, but you have to keep it up.

You barely have time for your vegetable garden and herb wheel. Holly Berry spent most of her time gardening. It was her life."

"You're good at design. What do you think?"

Smokey takes the papers from Autumn and looks them over. "Well, the more you have off the ground, the less weeding you'll have to do. You could put in walkways, so you get the separation between the plantings you want. You could also use thrift store finds as unusual planters and garden ornaments."

"I once saw a fence hung with old watering cans used as planters. It was really cute. Do you mean like that?"

"That could work," says Smokey. "But I'm sure we can come up more ideas. Go to some thrift and antique stores. Don't go in looking for anything specific. Just see what's there and try to envision what role it could play in your garden."

"I'm not sure I could look at one thing and think of how it could be used in a totally different way. You're the one who's good at that. Why don't you come shopping with me?"

"Now?"

"Why not? It's Sunday. The restaurant doesn't open until late afternoon."

"I guess we could. I need to get a few notebooks while we're out now that I'm signed up for business courses. Yesterday morning I had no thought of going back to school and today I'm shopping for school supplies."

"You never know what's right around the corner," says Autumn.

Stops at a few thrift stores score them some old watering cans and a few pairs of brightly colored galoshes to use as planters. While browsing in an antique store, Smokey spies a vintage sink. "How about this?" she asks.

"For the garden?" asks Autumn, perplexed.

"Yeah. It would make a great planter."

Skeptical, Autumn looks it over. She likes the sink. It's a farmhouse pedestal style, white enamel with two metal taps and a gracefully curving faucet. It's large enough to have been used in a kitchen. But she can't picture it as a planter.

"Oh, look. You could get this to go with it." Smokey leads her to a cast iron stove. "If you take the tops off the grates, you could put planters in here. And all these doors below could be opened, and you could have plants spilling out of them."

Autumn can see the wheels turning in Smokey's head.

"Oh, I know," says Smokey. "I'll design a garden for you using vintage kitchen appliances. We could put it behind your veggies and herbs. It could be set up just like it's an actual kitchen, but all the appliances hold flowers."

Autumn begins to warm to the idea.

"I'll tell you what," says Smokey. "I'll draw up a design combining your love for cooking with gardening. And it will be a lot easier to care for because it will be off the ground so more like taking care of houseplants. Best of all, it will be unique. I know it's nothing like what Holly had, but it will be distinctive to you."

"I can't wait to see your design," says Autumn.

"Let's try another antique store for some more ideas."

Just as they are getting back into Autumn's car, Smokey gasps.

"What?" asks Autumn.

"It's those two cats I see everywhere."

"Where?" asks Autumn, searching the parking lot.

"In that car," says Smokey pointing to a small blue sedan parked at the other end of the lot.

"Are you sure?" asks Autumn. "It's hard to see them clearly from here."

"I'm pretty sure."

"Hmm..." says Autumn. "It is strange that they keep following you around."

"Yeah. It's creeping me out. Let's go. There's a nice antique store in West Lake. Let's try there."

Autumn pulls out of the parking lot and heads for the highway. This store, being in West Lake, is much more expensive.

"I don't think I can afford anything here," says Autumn.

"That's okay. We're just getting ideas. You can't plant until spring anyway. And you'll want it designed before you make any purchases, so you'll know exactly what you'll need."

They browse the store, finding several more antique stoves and sinks along with a few vintage refrigerators, iceboxes, cabinets, and dry sinks.

"You could use a dry sink for a potting bench," says Smokey. "It would fit the theme."

"The more you talk, the more I'm liking the idea, but will all this stuff be okay outdoors? It's going to get wet when it rains."

"It's not exactly dry in a sink! I'm sure we can make it work."

As they finish perusing the store and head back towards the door, Smokey stops short. "It's them," she whispers. "Over there." She nods towards two cats with their backs to them who are looking at a gramophone.

"Are you certain?" asks Autumn. "Did you see their faces?"

"I saw them in the other parking lot and now they're here."

Autumn wonders if Smokey is so anxious about the cats she thinks are following her that she's starting to see them everywhere.

"Well, we've got enough ideas for today. Let's go get your notebooks and head home," says Autumn.

"Yeah. Let's." Smokey can't take her eyes off the two cats. Autumn has to tug her arm to keep her from walking into a display stand.

Back in the car, Smokey says, "I wonder why they follow me, but never say anything. And it's so weird that they look so much like Mama and Papa Cat."

"One of them is definitely a Russian Blue," says Autumn. "And you know you Blues all look a lot alike. The other is part Maine Coon, like me."

"Yeah, but not calico. More of the reddish fur color like Mama Cat."

"That's because he's a man cat. Almost all calicos are female. Have you thought of talking to them?" asks Autumn.

"Jasmine asked me that, but like I told her, I don't know what to say to them."

"How about 'why are you following me around?'"

"I don't want anything to do with them. I think it's very weird. Jasmine said I should file a report with the Police Dogs, just so they have it on record, but what can I say? That I keep seeing these two cats, but they never say or do anything to me?"

"That's why I think you should talk to them directly."

"I just wish they'd go away."

Chapter 5
The Shock of a Lifetime

Smokey finishes scribbling the final notes at the end of her Introduction to Business course. Having enrolled late, she's missed the first two classes, but the professor assures her she'll have no problem catching up. Dusty, who took this course last year, gave her the notes she took from the first classes since she had the same professor, and the syllabus hasn't changed. Smokey thinks she will enjoy the course, but wishes Abigail wasn't putting so much on her at work, too. She is also signed up for an accounting course. Her workload will be heavy for the next few months.

After tucking her notebook into her backpack, she leaves the classroom hoping to find Dusty. They'd met up when she got on campus, both of them having a course tonight in the same building. As she starts down the hallway, she is stopped cold by the sight of Dusty talking with two cats – the ones who have been following her.

Does Dusty know them? she wonders. She's still several steps away, and they haven't noticed her. Finally, the two mystery cats walk off in the opposite direction while Dusty heads towards Smokey.

"Who are those cats?" asks Smokey. "They've been following me around. Do you know them?"

"No. They just stopped me in the hallway. They asked a lot of questions about you."

"Like what?" Smokey starts to tremble.

"They wanted to know if you have any littermates and who your parents were. I told them you have one sister, but she's not from the same litter. I said I didn't know anything about your parents. I asked why they wanted to know, but they were very evasive."

"How did they know you know me?"

"They saw us come in together."

"I've had enough of this," says Smokey. "I'm going to find out why they're following me right now." She hurries down the hallway.

"I'll come with you," says Dusty scurrying after her.

The strange cats have reached the door leading to the parking lot and are about to exit. Smokey breaks into a run, ignoring the surprised looks of other students. She rushes out after them.

"Hey," she calls. They stop and turn in her direction.

"If you want to know about me, why don't you ask me?" she yells though she's standing right in front of them.

They turn to look at each other but don't speak.

"Well?" she asks as Dusty comes up behind her. "And why have you been following me around? Don't try to deny it. You're everywhere I go. At work, at the store, at Meowers, and now here. What do you want?" Smokey can't keep the agitation from her voice.

The two cats stand mute, glancing back and forth between Smokey and each other.

"Well?" Smokey demands. "I'm very close to filing a complaint with the Police Dogs."

Both look taken aback. Finally, the Maine Coon speaks. "We're sorry," he says. "We didn't mean to frighten you. We just wanted to be absolutely certain you're who we think you are before we approached you."

"Who do you think I am?"

They look at each other again and nod. This time it's the Russian Blue who speaks. "We think you're our littermate."

Speechless, Smokey stares at them, her mouth agape.

"Smokey," Dusty says in a near whisper. "Are you okay?"

"Impossible," Smokey hisses, ignoring Dusty. "My littermates were all killed by hawks."

"So you thought," says the Maine Coon.

Fury replaces shock. Ever since Oneness Park has been in the news, much has been written about her as one of the principal players. They've undoubtedly read about her background and are playing some kind of cruel game.

"What do you think you'll gain from making me or anyone else think we're related?"

The two cats look at each other again. "The reunion of our family," says the Russian Blue. "Or at least what's left to reunite. We thought you'd been taken by the hawks. Winthrop, too."

Again, Smokey gasps. One of her littermates was named Winthrop and she's certain she never gave any of their names to the press. Autumn knows their names, but never met them. She wouldn't have mentioned them in any of her interviews either. How could they know?"

"Can we go somewhere else to talk?" asks the Maine Coon, nodding towards the many students passing them headed for their cars. "We'll explain everything to you."

"There's a little café on campus," says the Russian Blue. "We noticed it coming in. Why don't we go there?"

Smokey's not sure if they're con artists, or just delusional. She does, however, want to get to the bottom of this.

"First, tell me your names," she says.

"I'm Sasha," says the Russian Blue.

"I'm Marlon," says the Maine Coon.

A chill runs through her. Those were her littermates' names, but that doesn't prove anything. If they know Winthrop's name, they would know the names of the other two as well. She wants to get a better look at them even though she's not sure she would recognize them now if they really are her littermates. But she can't tell here, with only the parking lot lights.

"Fine. We'll go to the café. But I'm warning you. If you don't convince me, I'm going straight to the Police Dogs."

"Do you want me to come with you?" asks Dusty.

"You don't have to," she says.

"I'd rather you didn't go alone. Besides, Autumn would never forgive me if I left you and something happened."

"Well, if you want to," says Smokey, secretly relieved not to be left on her own with these two strange cats.

They walk to the café and take seats at a corner table. Here, with better lighting, Smokey studies their faces. They do look a lot like how she remembers Marlon and Sasha. She even wonders if she sees traces of her parents in them.

Dusty has gone to get them each a hot mulled cider.

"So?" says Smokey. "What's your story?" She refuses to give an inch in case they are con artists, the most likely scenario.

"Smokey, we truly never meant to frighten or upset you," says Sasha. "We're very sorry."

"That's right," Marlon agrees. "We didn't want to say anything to you until we were sure."

"Are you're sure now?"

They look at each other. "We think so," says Sasha, "but we wouldn't have said anything yet. You confronted us so, here we are."

Dusty returns with a tray of mugs filled with fragrant, steaming cider each with a cinnamon stick poking out. After setting them in front of each cat, she takes her place next to Smokey.

"Why do you think you're my littermates?" Smokey asks. "And why now? After all these years?"

"We thought you were dead until recently," says Marlon. "We heard about you on the news when all the hubbub was going on over the park."

"We didn't suspect right away," says Sasha. "We saw you on TV and knew you were a Russian Blue, but you know how we all look so much alike. But your name – Smokerina. Smokey is a common name, though usually more for males, but Smokerina isn't that common. Still, we couldn't believe you were really alive."

"But then after plans for the cat park were dropped and Oneness Park for all the furs and feathers came into being, the press started doing stories on every fur and feather involved in it," Marlon picked up. "We heard how you and your littermates had been feral, and the others were all taken by hawks, and you were the only one to survive. We could hardly believe it. We kept talking about the possibility. After all, we didn't see the hawk actually go off with you. We just always assumed that's what happened to you and Winthrop."

"That's when we decided to look you up," says Sasha. "But, like we said, we didn't want to say anything until we were sure. How did you get away?"

Smokey thinks back to that terrible day. She and her littermates had been huddled together under a bush while their parents went hunting. It was the first time Mama Cat had left them alone since the moment they were born.

Smokey had thought the others were all asleep. Suddenly, there was a tremendous rustling and shaking of leaves before a pair of sharp yellow talons sliced through the bush. Smokey ran without thinking as fast and far as she could before she collapsed. She never saw what happened to the others. All she remembers is Mama and Papa Cat calling frantically for them. She followed their voices until she made her way back to them. None of the others were under the bush and there was no trace of them anywhere.

Smokey told her parents what had happened. Mama and Papa Cat took turns searching for days, maybe weeks. The only thing they could conclude was that the hawks had taken them. But like Marlon, she never actually saw the hawks grab any of them. She's not even sure how many hawks there were. They were so big and made such a racket, she thought at the time there'd been hundreds of them. She knows that couldn't have been true, but she always thought there were at least a few. Now she realizes she only saw one set of talons. Maybe there was only one and she and her littermates managed to scatter before it could get them. Or maybe it only got Winthrop.

"How did you get away?" Smokey asks, still skeptical. "I thought you were asleep when the hawks came."

"Who could sleep through that?" asks Marlon.

"We ran," says Sasha. "Only in the other direction. I'm pretty sure there was only one hawk. If there'd been more, they'd certainly have gotten at least one of us."

"Winthrop?" she asks.

"We don't know," says Marlon. "We assumed it got both of you. But it didn't get you so now we don't know what to think about Winthrop."

"What happened after you ran? Why didn't you come back? Mama and Papa Cat were devastated."

Both Marlon and Sasha stare into their mugs. Finally, Sasha breaks the silence. "Smokey, we were terrified baby kits. We ran until we were completely lost. We didn't know where we were or how to get back. I'm just grateful we stayed together."

"How did you survive?" Smokey asks, beginning to admit to herself that it might not be completely impossible. For so long she has wished she could have her littermates back. She dreams about them sometimes. She wants to believe these cats, but it seems too good to be true.

"We wandered around for a long time," says Marlon. "We were looking for Mama and Papa Cat, but we had no idea where we were or where we were going. I think we roamed for a few days."

"It was so scary," says Sasha. "We were hungry and frightened. We didn't know what would become of us."

"Maybe after two or three days," says Marlon, "we heard an owl hooting. We thought it was after us, so we tried to find a place to hide, but we were in an open field. There was nowhere to go. It swooped down and landed right in front of us. We thought we were goners, but she just cocked her head and asked if we were lost."

"Mama and Papa Cat had taught us not to talk to strangers, but we were desperate," says Sasha. "We told that owl everything. She was so kind. She told us to climb on her back and she flew us up to her nest inside a tree. We were scared because we knew owls were one of the animals we'd been warned about, but she was so sweet and gentle that we trusted her."

"We were lucky," says Marlon. "She was a very unusual owl. She took wonderful care of us. When we were older, she told us that she'd always wanted owlets, but since she never married, she hadn't had any. We became her adopted babies."

"You mean she didn't try to find Mama and Papa Cat for you?" asks Smokey. "She didn't go to the Police Dogs or anything?"

"Oh, she looked for Mama and Papa Cat for a long time," says Sasha. "She flew us around on her back so we could try to spot them. She asked her friends to look for them, too, but no luck. I don't know if she went to the Police Dogs, but she might have. She tried everything she could to find them."

"What we didn't know until we got older was that we had wandered all the way to West Lake. Where we had her looking wasn't in the right area at all, but we were too young to realize it. Anyway, we ended up staying with her and she raised us like we were her own."

"Her name was Ophelia McGivney," says Sasha. "We grew to love her very much. She kept hawks and other predators away from us. It wasn't long before they all knew not to mess with us. We had a good life with her. She did her best to teach us cat things, though there are probably gaps in our education. But all in all, she was a great foster mom."

Dusty nudges Smokey's paw and gives her a look that clearly asks whether she believes them. Smokey doesn't know what to believe. She has to find a way to figure out if they're telling the truth.

"What do you remember about Mama and Papa Cat?" she asks.

"Mama Cat was named Lucy and Papa Cat was Sebastian," says Marlon.

"Mama was a Maine Coon and Papa was a Russian Blue," says Sasha.

This is correct, but Smokey needs something more personal.

"Tell me about something that happened when we were little, before the hawk."

The two cats sit quietly. She's not sure if they'll have any memories of that time. Her own are very limited.

Finally, Marlon says, "I remember that I once slipped on a muddy incline and fell into a pond. Papa Cat jumped in and pulled me out."

Smokey's breath catches. She remembers it, too. No one else could possibly know about that, but she has to be absolutely certain. "Can you describe the surroundings?"

"I remember that we were walking in a line, Papa Cat in front of us and Mama Cat bringing up the rear. The grass was wet. It must have rained the night before. When we got near the pond, there was mud, but it was hard packed. My paws kept slipping on it probably because of all my floof." He holds up a paw even more floof-covered than Autumn Amelia's. "All of a sudden, I couldn't get my footing at all. I slipped backwards. I bumped into something on the way down, but I don't know what. The next thing I knew I was in the pond. I couldn't swim. I just sank. I tried to meow, but only got a mouthful of pondwater. I remember a big splash, then Papa Cat hauling me out of the water and back up the incline. He carried me until we were away from the mud. That's all I remember."

Tears are streaming down Smokey's face. "I know what you bumped into on your way down," she says. "It was me. I was right behind you, but you went sideways so you only knocked me over but not into the pond."

"You remember, too!" Marlon shouts. His eyes light up as do Sasha's.

"Oh my catness!" says Smokey. "You really are Marlon and Sasha!"

Chapter 6
First Date

"I hope you don't mind doing this," says Buster. The two of them are on their way to shop for home décor.

After Buster returned her food carrier on Monday morning, rhapsodizing over the best tuna sandwich he'd ever tasted, he'd invited her to go shopping with him.

"I'm all unpacked," he'd said. "It didn't take long. As I feared, the house looks terribly sparse, but I don't know what to get to cheer it up."

Autumn told him she'd have time on Tuesday afternoon. So, after she sent the Squirrel brothers off with her final delivery, she quickly cleaned up her kitchen and headed to Buster's house.

"I offered, remember? Do you have a theme in mind?" she asks.

"A theme?"

"Yes. An idea to build your decorating around," Autumn explains, marveling at how much she's absorbed from Smokey without realizing it.

"I never thought of it."

"Tell me some things you like, then. I know boating is one. You could do a nautical theme."

"Oh, now I know what you mean," he says. "I don't want nautical. That's what my parents have. I'd like something different."

"Okay, then what other things do you like?"

He thinks for a moment. "Well, I love the woods. I go walking in the woods a lot."

"That's great. We can do a woodland theme. Anything else?"

"I do like sports, especially brusselball, but I don't want a sports theme in my house. Let's see, what else?"

"Do you play?" asks Autumn.

"Brusselball? Yeah. Not on an official team or anything, but I do enjoy a pick-up game from time to time. I like watching the leagues play, too. I'm a fan of the Faunaburg Furs."

"That's the team Smokey's friend Jasmine and my friends, Sukey and Tamarind play for. They're great."

"They sure are. Especially Jasmine. She's the best player on the team. Do you play?"

"Like you. Just pick-up."

"I've heard a story about you picking brussels sprouts and cooking them and that sometimes you wander off the field during a game to graze. True or urban legend?"

Autumn feels herself blush under her fur. She steals a glance at Buster. His eyes are twinkling. "True, I'm afraid. But I don't graze. Even I wouldn't eat raw brussels sprouts. I have been known to harvest them, though, to cook later."

Buster breaks into a hearty laugh. "I'll bet you can make even brussels sprouts delicious."

"They're not bad," she says with a shrug. "So, do you want a woodland theme?"

"Sounds good to me, but I have no idea what to look for. Do you?"

"Sort of. It's kind of a *we'll know it when we see it* thing."

They peruse several stores and return to Buster's house with an armload of shopping bags. They spread out everything on his living room floor trying to decide what to put where.

"These would look nice on top of your bookcase," Autumn says, picking up a set of bronze candleholders etched with tree-shaped cutouts that allow light to flicker through them. She sets them together on the bookcase, then looks down at the stuff on the floor. "Now, what to go with them?"

"How about these?" asks Buster.

"Perfect. What books do you want to put between them?" she asks, taking the large leaf-shaped bookends from him.

"Hold on," he says and leaves the room. In a moment he's back with a small stack of books on hiking, forests, and trees.

"You really do like the woods, don't you?" says Autumn, looking over each book as she places them between the bookends.

"Yeah, I do. I've always wanted to live in the woods. That's one of the reasons I chose this house. The woods are behind it."

"I love nature, too" says Autumn. "The woods are behind our house, too, but I've never gone hiking or camping, though I'd like to. I love to be outdoors. Smokey tries to keep me cooped up inside. She thinks it's too dangerous out there."

"It can be if you don't know what you're doing. I could teach you."

"I would love that. You must like the ocean, too, since you have a boat."

"Yes. I sense that you do, too."

"Love it. I even like to swim."

"Seriously? I can swim, but I don't care for it. I learned when I was a kit. My parents insisted. They have a boat, too. I grew up around boats and spent a lot of time on them. At least I did while I lived on Niptucket. Once I moved my business to Faunaburg, I had to curtail my boating. Business is better in Faunaburg, but I don't get out on the ocean nearly as much anymore. I hope I get one or two more chances to take the boat out before it gets too cold and has to be put away until next year."

Autumn and Buster continue to chat while they finish decorating his living room. When the last item is put in place, Autumn says, "I think we've got a very good start, don't you?"

"I do. It looks great. I never would have thought of using a theme. I really appreciate your help."

"I enjoyed it."

"Autumn, I'd like to take you to dinner to thank you for all your help."

"That's very nice of you," says Autumn, "but I was happy to do it."

"Okay. Then I'd like to take you to dinner to spend more time with you."

"Oh," she says. "I...um...well..." Suddenly her mind is racing. She very much wants to go to dinner with Buster, but she doesn't want to embarrass herself or him. At this moment, she hates more than ever her problem with unconsciously eating whatever food is at paw. She thinks she can force herself to stay out of the restaurant's kitchen, but she's not so sure about being able to control taking food from passing trays without even realizing she's doing it. How can she explain?

"I'm sorry," says Buster. "That's probably a busman's holiday for you, isn't it? You run a restaurant. I wasn't thinking."

"No, it's not that," says Autumn. "I love restaurants. It's just that I...um...I...um..."

Buster's expression goes from perplexed to dawning realization, to deflation.

"Oh. Oh, I understand. I'm so sorry. I thought you were interested. I guess I got my signals crossed. Forgive me, please."

"No! No, that's not it, either," she says, feeling that she's making a terrible mess of this. "I am interested, and I would love to go to dinner with you. It's just that I..."

Either he'll like her despite her quirks, or he won't. Better to know now. Autumn takes a deep breath. "Remember when you asked if I wander off the field to pick brussels sprouts and I said yes?"

"Yeah."

"Well, that happens when I start thinking about what I can do with them. Before I know it, I'm in the brussels sprouts field without even knowing how I got there. But that's not the only time it happens. Whenever I cook, especially when I'm coming up with new recipes, I eat without realizing I'm doing it. It gives me inspiration, but it's totally unconscious. Unfortunately, when I'm in a restaurant, I become overwhelmed by the aromas, and I might take something off a patron's plate as I pass by or off a waiter's tray as it's carried past my table. I don't mean to do it. It just happens and I can't help it. I don't want to embarrass you."

Buster's expression changes again. Autumn's not sure how to read it. It looks like awe, but how can that be? She'd expected surprise at best, revulsion at worst. But awe? That makes no sense.

"You must be incredibly gifted," he says.

"Huh?"

"You get inspiration for your recipes from eating, and you eat without even knowing it?"

"Yeah."

"That makes me think of artistic geniuses. I've heard that some of them do things like that. It's part of their process and what makes their work so brilliant."

"It is?"

"Yes. And you're well known to be a culinary genius."

"I am?"

"Every fur and feather says so. I still want to take you out to dinner if you'll go. Will you?"

"You really still want to go with me?"

"I do."

"Well then, okay. But if you see me going for some other fur's food, would you, please, stop me? I know it's terribly rude and I don't want to do it."

"I would be honored. Where would you like to go? I'm not familiar with the places around here."

"Top Cat is the nicest restaurant in Wild Whisker Ridge."

"Top Cat it is. I'll need to change first."

"Me too," says Autumn looking down at her jeans and sneakers. "I'll run home and put on something nicer."

"I'll pick you up in about half an hour, okay?"

"Perfect," she says.

Later, after a lovely dinner, Autumn sits on her couch reveling in the memory of a perfect evening. The food was wonderful, Buster was charming, and their conversation was so absorbing that, marvel of all marvels, Autumn never once reached for food that wasn't on her own plate.

When the front door opens and Smokey steps inside, Autumn leaps from the couch and runs across the room.

"Smokey," she says. "You'll never guess what happened. After Buster and I finished shopping and decorating his living room, he asked me out to dinner. Don't worry. I told him what happens to me in a restaurant. He said it's a sign of genius. I'm not sure about that, but he didn't think it was awful, that's what matters. So, we went to Top Cat. And you will never believe it. I didn't take any other fur's food. I was so interested in Buster I didn't even notice the food around me. Well, except my own. It was delicious. I had herb-crusted steak with gorgonzola sauce, garlic whipped potatoes, and green beans. Buster had seared scallops and lemon risotto with grilled asparagus. Everything was great. We shared a peach mango cheesecake for dessert."

Smokey stares at her, looking dazed.

"And we're going out again. He's taking me to an outdoor concert on Saturday night. I know I'm supposed to work, but Sally can handle it for one night. I'm so excited. Isn't it wonderful?"

"Okay," Smokey mutters.

"Okay?" Autumn cocks her head. "Smokey, are you alright?"

"Autumn, something happened tonight. I need to talk to you about it."

"Oh." Autumn puts a paw to her mouth. "Let's sit down."

Smokey follows her to the couch. "Do you remember those two cats who kept following me around?"

"Sure," says Autumn. "Did you see them again?"

"Yes. This time I talked to them."

"What did they say?"

"They said they are my littermates, Sasha and Marlon."

Autumn's eyes widen. "How cruel."

"That's what I thought at first, but they told me things no other furs could have known."

"You said your littermates were taken by hawks and you were the only one who escaped."

"That's what I always thought. But I never saw the hawk actually grab them because I ran and never looked back."

"But you saw the hawks, right?"

"I saw the talons of *a* hawk. I thought there was more than one, but maybe there wasn't. It was after us, but I can't say for certain that it got any of us."

"But the others were never found. How did they explain that?"

Smokey tells her the whole story. As she listens Autumn feels stunned.

"So, you think it really is them?" she asks when Smokey finishes.

"I think it has to be. I can't figure any other explanation for how they would know about Marlon falling into the pond. And in such detail."

"Wow!" says Autumn. "I can hardly believe it."

"Me either. And it makes me wonder if Winthrop could be alive. It's a slim hope, but if Sasha, Marlon, and I all got away, maybe he did, too."

"How can you find out?"

"I don't know, but Marlon and Sasha want to look for him and asked if I'd help. Of course, I said yes."

"Are you sure about these cats, Smokey? Could they have found out about your littermates somehow? Maybe you just wanted it to be true so badly that it only seemed like they knew details."

"I don't see how they could have found out about that incident at the pond or especially about Marlon colliding with me when he slipped. You can ask Dusty. She came with us to the café and heard the whole story."

"This is totally blowing my whiskers off," says Autumn, shaking her head. "When are you going to see them again?"

"Saturday. I invited them here. I thought you'd like to meet them. They're your brother and sister, too, even if they aren't your littermates."

"I would love to meet them. I'll cancel my date with Buster. I'm sure he'll understand. Oh, my, and I thought I had big news."

Smokey puts a paw to her head. "I'm sorry. I wasn't paying much attention to what you said when I first came in. You went out to dinner? Where did you go?"

"Top Cat. It was great." Autumn recounts her dinner with Buster again.

"Wonderful, Autumn," says Smokey. "Just promise you won't rush into anything. You don't know him well yet."

"I know," says Autumn, feeling a bit hurt. "But I want to get to know him better."

"Take it slow, that's all I'm saying." Smokey sighs. "I have to get up early for work so I'm going to bed. Oh, don't cancel your date. Marlon and Sasha are coming for lunch. You can still go out in the evening."

Chapter 7
Commiseration

Autumn Amelia sits in her office typing up menu ideas for Abigail from her online search.

There's a knock on her office door. "Come in," she calls.

"Hi Autumn. I hope you don't mind me dropping in on you at work."

"Dusty! Have a seat."

"I was wondering how you're doing. I'm sure Smokey told you all about what happened after class last night."

"She did. I still can't wrap my head around it. She asked me not to tell anyone yet. She's still trying to process it."

"It's surreal, isn't it?"

"That's a good word for it. Do you think those cats were telling the truth?"

"I wasn't sure at first, but after Marlon talked about that incident at the pond and Smokey remembered it the same way, I guess I have to believe them."

"What were they like?" Autumn asks.

"I thought they were strange at first, but I guess that's because the whole situation was strange. They were actually very nice. Once Smokey was convinced they were for real, the three of them were all crying and hugging each other. I wasn't sure if I should slip out or not, but I wanted to be sure Smokey was okay, so I stayed."

"She seemed pretty dazed when she got home."

"She probably still is. I feel stunned and it's not even my family." Dusty places her portfolio on Autumn's desk.

What's that?"

"Sketches and computer-generated images of the wedding gown and bridesmaids' dresses Abigail wants me to make for her."

"It looks pretty thick," says Autumn.

"That's because she has changed her mind so many times. She can't decide on a dress, and I can't start sewing until she does. I thought she was finally settled a few weeks ago, and I started working on her gown. The next thing I knew she came bursting into my sewing room saying she didn't think that one was right after all. Honestly, I hope she doesn't think I'm going to make all these dresses overnight. I'm really starting to lose patience with her."

"Isn't Greyson helping? I thought that once he got here, she would settle down."

"She won't let him know anything about the wedding dress. Bad luck, you know."

Autumn titters. "And the bridesmaids' dresses? Does she at least know what color she wants?"

Dusty heaves a heavy sigh and rolls her eyes. "She's changed her mind about that a million times, too. They have to match or at least go with her flowers, but she's totally indecisive on those. First it was pink roses, then it was tiger lilies, then lavender, then yellow roses. Now she's up in the air again. I've tried to tell her that the wedding is too close to keep changing her mind, but she can't seem to help herself. I hope she gets through it without having a breakdown."

"If she doesn't give the rest of us one first," says Autumn. "I hope Greyson succeeds in calming her down. She told me how anxious she is for everything to be perfect. I can't imagine what she thinks perfect is, though."

"That's the problem," says Dusty. "I don't think she knows, either. Perfect is just some elusive ideal in her mind. I'm going to get Greyson alone as soon as I can and tell him to convince her that she has to make final decisions now and whatever she chooses will be perfect."

"Good luck to you and Greyson."

"Thanks."

"Can I see the portfolio?" asks Autumn.

"Sure." Dusty opens it and turns it towards Autumn.

"That was the first dress she picked," Dusty points to a picture in the portfolio. It's an intricately beaded gown with an appliqued tulle and a voluminous skirt. "I ordered over five thousand beads and sequins for that gown. The day after they arrived, she said she didn't want it, after all. I hope I can find a use for them."

"You will," Autumn assures her as she flips through the pages. "I can't understand what she could find wrong with any of them."

"She can't even decide on a style. Look at them. There's a ball gown, an A-line, a sheath, a column dress. Autumn, I'm going crazy. That's why I came here. I had to get out of the apartment. Greyson is off meeting with Max about tending bar. I was home with her, and she kept bugging me to show her more styles. I finally told her I had to go shopping and left her looking at dresses online. What am I going to do?"

"I think you need to flat out tell her that if she doesn't pick something, and stick with it very soon, she won't have a dress to wear for her wedding. And, if she doesn't agree to one of these menus," she taps her paw on the printouts in front of her, "I'll tell her she'll just have to order take-out from On The Side."

Another knock sounds at Autumn's office door. "Come in," she calls.

It's Sukey. "Autumn, oh, hi Dusty. Remember when Abigail decided on a wedding cake?"

"Uh-huh," says Autumn. She can guess what Sukey is about to tell her.

"Well, she just called me. She's changed her mind again. If I didn't think she'd stick you with making the cake on top of all the other cooking you're doing for her, I'd tell her to shove it in her litterbox and find another baker."

"You'd better come in and sit down, Sukey," says Autumn. "Dusty and I were just commiserating over Abigail's chronic fickleness. You can join us."

"We need a plan of action," says Sukey. "If this wedding is ever going to happen then we have to force her to get her act together." Sukey turns to Dusty. "She's your sister. What do you think we should do?"

"I had Greyson come up here hoping he could do something."

"Dusty, you said Greyson is talking to Max right now?"

"Yes."

"I'm going to call him while he's not with Abigail." Autumn pulls out her cell and gets him on the phone.

"Hi, Greyson," she says.

"Hi, Autumn. How's it going?"

"Not great. We need to talk. I've got Dusty and Sukey in my office right now. Abigail is driving us all up the curtains."

"I know. The florist called this morning while I was at her apartment. Apparently, she's changed her mind about the bouquet and the floral arrangements several times, too. Listen, I've just finished talking to Max. He's all set to tend bar at the reception. I'm heading over to talk to the DJ now. I'll get back to you. Meanwhile you ladies relax. I will find a way to straighten it all out."

"Thanks, Greyson. We're counting on you."

She relates her conversation to Dusty and Sukey who look guardedly relieved.

"Now, I've got some news. I met the most wonderful cat. His name is Buster, and he just moved in down the street from us." Autumn tells them about everything that happened yesterday, the euphoria returning just from talking about it.

"He sounds wonderful," says Sukey. "What does he do for work?"

"He owns a printing company."

"Wait," says Dusty. "Is his last name Parker?"

"Yes," says Autumn.

Seeing Dusty's stricken look, she asks, "What is it?"

"He's doing the invitations for Abigail."

"Doing them?" asks Sukey. "Shouldn't they have gone out already?"

"Yes, but Abigail keeps changing her mind. First it was the paper stock, then it was the design, now she's redoing the wording. Oh, Autumn, don't tell him your best friend is her sister until after the wedding or he might run in the other direction and never come back."

"He already knows," says Autumn. "I thought I saw his whiskers tremble when Smokey mentioned Abigail."

"Well," says Sukey, throwing up her paws. "He can join our club!"

Chapter 8
Getting to Know You

"They're here," Smokey calls to Autumn as she welcomes Marlon and Sasha.

Autumn, who has taken an entire Saturday off from work, is in the kitchen preparing lunch.

"Come in," says Smokey. "My sister has lunch almost ready." It feels awkward. Marlon and Sasha are her littermates, but she barely knows them. And now she has to introduce them to their other sister, the one they didn't know existed.

"Would you like a drink? There's fruit juice, seltzer water, ice water, coffee, tea."

"Ice water is fine," says Marlon.

"For me, too," says Sasha.

"Have a seat," she says indicating the couch. "I'll be right back."

Smokey enters the kitchen as Autumn is stacking plates and utensils on the table.

"I thought we'd eat in the dining room rather than the kitchen," says Autumn.

"Sure," says Smokey, pouring two glasses of water.

"Smokey, are you okay?" asks Autumn.

"It all seems so weird. I feel like I'm in a dream. I'm going to wake up any minute, but I'm not sure if I want to."

"What do you mean?"

"I've always wished my littermates were alive, but never believed it was possible. Now that they're here, I hardly know how to act around them. We don't know anything about each other. What if I don't like who they are now? What if they don't like me?"

"Of course, they'll like you. Give yourselves time to get to know each other. That's what I'm going to do. Come on, introduce me."

As Smokey returns to the living room with Autumn in tow, the two cats stand up. She hands them each their glasses of ice water, then says, "Sasha, Marlon, this is my sister...well, your sister, too, Autumn Amelia."

"Pleased to meet you," say the cats, shaking Autumn's paw.

"Hi!" says Autumn. She throws her arms around each one in turn. "Are you hungry? Lunch is almost ready. I made salmon macaroni and cheese, salad, and rolls. I hope you'll like it."

"It sounds wonderful," says Sasha.

"I'll set the table set and then we can eat."

"Well..." says Smokey. "Umm...did you have any trouble finding the house?"

"No. GPS got us here with no problem," says Marlon.

"Good." *Now what?*

"Autumn is a fantastic cook."

"We know," says Sasha. "We've eaten at Mama Cat's Kitchen."

"You've been to Oneness Park?"

"Yes. We love it. You did a magnificent job," says Marlon.

"Thank you, but it wasn't just me. A lot of furs and feathers were instrumental in creating the park. I'm glad you like it."

"Lunch is served," calls Autumn.

"This way," says Smokey, leading them to the dining room.

"We don't use this room much," says Autumn as they take their seats. "Just for special occasions. And I can't think of anything more special than this."

Marlon and Sasha smile at her, though Smokey thinks they feel as awkward as she does.

"So, what do you do for work?" asks Autumn, passing the serving dishes around the table.

"I'm an interior decorator," says Sasha.

"Really?" asks Smokey. "Where do you work?"

"I used to work for Nesters Decorating Company, but about a year ago I started my own business. It's called Hoot and Purr Decorating. I specialize in interiors for owls and cats."

"I'd love to see some of your work," says Smokey. "Do you have pictures?"

"I can show you some on my phone after lunch."

"What do you do for a living, Marlon?" asks Autumn.

"I'm a firefighter."

"In Faunaburg?"

"No, in West Lake."

"He's being modest," says Sasha. "Marlon is the Captain of the West Lake Fire Department."

"Wow!" says Smokey. "That's wonderful."

Marlon shrugs. "Thanks. I'm lucky to have a great crew."

"Autumn, this is delicious," says Sasha.

"It certainly is," Marlon agrees.

"Thank you. I'm so sorry you never got a meal by Mama cat. She was a wonderful cook. She taught me."

Smokey winces. She's not sure if bringing up their parents is okay. But then Autumn always was one for laying all her jingle balls on the table.

"I'm eating her cooking now," says Sasha, "since you learned from her."

"It's amazing that we are all here together," says Autumn. "I feel Mama and Papa Cat are here in spirit, too. It's like a miracle."

"Well," says Sasha. "We're not *all* here."

"That's one of the things we hoped to discuss today," says Marlon. "Sasha and I would like to see if we can find out if Winthrop is still alive."

"Smokey mentioned that," says Autumn. "What do you plan to do?"

"We thought we could brainstorm some ideas," says Sasha.

"We thought of putting something out on social media," says Marlon. "You know, to see if any cat comes forward."

"Since you've both been in the news so much," adds Sasha, "maybe you could ask the paper to do a story on our reunion. Mention that we're still looking for Winthrop. Maybe he'll read it and contact the paper."

"I'm sorry," says Smokey, "but I don't think those are good ideas." Tears prick her eyes as she sees their crushed looks.

"I can see that turning into a media circus," she explains. "We'd probably get many cats coming forward. One might be Winthrop, but how would we know?"

Marlon nods. "You're probably right."

"What about the Police Dogs?" asks Autumn. "Maybe they could find Winthrop."

"I doubt they would take it on," says Sasha. "He's not wanted for a crime, and he's not really considered a missing creature."

"He's missing from our family," says Autumn.

"Yes, but it's not the same," says Smokey.

"Hey," says Marlon. "I have a friend in the Faunaburg Fire Department whose cousin is a private investigator. Maybe we could hire him."

"That's a great idea," says Autumn. "Smokey, what do you think?"

"Is he good?" she asks.

"Well, his cousin thinks so and I trust him."

"I think it's worth a shot," says Sasha.

They all look expectantly at Smokey as she turns the idea over in her mind.

"He'd be discreet?" she asks, not wanting her front yard turned into a haven for reporters.

"I'm sure in his line of work he has to be," says Marlon. "He's a Shih Tzu named Archer and, according to my friend, he's extremely tenacious. Oh, and he has won an Outstanding Investigator Award."

Smokey feels excitement rise in her chest. "Okay," she says, "I'm in."

Cheers break out around the table.

"I'll text my friend right now and get his cousin's contact information," says Marlon, pulling his cell phone from his pocket.

At the same moment, a call comes in on Autumn's cell.

"It's Greyson," she says. "I'll take it in the kitchen while I'm getting dessert."

Smokey gathers the lunch plates and stacks them along with the serving dishes at the end of the table.

A few minutes later Autumn returns with a tray of apple spice cupcakes with cream cheese frosting, a tub of vanilla ice cream and a stack of dessert dishes. As she finishes handing a plate with a cupcake and a scoop of ice cream to each cat, Marlon's phone buzzes.

"The contact info," he says. "Should we call him after dessert?"

"Yes," says Smokey. "Put him on speakerphone so we can all talk to him."

After they finish eating, Marlon places the call then lays the phone in the center of the table. They all stare at it like it contains the secrets of the universe.

"Archer Investigations, Archer speaking." As the gruff voice emanates from the phone, Smokey feels both excited and disoriented. Is this happening?

After they explain, Archer tells them he's willing to take on their case. They will need to sign a contract that outlines his fee and all the expenses they'll be expected to cover. He will update them every day that he performs work on their case. Each of them agrees to swing by his office in Faunaburg to sign the contract and to split the costs among them.

After the call ends, no one can contain their excitement.

"I can't believe after all this time, we might all be back together again," says Sasha.

"I don't want to dampen the mood," says Marlon, "but remember, that the hawk may have gotten Winthrop, or he may not have made it after running away. We must be prepared for that."

"Well," says Sasha, "at least we'll know."

Smokey agrees. She desperately needs to know what happened to Winthrop.

After Marlon and Sasha leave and Smokey and Autumn are doing the dishes, Smokey asks, "What did Greyson call for?"

"He asked me to meet him at Miguel's private club at ten o'clock on Tuesday morning."

"Why?"

"I'm not sure, but he told me to bring everything I have regarding the menu for the wedding reception."

"Mysterious," says Smokey.

"I guess. Come upstairs and help me pick out what to wear tonight for my date with Buster."

Chapter 9
The Concert

"I'm surprised you've never been to any of the Concerts on the Common," says Buster as he and Autumn cross the street. They carry the snacks and drinks they've purchased from a street vendor as they make their way to a spot on the grass not far from the bandstand.

"Until I started working in Faunaburg, I didn't get into the city very often."

"Have you ever heard Wilbur sing?" asks Buster as he spreads out his blanket for them to sit on.

"Only once when the local radio station did an interview with him and played some of his songs. He has a great voice."

"He's even better live. Too bad this is the last concert of the season. It will soon be too chilly to sit outside in the evening."

"There's something fun to do in each season," says Autumn. "I like fall the best."

"It's certainly the prettiest," says Buster, gazing into her eyes. "That must be why you're named for it."

Autumn drops her gaze. Smokey is usually the one who gets all the compliments for her looks.

Buster lifts her chin with his paw. "You know you are a lovely cat, don't you?"

She shrugs. "If you say so."

"I do. So, what do you like about the fall?"

"The brilliant colors of the leaves and the brisk air. I love in-season foods like apples and pumpkin. I like going to orchards and picking apples. And I especially love Hunter's Moon Night. That's my favorite holiday."

"Mine, too. What are you doing for it this year?"

"I've been so busy with the restaurant and Abigail's machinations over the menu for her wedding reception that I haven't even thought about it."

"Is Abigail driving you up the curtains, too?"

"She certainly is. I've heard she's doing the same to you with the invitations."

"Her wedding is at the end of November. Those invitations should have gone out a long time ago. I've told her at this point it will be a rush order. She wants everything to match – flowers, decorations, invitations. I wish she'd make up her mind."

"The problem is when she changes her mind on one thing it necessitates that everything else change. I sure hope Greyson can set her straight."

"You mean her fiancé?"

"Yeah. He's my cousin. I'm meeting him at Miguel Gato's private club on Tuesday at ten. I'm to bring everything regarding the menu."

"That's interesting. He called me at work on Friday and asked me to come to Señor Gato's club, too."

"I wonder what he's up to," says Autumn.

"Is Greyson good at managing things?"

"Very good. He recently retired as CEO of PAWS UNITED."

"Seriously? They are a pawsome organization. I look forward to meeting him. And to seeing Miguel's. I've never been there. Have you?"

"Yes. I went to lunch there with Smokey, Greyson and Abigail once. That's where I met Sukey and Sally. They're now the pastry and sous chefs at Mama Cat's."

"Miguel doesn't mind that they left to work for you?"

"No. He knows what Gustav is like."

"Who's Gustav?"

"Miguel's chef." Autumn proceeds to regale Buster with the story of her visit to Gustav's kitchen and her improvement of his world-famous sauce. By the time she finishes Buster is wiping tears of laughter from his eyes.

Just then the warm-up act, The Rootin'-Tootin' Rottweilers take the stage and begin blasting out their big band sound. Once their set finishes, the announcer climbs the stairs to the bandstand to introduce Wilbur the Singing Otter. From the other side of the bandstand, a dashing otter dressed in formal evening attire with a striking red vest under his dinner jacket takes the stage.

Wilbur is a true crooner with a voice as smooth as butter. The Rottweilers, who are backing up Wilbur for tonight, tone down their sound to match.

Autumn is entranced. Before the evening is over, she finds herself comfortably leaning against Buster, his arm around her shoulders, melting into the romance of the soft evening breeze, Wilbur's dulcet voice, the gentle music, and the joy of a new relationship.

Chapter 10
Heart to Heart

"I'll be gone most of the day tomorrow," Abigail says intercepting Smokey in Fluffington's lobby when she arrives at work. "I'm meeting Greyson at Miguel's for brunch. After that he wants to spend the afternoon going over wedding plans. I'm not sure what could take so long. I'm doing most of the organizing. But he was insistent that I clear my calendar for him, so I've decided to humor him," she says escorting Smokey to her office. Smokey puts her jacket and purse away and follows Abigail to the coffee maker.

Smokey decides to keep the fact that both Autumn and Buster will be at Miguel's to herself. Abigail doesn't seem to know, so she assumes Greyson wants it that way. *I wish I could be a flea on a fur for that meeting,* she thinks.

"You'll have to handle the new client meeting on your own tomorrow," Abigail continues. "But I can always tell Greyson to reschedule."

"I'll be fine," says Smokey, excited by the opportunity to lead a new client meeting on her own. "You needn't worry."

"That's good, but let's spend some time after lunch going over it. And you can always call or text me with any problems."

Fluffington's would have to be on fire for her to call or text Abigail. She's more than ready to be a full partner. If only Abigail would let her.

"How are your courses going?" asks Abigail.

"Fine. Dusty loaned me her notes from the classes I missed."

"Oh, good. Dusty has done well in all her courses so I'm sure she must have taken excellent notes. But you know you can always ask me if you need extra help."

"Thank you, Abigial." *Not likely*, thinks Smokey. Abigail is a brilliant businesscat, but she is such a wreck over making sure Smokey knows everything that Smokey now resents her. This is no way to form a partnership.

"Abigail, there is something I'd like to discuss with you."

Abigail's face lights up. "Of course, Smokerina. Let's go in my office."

"Could we use the conference room?"

Abigail looks puzzled. "I suppose so," she says, following Smokey down the hallway.

They can sit side-by-side in the conference room. Smokey wants Abigail to see her as an equal.

"Abigail," she begins after they're both seated. "Are you certain you want me to be your partner? Please, tell me if you're not and we will dissolve the partnership. I won't be angry." *Well, maybe a little and I will be hurt, but I'd rather deal with that than viewed as subpar.*

"What?" Abigail gasps. "Of course, I want you as my partner. I wouldn't have asked you otherwise."

"I'm glad to hear it. So, you think I am qualified and capable?"

"Yes. Why would you think otherwise?"

"Because you've been acting as though you regret it."

"I have?" Abigail looks shocked. "How?"

"When I was a senior architect, you let me do most of my work on my own. Now you're constantly looking over my shoulder and burying me in the details of every account Fluffington's has ever had."

"I've had decades of experience. You've never owned a company. If this is about the courses –"

"It's not about the courses," Smokey interjects. "That was a very good idea, and I'm glad you suggested it. It's more the feeling I get that you don't think I'm truly capable. I mean, just now you asked me if I thought I could handle a new client meeting on my own and even offered to cancel your plans with Greyson – important wedding plans. I've never run a new client meeting before, but I've been in plenty of them. For what reason could I not be able to lead it?"

"I know you can. I just wanted to be sure you were comfortable doing it."

"If you thought I wouldn't be comfortable, why would you want me to be your partner? It's not the most difficult aspect of my position. Abigail, I am quite confident in my abilities."

Abigail stares into her coffee cup. After a moment, but without looking up, she says, "I know you are. You're very much like I was at your age." She raises her head and looks Smokey in the eye. "I made a lot of mistakes. In the beginning, I had some rough times. I wanted to impart some of what I learned so you don't have to make the same mistakes."

"I understand and appreciate that, Abigail. But you had to build Fluffington's from the ground up. I'm stepping into an established, successful business with several years of experience behind me. I've learned a great deal from you. I will make mistakes of my own, but I'll learn from them just like you did. What I need from you is your vote of confidence."

"I do have great confidence in you."

"Thank you."

Abigail shifts her gaze to the huge glass windows of the conference room's walls. "Smokerina, it's not you at all. It's me."

"What do you mean?"

Abigail's gaze moves to her lap. "I've been solely in charge of my business and my life since I crossed into adulthood. And that was a long time ago. Now, everything is changing. There's no part of my life that's in my control anymore. Once Greyson and I are married my living arrangements and day-to-day life will change. And Dusty. Why, I can't keep up with all her comings and goings. She's finally coming into her own, but I feel like I'm living with a different cat. Now she's informed me that she's going to get her own apartment. By the time Greyson and I return from our honeymoon she will have moved out. And of course, I'm slowly letting go of the business I built from scratch."

She looks up at Smokey.

"I've chosen the best successor possible," she says, placing a paw over one of Smokey's. "I have confidence in you as a partner and as the future owner of Fluffingtons."

Smokey swallows a lump in her throat.

"I'm floundering. If I'm not the head of Fluffington ArCATechture and if I'm not in charge of everything around me, then who am I?" Her eyes glisten.

"Abigail," says Smokey leaning towards her. "No one has forced you to get married or to make me your partner. *You* chose those things. Now you're on a great new adventure. You and Greyson. The rest of your life, together. Think of all you two can do. You both love to travel. Now you can do it to your heart's content.

"You don't have to worry about Dusty needing you all the time. You can rest easy knowing she's making her own way in the world.

"And I promise, you won't have to worry about Fluffington's. I'll uphold the highest standards of Fluffington's. Let me get started, maybe, even making a few mistakes."

Abigail manages a smile. "You're right, Smokerina. I know you will do a superb job. Is all this why I've been so indecisive about the wedding plans? I know I'm driving everyfur to distraction over it. I'm going to have to make some decisions and stick with them. I just hope I can."

"Why don't you try taking your mind off work? Let me try my paw at it by myself for a while. Focus on the wedding preparations without any distractions." At the hesitant look on Abigail's face, she quickly adds, "If anything major comes up I *promise* I will contact you. Deal?"

Abigail leans back in her chair. "Deal."

Chapter 11
The Intervention

Autumn Amelia rides up in the elevator with Buster, Sukey, Dusty, and two others she's never met, a snowy egret named Elaine, and a ferret named Phil. Elaine is the florist and Phil is the photographer for Greyson and Abigail's wedding.

"Welcome," says Greyson as they enter Miguel's private dining room. "Thank you all for coming. Please take a seat." He motions them to a long table. A contrite-looking Abigail Fluffington sits at the center, with a notepad and pen before her.

Greyson introduces himself to those he's not yet met, then says, "I've asked you all here so that we can get this wedding straightened out once and for all. Abigail has agreed that whatever is decided in this room today is final. So that everything coordinates, each of you will know what the other is doing. A buffet is set up over there," he points to two long tables against the wall. "Help yourselves to brunch."

Autumn smelled the food before she was even off the elevator. Delicious aromas are wafting towards her. She resists but knows she won't last long.

Abigail speaks next, "I know this is unusual, but I'm having some trouble making decisions."

A few barely concealed snorts are heard at the table.

"I know," she says. "I've been terribly difficult to work with. I'm truly sorry and I do appreciate the willingness of all of you to come. I chose each of you because you are all known to be the best in Faunaburg at what you do. Whatever we decide will be amazing. Shall we get started?"

Portfolios are opened on the table.

"What's the WiFi password?" asks Phil, taking out his laptop.

"One moment. I'll find out," says Greyson, heading for the kitchen.

Autumn, unable to keep her mind or her eyes off the buffet table, drops some of her notes on the floor.

"Hungry?" Buster whispers as the both lean down to pick them up.

Autumn nods. The aromas have her head spinning.

"I'd like to get something from the buffet," he announces.

"Me, too," says Phil.

"By all means," says Abigail.

The entire entourage eagerly heads for the buffet. "Thank you," Autumn whispers to Buster.

The spread is eclectic, reflecting the tastes of all gathered, including several fish dishes along with bacon, eggs, and fresh fruit.

When Greyson returns, he has Miguel Gato with him. Miguel welcomes everyone to his club then hands out cards with the network and password on them.

"Were you hiding in the kitchen, Miguel?" asks Sukey.

"If I were to hide, would it be in the same room as Gustav?"

Sukey bursts into laughter. Chef Gustav was her boss before she moved on to Mama Cat's Kitchen. "He's still his old, cranky self, then?"

"Crankier. Which, of course, means he's turning out scrumptious dishes."

"And destroying his new sous chef's will to live?"

"That too, no doubt. How is Sally, speaking of sous chefs?"

"She's very well. I'll tell her you were asking for her."

"And now, Greyson and I will leave you all to your business. Enjoy the brunch."

"I will return to pick up my lovely bride-to-be in a few hours," says Greyson. "I hope that will give you all enough time."

"It's a deadline," says Abigail. "Ta-ta, Greyson and Miguel."

Greyson leans down to kiss her cheek then departs with Miguel.

Abigail gives her full attention to the others at the table. "I'm looking for a balance of elegance, sophistication, and romance. Shall we start with the floral arrangements?" She says, nodding towards Elaine.

The snowy egret sets aside her lobster omelet, wipes her bill, then pulls some photos from her portfolio. "There is no flower more elegant, sophisticated, or romantic than the red rose," she says. "Do any of these appeal to you?"

They all look at the pictures. Each is a bridal bouquet of red roses, one interspersed with white baby's breath, one with a dot of white inside each rose, one that is a long spray of roses, and one of red roses atop a set of deep green leaves. Abigail carefully looks over each picture. "This one," she says, tapping the one with the green leaves. "It's perfect." Abigail sits up very straight and slides the photo towards Elaine with her paw.

Elaine pulls out another photo. "To match, we could put white tulle at the end of each pew in the chapel. Tied into each would be a single red rose backed by two deep green leaves."

"Splendid," says Abigail.

"For the other chapel decorations, I was thinking of rose bouquets in varying hues of red with some white interspersed so that it's not too monochromatic."

"Very good," says Abigail. "Just don't stray into pink. Pink is definitely out."

"Not to worry. There are several shades that won't approach pink. I'll be sure to include the greenery and a dash of white here and there. The chapel at Oneness Park isn't large so we don't want to overdo it anyway. Now, for the reception, I was thinking that rather than vases of roses on each table we could do ecru table runners with roses and greenery embedded in them. Since it's an evening wedding, I could add a string of small white lights in each."

She lays a photo on the table. They all ooh and aah.

"Lovely," says Abigail. "I much prefer that to vases. It's different and being low it won't be in the way of conversation across the table. Autumn, what do you think? Would that work on your tables?"

"That would look beautiful."

"Then it's decided."

Elaine continues. "For the head table I'm thinking of a large spray of roses atop deep green leaves in the center flowing out at either end and down the front. I assume you will have white table linens?" she asks.

"Oh dear. Who provides linens?"

"Don't worry," says Autumn. "Mama Cat's has lots."

"Thank you," says Abigail. "We'll go with them. I don't think I could handle having to coordinate with yet another vendor."

"Are we definite on all the floral choices, then?" asks Elaine.

"Yes," says Abigail.

"Very well." Elaine gathers up her photographs, placing the ones Abigail has chosen in a separate section of her portfolio, then resumes eating her lobster omelet.

"Buster," says Abigail. "Now that you know exactly what the flowers will be, can you produce an invitation that will match?"

"Certainly." He pulls up something on his laptop, then turns it towards her. "Do you like any of these?"

Autumn leans in to see, too. There are several invitation templates with red roses. One stands out to Autumn, and it's the one Abigail taps with her paw.

"Look," says Abigail. "Elaine, the roses on the invitation look like my bouquet!"

Elaine cranes her long neck towards Buster's laptop. "Exactly," she says after examining the red roses underpinned with deep green leaves set on a black background. "There's even a hint of white amongst the roses like the chapel design."

"That's it then," says Abigail. She decides on the cardstock. Buster types the wording for the invitations and promises to start on them the minute he gets back to his office.

"Phil," she says, turning to the ferret who has been furiously banging away on his keyboard, "I believe I will take your full package. I want pictures of the rehearsal dinner, preparations the day of the wedding, the ceremony, and the reception. You will be sure to include the floral arrangements in the photos?"

"Of course. Would you like a photo of your invitation for your online photo album as in the physical album?"

"Yes, wonderful. Please, coordinate with Buster."

"Will do," says Phil. "How about this for an album cover?" he asks, turning his laptop towards Abigail who clasps her paws over her mouth in surprise when she sees a cover that looks amazingly like the invitations, black with red roses and greenery.

"Oh, my. That's perfect," says Abigail. "I'm so grateful Greyson thought to get us all together for this. Just look how we're working to coordinate."

"I have an idea," says Sukey. "Phil, may I borrow your laptop for a minute?" she asks.

"Sure."

"Go on, Abigail," says Sukey.

Abigail turns to Autumn. "Let's get the menu settled, then the cake. I can always connect with Dusty at home if we run out of time."

"Oh, no you don't," says Dusty, pulling a fabric bag from the floor and setting it in the middle of the table. "At home, it's too easy for you to take forever," she says, standing now with paws on her hips. "When I get back to the apartment, I plan to start sewing immediately. If you haven't decided by the time we're finished here, you'll wear whatever I come up with and so will your bridesmaids."

"Well," Abigail huffs. "That's forward of you, Dusty."

Autumn exchanges an amused glance with Sukey. "We don't mind waiting," they declare together.

"Thank you," says Dusty. "Now, Abigail, would you kindly tell me which of these wedding dresses you want?"

Dusty sets four paw-drawn designs in front of her sister. With a sniff, Abigail pulls them closer and inspects each one. The others wait in silence. Autumn can tell that each one is completely different from the others.

"Well?" asks Dusty after too much time goes by.

"I'm trying," says Abigail, a pained edge to her voice.

"Think out loud," Elaine suggests.

"They're all what I want, elegant, sophisticated, and romantic. But each one has an element that I especially like."

"Go on," says Dusty. She takes a sketch pad and pencil from her bag.

All watch intently as Abigail points out her favorite features of each gown, then stare in amazement as Dusty quickly dashes off a new design. When she slides it across the table, Abigail lets out a gasp.

"Perfect. You're a genius!"

"Gifted," she corrects with a shrug. "On to the bridesmaid's dresses."

While Dusty pulls out fabric samples and drawings, Autumn reaches for the image of the bridal gown. A full-length dress that extends to the floor but has no train. The skirt bells out slightly and the bodice is a wrap-around crossing over the chest with a wide asymmetrical waist and three-quarter length sleeves. It is elegant, sophisticated, romantic and exactly right for a mature bride.

Sukey glances at the drawing. "I have a necklace you can borrow," she tells Abigail. "A gold chain with a red rosebud pendant. It will land in exactly the right spot with that neckline."

"Thank you, Sukey," she says. Then, "I got your name right this time?"

"You did," she says.

Choosing the maid of honor and bridesmaids' dresses goes smoothly now that they know the floral theme. Dark green is chosen for the bridesmaids. To set the maid of honor's dress apart, Dusty will add small sprigs of white like that to be added to the chapel's flowers.

"Phew!" says Dusty when they finish. "I am so glad Greyson and his groomsmen are renting their tuxes."

Abigail turns to Autumn. "Now for the food," she says.

"We'll start with a cocktail hour while you and the wedding party are with the photographer. Here is a list," she says passing a paper to Abigail. "Please pick what you'd like my waitstaff to pass around."

Abigail looks it over. "It's hard to choose. What do you suggest, Autumn?"

Autumn sighs. "If it was my wedding, I would go with these four," says Autumn choosing at random. She just wants Abigail to make a decision.

"Hmm…" says Abigail. "Maple glazed scallops with apples and bacon, crostini with white fig jam, mushrooms stuffed with crabmeat and herbed cheese, and roasted pears in phyllo cups. Yes, we'll go with that. What's next?"

"There will also be a stationary option with a variety of cheeses, fruits, baguettes, and crackers. And, of course, Greyson's shrimp," says Autumn.

"Now for dinner. The wedding is late in November and soup is so warming. I could do a butternut bisque or a cream of mushroom. The soup will be followed by salad."

"Tell me the main course selections. I want to know those before I decide on the soup."

"You will have options for the main course on the RSVP card, I assume?" Buster interjects.

"I forgot about that," says Abigail.

"That's why I'm still here," he says, smiling broadly. "The cards will match the invitations. I need to know what to put on them for dinner options."

"Three options," says Autumn, "a meat, a fish, and a vegetarian. For the meat, sliced tenderloin of beef with a wine glaze and sauteed onions and mushrooms. For the fish, seared sea bass with garlic lemon sauce. And for the vegetarian, butternut squash ravioli with white wine sauce."

"Then I think we'll go with cream of mushroom for the soup," says Abigail.

"Excellent," says Autumn, relieved that Abigail didn't notice that she had given her no other choices on the entrees. "Each will be served with roasted potatoes, haricots verts, and steamed baby carrots. Since there will be wedding cake and the groom's cake, we'll keep desserts to a minimum, but we could put out a few selections on a side table. How about crème brûlée topped with berries in ramakins, eclairs, and chocolate mousse?"

"Wonderful," says Abigail. "Buster, did you get the main course options?"

"Yes."

"Great. All that's left is the cake."

Sukey turns Phil's laptop towards Abigail. "Feast your eyes on this," she says.

Abigail gasps. "That is stunning!"

They all clamber to see. Sukey turns the laptop around. A chorus of *wow!, gorgeous!, amazing!, and oh my catness!* sweeps the table as they gaze at an image of a cake in six separate tiers. The largest cake is front and center, behind it are two equally sized, slightly smaller cakes on raised crystal cake plates. Behind those are two smaller cakes on taller cake plates, and in the back is one small cake on the highest crystal plate. Each is frosted white with a spray of roses atop green leaves that cascade gently down the sides. Beside each cake are crystal candle holders in graduated heights and standing a bit higher than each cake tier. The topper sits on the largest cake.

"The roses in this picture are yellow, but imagine them in red," says Sukey. "Elaine, if you send me a picture of Abigail's bouquet, I'll try to match the frosting as closely as possible."

Autumn glances at Abigail. Tears shimmer in her eyes, a beatific smile graces her Persian face. Autumn nudges Sukey.

"You like it?" asks Sukey.

"It's perfect," says Abigail, her voice a rapturous whisper.

"I assume a whitefish frosting will suit?"

"Very nicely."

"Settled. Now all that's left is the groom's cake. You mentioned whimsical?"

Abigail looks concerned. "Though I'm not sure what that would be. I don't suppose you could make a shrimp-flavored cake, could you?"

"Ah, yes. Greyson's legendary love of shrimp," says Sukey. "Hmm..." She googles something then scrolls for a moment. "Something like this?"

She shows the screen to Abigail who bursts out laughing. "That's it! The only pink allowed in the wedding."

The cake on the screen is in the shape of a giant pink shrimp.

"I'll just need to order a mold," says Sukey. "I'll use shrimp to flavor the cake and the frosting."

"Don't anyone tell Greyson," says Abigail. "I want it to be a surprise. Now, I think we're finally finished.

This has been such a long, difficult ordeal. Before you go, join me in a toast." She goes behind the bar.

Returning with a bottle of nip-pagne and a tray of glasses, Abigail pops the cork, fills the glasses and passes them around. "Miguel and I go way back," she assures them. "He won't mind that I've helped myself. Now," she says standing at the head of the table and raising her glass. "To each one of you. Thank you for coming, for working together, and, most of all, for putting up with me. You are truly the best wedding planning team a cat could hope for."

As they down their nip-pagne, there is a palpable sense of relief permeating the room. When Greyson and Miguel return, Abigail and her cohort are laughing uproariously at the Pawbook reels of wedding bloopers on Phil's laptop.

Chapter 12
Revelation

"Smokerina?"

Smokey whips her head around to find Abigail and Greyson.

"Oh. Hi," she says.

Abigail looks up at the sign on the office door. "Why are you at a private investigator's office?"

"Um...I had to sign something. What are you doing here?"

"We stopped at the sandwich shop next door," says Greyson. He holds up the bag of sandwiches.

"How did the wedding planning go?" Smokey asks, hoping to change the subject.

"Wonderful," says Abigail. "We got everything straightened out. How was your new client meeting?"

"Great. Paulie Pomeranian is a perfect fit for that project given his specialty in designing mansions. He hit it off well with the client."

"Good," says Abigail, still eyeing her sideways. Greyson, too, has a look of speculation.

Smokey sighs. "You'll both find out soon enough, anyway," she says. "Can we go somewhere to talk?"

Greyson and Abigail look at each other.

"It's nothing bad," says Smokey. "In fact, it's incredibly good. Almost unbelievable."

"Well, now we're hooked," says Greyson. "Let's sit over there." He indicates the tables and chairs on the patio outside the sandwich shop.

"Have you had lunch?" he asks once they take the table furthest from other diners.

"No, I haven't. I'll go order something."

"Allow me. We need drinks, anyway. What would you like?"

"Tuna," says Smokey. "And a cola."

"Just a spring water for me," says Abigail.

Greyson disappears into the shop. Abigail turns to Smokey. "Do you want to wait until Greyson returns to tell us what's going on?" she asks.

"Yes. But I'd love to hear about the wedding plans while we're waiting."

Abigail regales her with the intervention staged by Greyson. "Don't mention anything to him about his cake," she finishes. "It's a surprise."

"I won't," says Smokey just as Greyson returns with her sandwich and their drinks.

"Won't what?" asks Greyson.

"We were just talking business, dear."

"Okay, Smokey, time to spill the catnip. What's this big mystery?" asks Greyson.

Smokey takes a sip of her drink. "Do you remember that when I was born, I had three littermates?"

"Of course."

"And one day they were taken by hawks. I was the only one who got away?"

"Such a tragedy," says Abigail, patting Smokey's paw.

"Well," says Smokey. "I saw a hawk crash into the bush we were under, but I ran so fast I didn't see what happened. Since none of them were ever found, we assumed hawks got them all."

Greyson puts down his sandwich. "Is that why you went to a private investigator? You think they could still be alive? Smokey, I know losing your littermates was traumatic, but —"

"Two of them *are* alive. Autumn and I had lunch with them on Saturday."

"What?" Both Greyson and Abigail exclaim.

"Did you hire the detective to find out if they're for real?" asks Abigail.

"No. I'm sure they're my littermates, Marlon and Sasha. Together we hired a detective to see if we can find Winthrop."

"How did all this come about?" asks Greyson.

Smokey relates the entire story. When she finishes, they stare at her in astonishment.

"Dusty was at the café and heard all of this?" asks Abigail.

"Yes."

"She never said a word." Smokey's not sure if Abigail is more stunned by her revelation about her littermates or the fact that Dusty kept something so monumental from her.

"That cat has changed so much," Abigail says, her voice filled with wonder. "Ever since she met Autumn Amelia."

"Autumn can have a profound effect," says Greyson. "But about your littermates, Smokey. Do you think there's a chance that Winthrop is alive?"

"Marlon and Sasha are, so why not?"

"Why not, indeed," says Abigail, recovering her senses.

"And this Archer? He's good?" asks Greyson.

"He's supposed to be. He promised that if Winthrop is alive, he will find him. He showed me testimonials from previous clients. He even won an Outstanding Investigator Award. His fee seems reasonable. I'm comfortable with him."

"Okay," says Greyson. "This is rather staggering."

"It is. I should be overjoyed at finding two of my littermates, but I can't take it in yet. They seem to be feeling the same way."

"Probably that will change once you get used to it," says Abigail. "Greyson, we should invite them to our wedding! They're your cousins."

"Oh, Greyson," says Smokey. "That's right. I should have told you sooner. I'm so sorry."

"Totally understandable. I would like to meet them. I remember them from when we were all very young."

"Let me talk to Autumn."

"Where do they live?" asks Abigail.

"West Lake."

"Really? I went to Verdant University there. I haven't been to West Lake since I graduated. Greyson, let's find a nice restaurant there to take everyfur to for dinner."

"Good idea."

"The hard part will be finding a time when Autumn can go," says Smokey. "She's always either working or on a date."

"A date?" Greyson and Abigail ask simultaneously.

"Yes. With Buster Parker."

"The printer?" asks Abigail. "The one doing my invitations?"

"The same. He just moved onto our street. Autumn made him lunch the day he moved in, and they've been together ever since."

"Now that you say it, they did seem awfully cozy at the meeting. Well, that'll be another for a wedding invitation."

"Abby," says Greyson. "I'm sure Buster will be Autumn's plus one."

* * *

"What a pretty town," says Autumn as she and Smokey stroll down a tree-lined sidewalk in West Lake. "It will look spectacular in October after the leaves have turned." She pictures vibrant fall leaves fluttering to the cobblestone street against the backdrop of old brick buildings. "I wonder if Buster has ever been here."

"It's nice," says Smokey. "I still like the bustle of Faunaburg the best."

"You really are a city cat. Do you think you'll move there someday?"

"Would you mind if I did?"

"Not if that's your dream."

"Wouldn't you like to be closer to Mama Cat's Kitchen?"

"It's only about twenty minutes away. And I am decidedly not a city cat. But for a place like this," she says, gazing at the lovely old college town, "I might be enticed to move."

"It's a very wealthy town. Did you know Abigail went to college here at Verdant University?"

"I'm not surprised. That's one of the best. Didn't Chrissy say that the dog who bought her great aunt's house is a professor at Verdant?"

"Oh, that's right. Professor Chewy. I wonder what he's like."

They reach a building with a sign out front reading *The Falling Leaf Tavern*. They are meeting Greyson, Abigail and Smokey's littermates here for dinner.

"Why would they put a restaurant at the end of a street you can't even drive on? It's inconvenient." Because of the cobblestones, vehicles aren't allowed on the street, so they had to park in a lot reserved for those wanting to access Wayside Avenue.

"I think it's quaint," says Autumn. "Mama Cat's doesn't have a parking lot. You have to park in the lot for the park and walk over."

"But that's because it's a restaurant *in* the park. This is just a restaurant at the end of a street."

Autumn sighs. "It's part of the charm of this area. Look at the building. It has to be a few hundred years old. It might even be as old as Verdant. Come on, let's go in."

They step into the vestibule, a long narrow room. The walls are covered in photographs of West Lake and Verdant University's campus.

"Oh, look," says Autumn. "Here's a painting of this tavern from 1780. I told you it was old. Just think of all the history!"

"May I help you?" asks the hostess, a Turkish angora.

"We're meeting four other cats here."

"Greyson?" asks the hostess.

"Yes."

"Right this way."

They follow her into the main room to a large table near the back.

"Here you are," says the hostess.

Greyson and Marlon stand as they arrive. "Ladies," says Greyson.

"I hope we didn't keep you waiting long," says Smokey.

"Not at all," says Greyson. "Abby and I arrived at the same time as Marlon and Sasha. We were getting acquainted."

"I've been admiring the town," says Autumn. "It's charming."

"Thank you," says Sasha. "We've always loved it."

The waitress, a French Bulldog, arrives at their table. "Hi, I'm Rivet," she says. "Can I start you off with some drinks?"

They order drinks and an appetizer of artichoke dip and pita bread.

"Smokey told us all about what happened to you," says Abigail to Marlon and Sasha. "It's an amazing story."

"We're still caught in a sense of disbelief," says Sasha. "Though I think it's finally starting to sink in."

"I know," says Smokey. "I'm the same way."

"Maybe it will help if we keep getting together," says Autumn. "We should do some family things."

"That's a good idea, Autumn," says Abigail. "Greyson and I would love for you to come to our wedding," she says to Smokey's littermates. "It's at the end of November."

"The twenty-eighth," says Greyson.

"We're having the ceremony in the chapel at Oneness Park and the reception in the function room at Mama Cat's Kitchen," says Abigail.

Marlon smiles. "That sounds lovely."

"We'll put it on our calendars," says Sasha.

"Give me your addresses so I can send you each an invitation," says Abigail.

"What sort of family things do you have in mind?" Smokey asks Autumn.

"Maybe we could host a Hunter's Moon Night party at our house? We could invite friends and neighbors. It would be a good way for Buster and Professor Chewy to get to know their new neighbors and meet some of our friends and new family."

"Who is Professor Chewy?" asks Abigail.

"He just bought Holly Berry's house," Smokey explains. "He'll move in on the first of October."

"He teaches at Verdant University," says Autumn Amelia.

"A lot of the waitstaff here go to Verdant. I'll bet some of them know him," says Marlon.

Rivet returns with their drinks and appetizers. After they've all given her their dinner orders, Sasha asks, "Are you a student at Verdant?"

"Yes, I am."

"Do you know a Professor Chewy?"

"Sure do. Everyone knows Professor Chewy."

"What does he teach?" asks Smokey.

"Botany. He specializes in ethnobotany."

"Have you taken any courses with him?" asks Abigail.

"I'm majoring in astronomy, but I took an elective with him just so I could have him for a teacher. He's pawsome."

After Rivet leaves their table, Greyson says, "I'm not sure what ethnobotany is."

"I'll look it up," says Sasha, pulling out her cell phone.

"Well," says Autumn. "As a botany professor, he must have fallen in love with Holly Berry's gardens." Autumn goes on to regale them with a description of the flourishing flower gardens behind Holly's house.

"Here it is," says Sasha. Reading from her phone's screen, she says, "Ethnobotany is the scientific study of the traditional cultural knowledge and customs of a people regarding the medical, culinary, religious, and other uses of plants."

"That sounds fascinating," says Autumn.

"Speaking of plants," says Marlon, "Sasha and I were trying to recapture any of our memories from before the hawk. There is one we both remember but only a little. Smokey, maybe you can fill it in for us. It must have been a bad hunting day because there was nothing to eat, and we were all very hungry. I think we were living in the woods at the time because we both remember being near a fallen tree. Anyway, Papa Cat returned to us at that tree, empty-pawed. Then some other cat, a young cat, but not a baby like us, came by and dropped a bunch of dandelions and violets for us. I don't think he stayed long. We ate them. I remember I thought they weren't bad, and at least we had something in our bellies that night, so we didn't go to sleep with our stomachs growling. Do you remember anything about that?"

"Vaguely, says Smokey. "But nothing more than what you've just described."

Autumn watches as Greyson's paw stops in mid-air with artichoke dip dripping from his pita bread.

"Greyson?" Abigail asks. "Are you alright?"

They all look at him. He puts the appetizer down on his bread plate.

"That was me," he says. "I brought the dandelions and violets. We'd had them the night before and knew they were safe. My mama cat sent me over with a bag of them."

They all stare at Greyson, then at one another. Autumn notices a look pass between Greyson and

Smokey. She senses that he's acknowledging Marlon and Sasha to truly be Smokey's littermates.

"Autumn," says Smokey. "Your idea of a Hunter's Moon Night party is great. Let's do it." Turning to Marlon and Sasha, she says, "You'll come, won't you?"

"Of course," says Marlon.

"Actually," says Sasha. "If you don't mind, I'd like to help organize it."

"Great idea," says Marlon. "Let's all do it together."

"As a family," says Sasha.

At those words, Smokey bursts into tears.

"What's wrong?" asks Autumn.

"Nothing," she says. "I'm so...I'm so happy!" She throws herself into Sasha and Marlon's arms.

Greyson gets up along with Abigail. Autumn joins them. They stand together clustered in front of the three littermates. Even though their table is at the back of the tavern, there are a few other tables nearby. The three cats block the view of any curious onlookers so that Smokey, Sasha, and Marlon can have their moment and recompose themselves in private.

"Sorry. That was weird," says Smokey, looking abashed.

"Not at all," says Greyson.

"Don't be surprised if you have more moments like that," says Abigail. "What you three are experiencing is monumental."

They've all resettled when Rivet returns with their meals. As she's placing them on the table, she says, "Professor Chewy just came in. A lot of the profs like to eat here. He's in the booth near the front with Professors Bob and Gromit."

As they are leaving the tavern, they notice a booth near the front that contains two dogs and a mancat. One of the dogs is a French bulldog, the other is a Maltese Yorkshire Terrier mix.

"Excuse me," says Autumn. "Are you Professor Chewy?" she asks the Maltese Yorkshire. He is dressed in a brown tweed jacket and matching bow tie.

"Yes," he says, looking up in surprise.

"I'm Autumn Amelia and these are my sisters, Smokey and Sasha, my brother, Marlon, my cousin Greyson, and his fiancé, Abigail. Smokey and I live in Wild Whisker Ridge. You just bought the house of our friend, Chrissy. You'll soon be our new neighbor."

Professor Chewy's eyebrows raise. "Truly?" he says. "What a delight."

"I'll bet you love the Empress's gardens."

His look changes to confusion. "The Empress?"

"Oh, that's what we called Holly Berry. She was Chrissy's great aunt and lived there with her. Anyway, we'll be having a Hunter's Moon Night party next month, so I hope you'll come. We'll send an invitation."

"Autumn!" Autumn feels Smokey grab her paw, looks down and realizes she's holding a dinner roll.

"Oops!" says Autumn. "I'm sorry. I didn't realize I'd picked that up."

The other two professors look at her askance, but Professor Chewy smiles and says, "You go ahead and take that. I'll be happy to attend your party."

"That's great," says Autumn. Turning to the other two professors, she says, "Of course, you can come, too."

Chapter 13
Another Choice

"Hi, Jasmine," says Smokey when her friend answers her phone. "Can we get together for lunch this week?" Smokey is finally ready to share the news about her littermates and wants to start with her best friend.

"I'd love to," says Jasmine. "Let me check my calendar."

There's silence for a moment. Finally, she says, "This week is going to be tough. We're booked solid."

"Even at lunchtime?"

"Dash is an amazing publicist. We've been bursting at the seams with new clients. Louisa and I can barely keep up. We may have to hire a third."

"Wow. Congratulations."

"Thanks, Smokey. Let me see if I have time next week."

"How about Saturday? We could spend the day together here. Or I could go to your place."

"I can't. Louisa and I are having a strategy meeting on Saturday."

"Why not during the week?"

"We've both been staying late every night as it is. We've got to figure out how we're going to handle all these accounts. We don't want to turn away any prospective clients."

"I see," says Smokey, feeling her resentment towards Louisa rise again. She knows it's irrational, and she should be happy for Jasmine that Blue Landing is doing so well, but she can't shake her disklike of that great blue heron. From the moment she met Louisa,

Smokey thought she took the word 'great' a little too seriously.

"Sunday, then?" asks Smokey.

"Got to get some of my own errands done. We'll get together soon, once we've got our work situation under control. Seriously, this is a good problem to have, right?"

"Sure," says Smokey. "But something really huge happened in my life recently and I want to share it with you."

"What is it?"

"I'd rather not tell you over the phone."

"Okay, let's do Sunday. Do you mind coming over and doing some errands with me?"

"Not at all. See you at lunchtime?"

"Sure. Sorry, I've got to go. Louisa just popped her head into my office. Our next client is here early."

Smokey puts away her cell phone and stares at the files on her desk. Two of Fluffington's architects and Claudia, the receptionist, are due for their annual reviews tomorrow. Smokey will be joining Abigail for them. Now she's supposed to be preparing their personnel files. Instead, she keeps wondering why she has such negative feelings towards Louisa.

She first met Louisa at the gathering called by Jerome J. Ratley outside City Hall. She'd just become part of the web design team. Jasmine introduced her and the rest of the team to Smokey. Louisa been standing on one leg and stretched out the one she'd been holding up to shake Smokey's paw. Louisa hadn't said much.

Since that time Smokey has seen her only in the company of Jasmine. Each time, Smokey had had little success in engaging her in conversation. She was aloof with a regal attitude. At least that's how Smokey read it. Oh, she was polite enough, but standoffish. Louisa is not the sort Smokey ever would have expected Jasmine to hit it off with.

I just don't get it, thinks Smokey. Even if they make good business partners, why would Jasmine want to hang out with Louisa outside of the office? She didn't seem upset about meeting with her on Saturday and she'd sounded excited to go shopping with her when Smokey had called her before.

Will she take my place as Jasmine's best friend? I can't believe I'm thinking this. Am I in Junior High again?

Smokey opens Claudia's file and forces herself to focus on its contents.

She's halfway through when her office phone rings. It's Miguel Gato.

"I want to give Abigail and Greyson something very special for a wedding present. How about some help?"

"Do you have anything in mind?"

"Perhaps. Do you know where they're going for their honeymoon?"

"I don't think they've settled on anything yet."

"Could you try to find out and let me know as soon as it's definite? I thought I'd have some surprises waiting for them when they arrive."

"Sounds intriguing. I'll do my best."

"Thanks, Smokerina."

Once Smokey has finished with the personnel files, she takes them back to Abigail's office.

"Abigail," she says, setting them on her desk. "I think the reviews should go well tomorrow. They're all doing a fine job."

"Yes, they are. I've always been very careful when I hire. Have we talked about hiring? No? Sit down, Smokerina. We should go over what to look for when hiring for each position."

They spend the next hour discussing the best attributes for perspective employees. When they finish, Smokey asks, "Have you and Greyson decided on a honeymoon destination yet?"

"We have narrowed it down to a few. Take a look," she says pulling some travel brochures from her drawer.

Smokey picks up the brochures. There is one for Santorini in Greece, one for Tanzania, and one for Moracco.

"Which are you leaning towards?"

Abigail laughs. "I change my mind daily. It's worse than the wedding planning."

"What about Greyson? Which does he favor?"

"We chose three mutual favorites. That's how we got to these," she says tapping a paw on the brochures. "I wish I'd told him to pick one instead of three because now he says I have to make the final choice."

"Why not just pick one and save the others for another time?"

"Yes, but which one?"

Smokey shrugs. "Isn't there one that stands out?"

"They all do. That's the problem. Which would you choose?"

"I'd have to research them. Have you been to any?"

"I've been to Greece, but not to Santorini. I've not been to the other two. Greyson has been everywhere. That's why it doesn't matter as much to him. Oh, I know," she says, with the look of sudden inspiration. "You pick!"

"What?"

"Research them. Then you decide for us."

"But Abigail, you asked which one I would choose. I'd be looking for the things that interest me."

"Any one of them will be fantastic so you can't go wrong. I want it taken out of my paws. Now, I have work to do, so ta-ta."

Smokey returns to her office with the brochures. *How do I get myself into these things?* she wonders.

She's not sure which one she'd choose either. She picks up her phone and calls Miguel. Maybe he can help. He's been everywhere.

"Abigail says whichever one I pick is where they'll go," she explains.

"How did you get her to agree to that?"

"It was her idea."

"What are the choices?"

"Santorini, Tanzania, or Morocco.

There is silence for a moment. "Tanzania," Miguel finally says. And, I now have the perfect idea for their wedding gift. Give Abigail a few days before you tell her, so she thinks you put a lot of effort into it. Now, I need to call a zebra."

* * *

Jasmine stares at Smokey. "That is amazing, absolutely pawsome!"

Smokey is sitting on the chocolate brown sofa tucked between two built-in cabinets in Jasmine's living room. She loves Jasmine's apartment. It's nothing like Abigail Fluffington's luxury apartment, but then what is? Jasmine's place is small but filled with clean white lines interspersed with pops of color here and there. Sliding glass doors lead onto a balcony where they often sit in the warm months.

Jasmine had called her this morning to say she couldn't get together with her on Sunday, after all, and would she like to come to her apartment for dinner after work?

Smokey explained everything about her littermates while they ate. Now they are sitting in the living room enjoying a glass of wine.

"Winthrop could be alive, too? And you could find him?" Jasmine asks.

"It's possible."

"Wouldn't that be something! What about Marlon and Sasha? What are they like?"

"They seem great. Marlon is a captain in the West Lake Fire Department and Sasha is an interior decorator. She showed me photos of her work. It's terrific. She specializes in decorating the homes of cats and owls. You know how owls live in tree hollows? Well, I never realized how much room there is in some of them. The rooms are stacked one on top of the other going up the tree trunk. Some of the pictures she showed me had really cool spiral staircases. She uses a lot of wood in her owl house decorating. They're partial to it."

"Sounds fascinating. Would you consider doing architecture for owl houses?"

"I'd have to study it, but it might be very interesting."

"What did Autumn think of your littermates?"

"You know Autumn. She likes everyfur. We're having a Hunter's Moon Night party at our place. Sasha and Marlon are going to help us plan it. We're going to invite friends and neighbors so that our two new neighbors can get to know everyfur and feather. Especially Buster."

"So, things are going well for Autumn and Buster?"

"They seem to be."

"Still concerned? You were all wound up over making sure he was right for her."

"I'm trying to let her be her own cat and make her own decisions. Buster seems very nice. I think he really cares for her. She seems to be crazy about him."

"How exciting for her."

"I guess it is."

"You don't sound enthused. You do want her to be happy, don't you?"

"Of course. But it's a big change."

"Not all change is bad, you know."

"It's my nature to resist it. You help me see the good side of things. I've missed talking with you lately."

"I'm sorry about that. We're so busy with the new business."

"I'm glad it's a success. You are such a hard worker and very talented. You've got a great publicist, too."

Jasmine gives her a questioning look. "Thanks. But Louisa is a big part of our success, too."

"I'm sure," says Smokey.

"You don't like her, do you?"

"I barely know her."

"True. I wish you did. She's got great ideas for the business, she's smart, and she can be a lot of fun."

"Really?" Louisa, fun? That she can't picture.

"Why do you question it?"

"She seems standoffish to me."

"How so?"

"She hardly says anything. She stands around, barely moving."

"Smokey, she's a great blue heron! That's what they do." Jasmine laughs. "Not all the time. Mostly when she's contemplating something. It's how she comes up with her best ideas. I wish I could do it."

Smokey shrugs. "As long as she is a good business partner for you, that's what matters."

Jasmine's phone rings. "Just a minute," she says.

It's obvious from their conversation that it's Louisa. They chat for a few minutes, then Jasmine says, "Hey, Louisa, my friend Smokey is here. We had dinner together and we're catching up. Can we talk about this tomorrow?"

"She monopolizes your time, Jasmine?" The words are out of Smokey's mouth as soon as Jasmine ends the call.

Jasmine flashes her a surprised look. "Are you jealous?" she asks.

"Of course not!"

"You sound it."

"She could let you have an evening in peace."

Jasmine heaves a heavy sigh. "Smokey. Look at all the work you're doing for your new position. You've even gone back to school. Things will settle down eventually for both of us. Hey, I know! When that happens, let's make plans for you, me, and Louisa to get together. If you got to know her better, you'd like her."

"Maybe," says Smokey.

"It's not fair of you to judge her when you barely know her."

Smokey knows Jasmine's right. She doesn't even understand why she dislikes Louisa. "Okay," says Smokey. "Let's try it."

"Great! Now, tell me about your courses."

Chapter 14
Autumn's Decision

Autumn hasn't even rolled out of bed when her cell phone rings. It's Monday, one of the two days she bakes for Furry Confections.

"Hi Tabby," she says with a yawn.

"I'm sorry to bother you this early, but Alvin called in sick so I'm short a regular baker. Would you bake enough tuna chip cookies for the day first thing? I'll send the squirrel brothers to pick them up as soon as they're ready."

"Okay. Sure. I think I have the ingredients."

Autumn stumbles down the stairs, through the kitchen, and into the pantry, willing herself to wake up enough to know what she's doing. After checking her supplies, she tells Tabby, "I don't have enough tuna chips, but I'm good on everything else."

"Enough to get started?"

"Yes. Just not enough for a whole day."

"Okay. You get started baking and I'll send the squirrels over with more."

"Sure," says Autumn, dropping into a kitchen chair and laying her head on the table.

She soon starts snoring.

"This is for you, Autumn. Autumn?" Smokey's voice barely registers.

"Huh?" she asks, sitting up.

"Didn't you hear the doorbell?"

"No."

"It was the squirrels. They left this for you." Smokey places a bag of tuna chips on the table in front of Autumn.

"Oh. Yeah."

"Autumn, are you okay?"

"Tired. It was crazy all weekend at the restaurant."

"You should give up this baking job. You're exhausting yourself."

"I know, but Tabby will have her paws full with extra orders soon. Now that it's October, everyfur will want Hunter's Moon Night goodies for their parties."

Smokey grabs a bowl, spoon, and a box of Crunchy Purrs. "She handled it before you started working for her."

"But her business has grown since then."

"Because of you. Leave all your recipes with her. Your chefs at Mama Cat's have learned to make your recipes. I'm sure Tabby and her bakers can do the same."

Autumn doesn't respond. She knows Smokey is right. But she doesn't want to leave Tabby in the lurch with the approaching holiday.

"Don't forget," Smokey continues, pouring milk over her Crunchy Purrs, "you will be coordinating our Hunter's Moon Night party."

"At least I'll have a lot of help with that."

"You'll still end up doing most of the cooking. Then there's Greyson's and Abigail's wedding."

Autumn winces.

"And how will you make time for Buster? Monday and Tuesday are your only free days, so it's just a couple of evenings a week you've got for him.

Autumn grabs the box of Crunchy Purrs, dumps some on the table, and eats them dry.

"I just want to help Tabby get through the holiday."

"Good luck with that," says Smokey, carrying her empty bowl to the sink before she exits the kitchen.

Autumn swipes her phone screen, looking for the list of specialty items she knows Tabby will have texted to her. Her heart sinks.

12 Apple sardine blondies
12 Mini pumpkin and mackerel pies
2 dozen Maple cookies with ocean white fish frosting
5 Pumpkin catnip spice cakes
12 Apple cider cod muffins
4 Caramel-covered tuna bread puddings
2 Pumpkin trout bundt cakes with salmon frosting
5 Flounder apple crisps
 2 Loaves of baked halibut pumpkin bread

The list is double the usual size and it's not even close enough to Hunter's Moon Night for these to be for parties. While she's contemplating the best order for coordinating her baking, another text appears from Tabby.

I just got a request from a Robin family for a worm-berry cake for a birthday party. Please add that to your list. I'll send the squirrels back with some worms and berries.

"Sheesh!" Autumn says aloud. "How am I supposed to do all this?"

Is the worm-berry cake for today or tomorrow? she texts back.

It's for pickup tomorrow morning. You can make it last today.

Give me time to make the tuna chip cookies before you send the squirrels so I can send some back with them.

Autumn throws her apron over her nightgown then gets started on the tuna chip cookies. As she's mixing the dough, she hears the clack of Smokey's feet on the stairs.

"I'm leaving, Autumn. See you after work," she calls.

While the first batch of cookies is baking, Autumn sets out everything she will need for the day feeling as though she's sleepwalking. It's going to take half the morning to bake all the tuna chip cookies the bakery will need for the day. They're one of the biggest sellers. No matter how many are made, they sell out. It wouldn't be so bad if she was in the bakery's kitchen with their industrial ovens. She looks at the list again and wonders how she'll get to them all.

After the third batch of cookies comes out of the oven, Autumn texts Tabby again.

Are all the orders for today?

She goes to the pantry for a bag of moth flour. She sets it down on the table with a thud. A poof of flour explodes into the air making her cough and sneeze.

It's not until after the fourth batch of cookies is ready that Tabby texts her back.

The last four can wait until tomorrow.

Well, that's something, but it still leaves five recipes that she has to make today. No, six. The worm-berry cake.

She's just pulled the fifth batch of tuna chip cookies from the oven when the doorbell rings. She glances out the living room window as she heads to the door and sees Simon and Sam Squirrel's tandem bicycle in the driveway.

When Autumn opens the door, the squirrels start to say, "Good morning, Miss Aut..." then stop dead, their mouths hanging open. Simon falls backwards right off the front step.

"What on earth is wrong with you boys?" she asks. "Simon, are you okay?"

Neither speaks. They both continue to stare at her.

"Did you bring the worms and berries?"

"Uh-huh," says Sam. He holds up a bag. Autumn takes it from him.

"That's the worms," she says. "What about the berries?"

"Here," says Simon, getting up and handing her a small bucket.

"Thank you. Wait here and I'll get the cookies."

She leaves the worms and berries on the counter and returns with five boxes of tuna chip cookies.

"Here you, go," she says, handing the stack to them. They still haven't stopped staring at her.

"Miss Autumn," says Sam. "Are you a ghost?"

"You're all white and dusty," blurts Simon.

"I suppose I need to go clean up. Go on with those cookies," says Autumn. "Tabby is waiting for them. I'll see you boys when I've got more things ready to go."

After the squirrels leave, Autumn runs upstairs. Entering the bathroom, she looks in the mirror and nearly jumps out of her fur. Her face is covered in moth flour and there are remnants of the tuna chips she's been munching hanging from her whiskers. Quickly, she gets washed and dressed then runs back downstairs to the kitchen.

Next up are the apple sardine blondies. While she's coring and paring the apples, her phone rings. It's Rueben, a fox, one of the prep chefs at Mama Cat's Kitchen.

"Chef Autumn, we can't find the prep sheets anywhere," he tells her, referring to the papers that tell them how much of each food to prepare for the day.

"Aren't they on the bulletin board?" she asks.

"No, and they're not on the clip board either."

"They must be in my office then. Check my desk. I'll wait."

A few minutes later, Rueben picks up the phone again. "Not there."

"Is Sally in yet?"

"Yes."

"Put her on the phone, please."

"Good morning, Autumn," says Sally's perky voice.

"Good morning. Rueben says he can't find the prep sheets. I thought I posted them on the bulletin board like usual last night. I hate to ask you this, but can you write up new ones?"

"You wanted me to do the inventory this morning."

"Well, the prep sheets have to come first. Start on inventory afterwards. If you don't have a chance to finish, you can do it tomorrow."

"Okay. I'll take care of it."

"Thanks, Sally. You're the best."

With that issue settled, Autumn returns to the apple paring. No sooner are the blondies in the oven than she realizes she doesn't have enough mackerel for twelve mini pumpkin and mackerel pies. She texts Tabby asking her to send the squirrels back with some mackerel, then moves on to maple cookies with ocean whitefish frosting.

The cookies are baking, and Autumn is mixing up the frosting when Tabby calls.

"I don't have enough mackerel. I thought you had everything," Tabby tells her.

"That was before you sent me the list. I didn't know I was going to need it."

"I'll have to send the squirrels to the fish market. Will you need anything else?"

"I've got all the rest."

"Okay. I'll tell Simon and Sam to take the mackerel straight to you. Take however much you need. You can give them whatever else you have ready when they get there."

By the time the squirrels get to her house with the mackerel, Autumn has the cookies baked and frosted and three of the pumpkin catnip spice cakes in the oven.

She watches the squirrels breathe a heavy sigh of relief when she opens the door to find her presentable.

"I'm not so scary looking anymore?" she asks.

"Now you look like Miss Autumn again," says Sam.

"Yeah," says Simon. "Ghost Autumn scared us."

"Scared me, too, when I looked in the mirror," she says with a laugh.

"Miss Autumn, what are you going to do for Hunter's Moon Night?" asks Sam.

"We're having a party. Would you boys like to come?"

The two squirrels jump up and down yelling, "Yes! Yes! Party! Party!" then scamper to the nearest tree, chasing each other in a spiral up the trunk.

"Boys!" calls Autumn. "There's no time for this. Please, come down and take what I have ready back to Furry's."

They race back to her doorstep, coming to a sudden halt right in front of her.

"That's better," says Autumn, handing them everything that's ready to go. "I'll be sure you get invitations."

"Thank you, Miss Autumn," they say in unison before running off to secure the packages to the wagon attached to their tandem bike. "See you later," they call.

When Autumn returns to the kitchen, she realizes it's lunch time. After clearing a space on the table, she makes herself a sandwich and sits down to eat. She's about halfway through lunch when her cell phone rings. It's Buster.

"I hope I'm not disturbing you," says Buster. "I know you're baking for Furry's today."

"I'm taking my lunch break. What's up?"

"The weather is supposed to be nice tomorrow. I'm going to take the boat out. It might be the last time this year. Would you like to go?"

"Aren't you working tomorrow?"

"Normally, yes, but Scottie, my assistant can take over. It might be the last really nice day. What do you say?"

"Let me talk to Tabby. I usually bake Mondays and Tuesdays, but if she can give me tomorrow's list by this afternoon, I can work late and get it all done."

"Don't run your paws off. There's always next year."

"Don't worry," she says. "It will be worth it."

"Can I pick you up around seven thirty tomorrow morning?"

"Sure," says Autumn wondering if she'll even be able to prop her eyes open by then.

"Great! See you then."

"Oh my," says Autumn aloud. She calls Tabby to ask her to text tomorrow's list as soon as she has it.

"How will you get it to me?" Tabby asks.

"If I can finish everything in time, I'll have the squirrels bring it over. If not, I'll bring it myself. How late will you be there?"

"I can stay until nine or nine-thirty. Autumn, is Buster this special?"

"He really is, Tabby."

"Alright. I'll start sending the special orders for tomorrow. Just don't forget about the worm-berry cake."

"I'll get everything done and to you before you leave tonight."

Autumn flips into high gear as soon as she gets off the phone. She wishes she had a bigger oven. Then inspiration strikes. She packs up everything she'll need and heads for Mama Cat's Kitchen.

"What are you doing here?" asks Sally when Autumn arrives loaded down with bags of supplies.

"I need the industrial ovens."

"What about our patrons?" Sukey demands. "We need the ovens to cook for them."

"I'll use my section in the back," says Autumn. "Pretend I'm not here."

Tabby texts orders to her in dribs and drabs. Just as the restaurant staff is preparing for the dinner rush, Autumn's phone rings.

"Autumn, where are you?" asks a frantic sounding Tabby.

"At Mama Cat's Kitchen. Why?"

"I sent the squirrel brothers to your house, and they came back saying no one was there. I was in a panic."

I'm sorry, Tabby," she says. "I should have told you. I was in a hurry and not thinking."

"If you wanted to use bigger ovens, you could have come here."

Autumn feels her face flush under her fur. "You're right. I'm so sorry. Please, tell Simon and Sam not to go back to my house today. I'll get everything done and bring it to you before I go home."

"Do you have any birch tree bark?"

"Maybe. I'll check our inventory."

"I figured you wouldn't have any at home. That's why I sent the squirrels. We just got an order from a beaver who wants a peppermint birch bark pound cake."

"We make them here. I'm sure we have the ingredients. Just text me the order."

"Okay," says Tabby. "But next time, Autumn, please just come here if you need the bigger ovens."

"I will. Sorry, again," says Autumn.

After ending the call, Autumn feels like she's been reprimanded. That's hard to take while standing in the kitchen of her own restaurant.

Tabby is a business owner, too, she reminds herself. *She's just taking care of her own business.* Still, it rankles.

It's quarter of nine by the time Autumn finishes the last order, packs everything up, and heads for Furry Confections. She never stopped for supper. For once, she's glad she munches while she cooks, or she'd be ravenous.

On the drive back to Wild Whisker Ridge, she mulls over what to say to Tabby. She still hasn't decided by the time she arrives.

"That's everything," she says as she brings the last of the orders into the bakery. "Again, I'm sorry, but I need to let you know that I simply can't do the specialty baking for you anymore. I'll continue until you can find someone to take my place, and I'll give you all the recipes for my desserts. I hope you understand."

Tabby stares at her, dumbfounded. Finally, she says, "What took you so long?"

"What?" asks Autumn.

"I never thought you'd still be doing this over a year after starting Mama Cat's."

"Why didn't you say anything?"

"It's your decision. It was your specialty items that have put Furry Confections on the map. I can't tell you how pleased I am that you're going to leave your recipes with me. I'll put an ad online for a new specialty baker tomorrow. With your recipes to work with, I'm sure I'll be overloaded with applicants."

"So, you're not upset?"

"I honestly don't know how you kept up with it this long."

Autumn's stomach gives a loud growl.

Tabby's eyes grow wide. "*You* skipped supper to finish two day's work so you can go out with a mancat tomorrow?"

"Um...yeah. I guess I did."

"I made stew. There's plenty left. Come in my office and have a bowl." Tabby glances at her sideways and, giving her a soft hip check says, "And tell me all about this Buster."

Chapter 15
Smooth Sailing

Autumn stands on the deck of the Sea Nip letting the breeze flutter her whiskers. She breathes deeply of the salty air. Looking out over the expanse of blue, she feels free. No thoughts of work, party planning, or anything else. She's at one with the sea, the wind, and the sky. Her thoughts drift to the glass pirate ship in her closet, then to herself as Pirate Queen of the High Seas. In her imagination, she stands with feet firmly planted, a cutlass at her waist, and a spyglass in her paw as she calls orders to her crew.

"You look lost in thought." Autumn jumps as Buster strolls up beside her.

"I didn't mean to startle you," he says.

"I was daydreaming."

"About what?"

There is no way she's going to tell him, so instead she says, "About how beautiful the sea and sky are. Such incredible shades of blue." This isn't a lie. She had been thinking that before drifting into her pirate fantasies. These are tremendously private. She's never told a soul about them. Not even Smokey.

"There's only one thing that makes this scene more beautiful," says Buster. "Having you in it."

His eyes gaze into hers.

"Such a smooth talker," she says, teasing.

"Simply a truth-teller," he counters.

"Wait!" says Autumn, startled. "If you're here, who's at the wheel?"

"Buster laughs. "It's on autopilot."

"It can do that?"

"Yes."

"I don't know anything about boats."

"Would you like to learn?"

"I would love to. I've always wanted to."

"Well, now you can. Come with me."

Buster leads her to the helm.

"The Sea Nip has a center console," he explains. "It's where all the controls are located. Here is the radio, the trim control, the ignition. And, of course, this is the steering wheel."

Autumn looks at all the screens and buttons. "How did you learn to pilot a boat?" she asks.

"I practically grew up on my parents' boat. They taught me a lot, but I did take courses in boating safety."

"Wow." Autumn runs her paws lightly over the equipment.

"Would you like to try steering?" he asks.

"Are you sure it's safe?"

Buster laughs. "It's not like you're going to run into anything."

"What if I hit a whale?"

He laughs harder. "They're good at staying out of the way."

"Well, if you're sure." Her heart is pounding with excitement. She can't wait to get her paws on the wheel.

"I'll take it off autopilot and it's all yours."

"Is it like driving a car?" she asks.

"Not exactly. A boat depends on thrust for steering. Turning is different depending on how fast you're going. Here, take the wheel."

Autumn steps up, puts her paws on the wheel.

"We're going slowly now. Turn the wheel."

She does and the boat gently turns.

"Now, I'll increase the thrust," he says, moving a lever near the wheel making the boat speed up. "Try turning the wheel now. Gently."

Autumn turns to the right. The boat makes a more dramatic turn.

"That was smooth," says Buster. "You're a natural."

A smile spreads across Autumn's face. She loves the feel of the increased speed. "Can I try again?" she asks.

"Sure, but always remember to look around first. Make sure there are no other boats close by or big waves."

She looks in all directions, sees nothing but a shimmering expanse of blue, so turns the wheel to the left this time.

"Shall I speed it up more?" Buster asks.

"Do it!"

He increases the thrust so that they are zipping along the water.

"I'm going to turn now," she says. Careful to look around first, she turns the wheel even more gently than before.

"Great," he says. "I wasn't kidding. You really are a natural."

"I love this!" Autumn yells over the roar of the boat's engine as a sense of euphoria overtakes her.

"See that?" Buster calls, pointing ahead. "That's a channel marker."

She can barely make out something floating in the water.

"What's a channel marker?" she asks.

"An aid to navigation. It's like a road sign. It tells you where you are. Some are red and some are green. When heading into open water, keep the red ones on your left and the green on your right. Reverse that when heading inland. Think 'red right returning' and you'll remember it. Now, head towards the marker."

With slight adjustments to the wheel, Autumn steers in the direction of the red buoy marker. As she approaches, she turns the wheel just enough to pass by with the marker to the left of the boat.

"Brilliant!" says Buster. "It's like you've been boating your whole life."

Autumn is giddy with delight.

"Too bad it's the end of the season. But you could take the online course in boating safety during the off season. Then next year you'll be ready."

"I'll do that," she says.

"I'll be happy to help you study," says Buster.

"I'll have time now that I've quit baking for Furry's."

"When did that happen?"

"Yesterday. I'll keep baking until Tabby finds a replacement. That's only fair, but then I'm done."

"Good for you," he says. "Are you hungry? I packed a lunch for us."

"Sure." Her tummy has been rumbling for a while, but she doesn't want to tell him that.

Buster cuts the engine so they can drift while they enjoy their egg salad sandwiches and iced tea.

"It's such a warm day, it's hard to believe that Hunter's Moon Night isn't far away. The weather will surely have changed by then," he says.

"That reminds me," says Autumn. "We're having a Hunter's Moon Night party at our house. We specifically want you and Professor Chewy to come. We're going to invite other neighbors and some friends so that you can get to know them."

"That's so thoughtful of you. I'd be delighted. Can I bring anything?"

"I'll let you know after Smokey and I get together with Marlon and Sasha to plan."

"Who are Marlon and Sasha?"

Autumn figures it's okay to tell Buster. "It's an amazing story," she says, then launches into the entire account.

"Astonishing!" says Buster when she finishes. "I hope they find Winthrop."

"Me, too. Marlon and Sasha are Smokey's littermates, but they're also my siblings. It's surreal to find that they're alive and to meet them. Sasha had a good idea that we should work together on this party to start doing family things. But it feels weird when we barely know them."

"That will change over time, I think. You know, Autumn, I'm glad you quit the job with Furry's for your own sake, but I have to admit I have a selfish reason for being glad, too."

"Oh?"

"I hope it means that you and I can spend more time together."

Autumn smiles. "That was a consideration when I made the decision."

"I'm glad to hear that. I like spending time with you. You are the most interesting cat I've ever met. Not to mention the prettiest." He reaches out to stroke her fur. "I love your calico markings."

"Thank you."

"I'd like for us to be a couple. Would you like that?"

Autumn's heart flutters. "Yes, I would. Very much."

Buster smiles then closes his eyes half-way. Autumn does the same. Then his lips touch hers in their first kiss.

When Autumn returns to the cottage, she cannot imagine a more perfect day.

"Autumn," says Smokey, running to meet her at the door. "Archer called Marlon to say he has a lead on Winthrop!"

Chapter 16
Making Plans

"Winthrop's alive?"

Smokey watches Autumn's expression change from dreamy to surprised.

"Archer's not certain, but he found a cat who fits the description," Smokey explains.

"Let's sit," says Autumn. "I want to hear everything."

Once they settle on the couch, Smokey says, "Archer's been following up on some leads from chipmunks who live in Oakton. They know of a kitten who showed up there around the same time that Winthrop disappeared. He fits Winthrop's physical description. Apparently, he was taken in by squirrels."

"Is he still there?"

"They haven't seen him in a while, but he and the squirrels come and go a lot. One of them will call Archer as soon as they see him again."

"Oh, Smokey, wouldn't that be amazing!"

"I'm trying not to get my hopes up. It might not be him."

"What do Marlon and Sasha think?"

"The same. Hoping, but not expecting."

"Probably the best option."

"Yeah, but it's hard not to think about the possibility."

"Even if it's not him, Archer won't drop the case. He's a shih tzu. They never give up."

"True. Now, tell me about your day on Buster's boat."

"Oh, Smokey, Buster let me pilot. I loved it. I'm going to take boating safety lessons online and get a certificate. I think I could live on a boat."

Smokey can't keep her mind totally off the possibility of finding Winthrop.

"And now we are officially a couple. He even kissed me."

"What?" asks Smokey, fully reengaged.

Autumn sighs. "He said he wanted us to be a couple, and I said I wanted that to. So now we are. And he kissed me. It was pure heaven."

"Oh," says Smokey. "That's great. Don't go too fast, though."

Smokey's cell phone purrs. "It's Sasha," she says before answering.

"Smokey, when is a good time for all of us to get together to plan the Hunter's Moon Night Party?"

"Autumn's got the toughest schedule. Let me see what works for her."

Autumn thinks for a moment. "Have them come to dinner at Mama Cat's on Saturday. We can all meet in my office afterwards."

Sasha agrees. Smokey enters it into her calendar.

"By the way, Smokey, I told Buster about the party and about your littermates. That news nearly blew his whiskers off. I hope you don't mind."

"Tell whoever you want."

* * *

"That was a fabulous meal, Autumn Amelia," says Marlon as they gather in her office after dinner.

"I'm glad you enjoyed it."

"Let's get the party planned," says Smokey taking out a pad of paper and a pen from her purse.

"Oh no!" says Marlon, melodramatically slapping a paw to his forehead. "You too?"

"What?" asks Smokey.

"Sasha is Miss Super Organized, too."

Smokey and Sasha look at each other. Seeing that they've each pulled a pad of paper and a pen from their purses at the same moment, they burst out laughing.

"Littermates!" exclaims Autumn.

"Look alike and act alike," Marlon chimes in, a big grin splitting his face.

"Wait until you meet Smokey's friend Jasmine," Autumn tells him. "Another Russian Blue. Looks just like Smokey and ultra organized. Everyfur thinks they're twins."

"Great Creator help us!" says Marlon.

"Who will write everything down?" asks Sasha. "We don't both need to."

Smokey hates losing the feeling of control. Before she can say anything, Autumn says, "Both of you. You'll each have your precious list. Now let's get started."

Smokey asks, "Invitation list first?"

"Is there any fur or feather you'd like to invite?" asks Autumn.

"Not for this party," says Marlon. "At some point we'd like to have you over to meet our friends."

"We'd love that. Wouldn't we, Smokey?" says Autumn.

"Definitely."

"Okay, then we'll move right to the food," says Autumn.

"Before we do that, let's make headings for each thing we're going to discuss," says Sasha. "I'll put down invitations even though you'll be handling them. There's food, decorations, what else?"

"I was about to suggest we do that," says Smokey feeling her kinship with Sasha grow despite the eye rolls from Autumn and Marlon.

"Marlon," says Smokey. "Will you change seats with me? I'd like to sit next to Sasha so we can compare notes and make sure our lists match perfectly."

"Good idea," says Sasha.

Marlon, amused, swaps seats.

"If you've both got the heading FOOD on your papers now, can we get started?" asks Autumn.

"Go ahead," says Sasha. "You're the expert. Tell us what we should have."

"Oh, my catness, look at them," Autumn says, nudging Marlon.

Smokey and Sasha glance at each other. Both of them are sitting with the pad of paper in one paw and their pen poised over it ready to write.

"I'm seeing double," says Marlon.

"We're waiting," says Sasha, tapping one paw on the floor.

Suppressing a laugh, Autumn says, "Let's start with the traditional Hunter's Moon Night food. Pumpkin tuna cornbread, goat cheese cranberry cheese balls, ocean whitefish frosted apple cider donuts, cheddar cheese and catnip crackers, cranberry niptinis, and matatabi-spiked apple cider. And, of course, Hunter's Moon Night cake."

"Not all the guests are cats?" asks Marlon.

"No, it will be a mix. Cats, dogs, birds, rodents," says Smokey. "We'll need to be sure we have things they like, too."

"Of course," says Autum. "I'll make a sunflower seed, cranberry, pumpkin seed mix, mini mixed nut and peanut butter cakes, and bacon-wrapped apple slices."

"Don't forget shrimp for Greyson," says Smokey.

"Never," says Autumn. "There will be too many of us for a sit-down dinner, so I thought a buffet would be best. What do you think of a crab and pumpkin lasagna?"

Murmurs of *oohh, yum,* and *scrumptious* fill the office.

"I'll also make some meatball sliders, variations on the lasagna with acorns instead of crab for the rodents, and worms and berries for the birds, and some fried fish. Now for desserts. Pumpkin pecan cheesecake, cranberry tuna and sardine chip cookies, and salmon ice cream with matatabi shavings. Anything else?"

Smokey's mouth is watering just thinking about it. "Will you get Sukey and Sally to help you?" asks Smokey.

"They're going to be guests. I can't ask them to help. Maybe I'll hire one or two of my prep chefs. They'd probably like earning a little extra cash."

"Now for the decorations," says Sasha. "I was thinking of creating a display of pumpkins in various sizes and colors, and some orange, red, brown, and maroon balloons, made of crepe paper. That way they won't pop if someone accidentally puts a claw in them. We could have a nice bouquet of fall flowers on the table. Is there a good place to hang a Happy Hunter's Moon Night banner?"

"We usually put the moon up in a corner of the living room," says Smokey. "Maybe the banner could go on one of the walls."

"Can I come over and look around?" asks Sasha. "I'd like to get a look at the place with an eye for decorating."

"Can you come tomorrow?"

"Sure. Oh, this is really getting exciting!"

Smokey and Sasha both squeal in delight, their voices almost identical.

"Orange tablecloths," Sasha continues. "Autumn, do you have any brown serving dishes?"

"A few."

"Count them. We'll pick up some more. Smokey, do you want to go shopping?"

Smokey is ready to jump out of her fur with excitement. "Do I ever!"

"We'll do that tomorrow, too. Why don't we hold off on writing down the rest of the decorations until we're in the cottage and can decide what would work best?"

"Perfect," says Smokey. "What's left to plan?"

"How about entertainment?" says Marlon. "And what time should the party start?"

"Seven, if that works for you two" says Sasha. "Not too late for dinner, but not too early a start for a party that always goes past midnight."

"We have a recording of traditional Hunter's Moon Night songs," Autumn says.

"Since there will be several furs and feathers who don't know each other," says Smokey, "we should come up with a few ice breakers."

"I have a friend who's great at those," says Sasha. "I'll ask her."

"Sounds good," says Smokey. "We're all set for now and ready for invitations."

"We can pick some up tomorrow while we're shopping," says Sasha.

As they are ending the planning meeting, Marlon's cell phone rings.

"It's Archer," he says. "I'll put it on speaker phone."

"Hi Archer," says Marlon. "Perfect timing. We're all here."

"Good. The cat I think might be Winthrop is back in Oakton. Tomorrow, I'll talk to him and let you know what happens."

There is a collective intake of breath in the room. Sasha says to Smokey, "I'm glad we'll be busy. I don't think I could stand the wait."

"Paws crossed, but hopes not too far up," says Marlon.

* * *

After looking over the living and dining rooms in the cottage, Smokey and Sasha head out to BarkMart, the biggest department store in Faunaburg. In the car they chatter about the party and the decorations.

Smokey gets the strong feeling that they are both purposely avoiding the subject of Winthrop.

"They put the Hunter's Moon Night stuff out in August," says Sasha as they enter BarkMart. "Earlier every year."

"Good for us," says Smokey.

"Indeed," agrees Sasha, pulling the list they'd made at the cottage from her pocketbook. "Let's get started. We'll need a cart."

Smokey loses herself in the quest for party decorations, tablecloths, and serving bowls. Every time her mind wanders to Winthrop, she pulls it back to the task at paw.

"Oh, look at this," says Sasha, holding up a lighted maple tree. "We could set some of these on the buffet table. They go great with the lighted maple leaf garland."

"Perfect," Smokey agrees. "How many do you think we'll need?"

"Four should be enough," she says, adding them to their cart.

"I think the dishes are down this aisle," says Smokey.

Heading down the next aisle they find a huge selection of fall-themed serving dishes and dinnerware.

"Is Autumn making soup?" asks Sasha.

"I don't think so," says Smokey. "Let me look at my list." She pulls it from her purse. "No soup."

"Too bad. Look at this." Sasha holds up a soup tureen shaped like a pumpkin. "And these go with it," she says, pointing to a set of matching bowls with lids.

"They're adorable," says Smokey. "Autumn would love them. I'm going to call her."

After getting the okay from Autumn to add butternut squash bisque to the food list, they place the tureen and bowls in their cart.

"Oh, look!" says Smokey. "There's more in the same pattern. Here's a baking dish that's just right for lasagna. We'd better get three since she's making three different types."

"And serving bowls and platters," says Sasha. "Oh, and look, a cake stand, perfect for the Hunter's Moon Night cake. Should we get the whole set?"

"Yes," says Smokey. "But I think we should use paper plates for the food. Let's see if we can find some with a similar pattern."

After placing all the serving ware into the cart, they search through the sets of paper plates. A large blue wing crosses Smokey's paw.

"Excuse me, please," says the wing's owner.

Smokey looks up to see Louisa standing next to her.

"Oh," says Louisa. "You're Smokey? Jasmine's friend."

"Yes. Hi Louisa," she says, unable to make her voice sound friendly.

Louisa glances at Sasha. "This isn't your littermate, is it?" she asks.

Smokey takes a step back. Jasmine must have told Louisa.

"Hi, I'm Sasha," says Sasha, reaching out a paw.

"Louisa," she says, lifting a leg to shake. "Smokey's best friend, Jasmine, and I are business partners. We own Blue Landing Web Design. It's nice to meet you. Jasmine told me your amazing reunion story."

Smokey watches this exchange. Apparently, Jasmine is telling Louisa everything these days.

"Well," says Smokey. "We've got a lot of shopping to do."

"Of course. I won't hold you up. Give my best to Autumn Amelia."

"I take it she's not your favorite feather," says Sasha once Louisa is out of earshot.

"It shows?"

"In neon lights. Why don't you like her?"

"I'm not sure. That's what bothers me. There's just something about her that rubs my fur backwards."

"Jasmine must get along well enough with her if they've gone into business together."

"Mm. Louisa and Jasmine have become very tight," she says, nearly biting off the last word.

"Is that the problem?"

"What do you mean?"

"Jasmine is your best friend, but now she's gotten awfully chummy with the heron."

"They're business partners so they have to spend a lot of time together. I understand that. I don't know what it is."

"Maybe a simple clash of personalities, then. These plates are a pretty close match. What do you think?"

"Looks good. We'll need a lot. Cups and napkins, too."

Once back in the car, Smokey becomes very quiet.

"What are you thinking about?" asks Sasha. "Winthrop?"

"No. I was thinking about what you said about my not liking Louisa because she's getting close to Jasmine. You might be right."

"Really?"

"Jasmine asked me if I was jealous. I said no, but I'm starting to wonder."

"Doesn't Jasmine have any other friends?"

"Sure. Lots."

"Are you jealous of them?"

"Not at all. But I'm her best friend. Other furs and feathers who see us together for the first time think we're twins."

"She's a Russian Blue."

"Uh-huh. We do everything together. We tell each other everything. We're *best* friends."

"You think Louisa's trying to usurp your place? She must have her own friends. She probably has a best friend who's a heron or some other wading bird."

"I don't get to see much of Jasmine anymore. She's always with Louisa."

"She wasn't with her today."

"True."

"And neither were you. You were with me. I've just waltzed into your life, and I am trying to get close to you. Do you think Jasmine will become jealous of me?"

That thought has never occurred to Smokey.

"She's going to have to not mind being mistaken for triplets now." Sasha laughs.

Thinking of Jasmine being jealous of Sasha makes Smokey see the ridiculousness of the situation. "I hope she won't be," says Smokey.

"I assure you, I'm not trying to replace Jasmine or any of your friends. You wouldn't do that to me and my friends, would you?"

"Of course not."

"Exactly. I think since they are business partners, it's good that they get along well. It would be brutal if they didn't."

"You're right," says Smokey. "Jasmine wants me to get together with her and Louisa to get to know her better. I didn't want to, but maybe it would help."

"Why not invite her to the party? You'll have a little more interaction with her, but nothing overwhelming. Just spend enough time with her to have something to talk about when you get together with her and Jasmine."

Smokey thinks it over. "Good idea. Okay, let's invite her."

While carrying the party supplies into the house, Sasha's phone rings.

"Hi Marlon," she says, setting a shopping bag down on the table. "Did you talk to Archer? Okay. I'm at Smokey's. I'll put you on speakerphone so she can hear, too."

"I need to sit down for this," says Smokey. They both drop into chairs at the dining room table.

"Archer just called me," says Marlon. Smokey thinks she detects the slightest tremor in his voice. "He met with a cat called Platelicker."

"Platelicker?" asks Smokey.

Marlon clears his throat. "Archer is pretty convinced he's Winthrop."

Chapter 17
Getting the Best

When Autumn arrives at the Fluffingtons' apartment, Dusty meets her at the door.

"Let me show you how I'm coming on the dresses," Dusty asks. "I should have had at least six months, of course," Dusty fumes as she leads Autumn down the hallway to her sewing room. "I can't work on anything else until these are finished."

"Where is Abigail?" Autumn asks.

"She went to see Sukey. Something about the groom's cake."

Autumn hopes that when she goes in to work later, she won't find Sukey with her whiskers in a twist.

"What do you think?" Dusty asks, sweeping her paw towards the dress hanging in the center of the sewing room.

Autumn gasps. "Beautiful!" She moves closer but doesn't dare touch

"I still have a few things to do. Then the fitting for adjustments so I can move on to the bridesmaids' dresses. Thank goodness it's a small bridal party."

"Everyfur is going to look amazing," says Autumn.

"Have you thought about what you're going to wear?" asks Dusty.

"I'll think about that closer to the big day. Have you planned the shower? That is the maid of honor's responsibility, right?"

"I've been getting these dresses made. I'll give it some thought soon. When this wedding is over, I'll need a vacation."

"Just think," says Autumn, "once Abigail and Greyson leave for their honeymoon, you'll have the entire apartment all to yourself."

"I can't wait."

"Don't worry about the shower. I'll help you with it."

"Thanks," says Dusty, grabbing her purse. "Now, I want to hear all about you and Buster. Maybe I'll be making a wedding gown for you soon."

Autumn laughs. "Don't say that in front of Smokey. She keeps warning me not to go too fast."

"Good advice, but don't go as slowly as Smokey wants you to. She's as overprotective as Abby." Dusty heads across the hall. "I'll tell Darlene that I'm leaving. Do you want to say hi?"

"Love to. I haven't seen the mice in a while."

They troop into Dusty's bedroom and crouch near the little door in the baseboard.

"Darlene?" Dusty calls.

The door opens and a nose and whiskers pop out. "Yes, Dusty? Oh, hi, Autumn Amelia."

"Hi Mrs. Mouse," says Autumn. "How's the family?"

"All well, thank you. The kids are in school and Rodney's at work."

"Autumn and I are going to Tonk's Treasures to buy wedding gifts for Abby and Greyson. Do you need anything while we're out?"

"No, thank you, dear."

"Okay. See you in a while then."

"Nice to see you, Mrs. Mouse," says Autumn. "Give my best to your husband and kids."

"I will."

"What's going to happen to the Mouse family after you move out?" Autumn asks as they enter the elevator.

"Abby and Greyson told them they're welcome to stay. They plan to travel a lot, so they like the idea of having them here while they're away. Darlene and Rodney were very relieved."

"Are they coming to the wedding?"

"Of course. Now, come on," says Dusty as they exit the building. "Spill it on you and Buster."

When they reach Tonk's Treasures, Autumn has managed to get Dusty all caught up.

"I will definitely be making your wedding gown," says Dusty as they head into the store.

"Hey, ladies!" calls Tamarind, the store owner, as they enter. "It's been a while."

"Blame my sister," says Dusty. "She's finally made up her mind about the wedding and bridesmaids' gowns. Now I'm busting my tail to get them done. I'm sorry but I won't be able to bring you anything until they're finished."

"Bring the next batch when you can. Your stuff always flies out of here."

As Tamarind and Dusty chat about the clothing Dusty sells on commission at Tonk's Treasures, Autumn looks around the store. The first time she came here over a year ago, cats and a few dogs made up the entire clientele. Now that Oneness Park has brought all the furs and feathers together, she is gratified to see that the store is filled with diversity. Two rabbits are trying on hats with holes made specially to accommodate their ears, a duck and a muskrat are discussing makeup samples, and two mice are comparing paw lotions with a cat.

"You should try this," Autumn hears a goldfinch say to a crow. "It does wonders for your beak."

"I'll help you ladies in just a minute," Tamarind says, pulling Autumn's attention back. "I just have to ring up a customer."

Looking towards the checkout counter, Autumn sees an eagle waiting.

"Oh, you're going to love that, Helga," says Tamarind as she wraps a box of different colored talon polishes.

"Samuel likes the coral on me best," says the eagle. "But I'm rather partial to the caramel apple. I'm looking forward to trying some of the other colors in the collection.”

“Try this coffee beige,” says Tamarind, motioning towards one of the bottles. “That’s a perfect color for you.”

“It does look good, doesn’t it? I’ll try it on as soon as I get home.”

Once the eagle has departed, Tamarind returns her attention to Autumn and Dusty. “Okay, do you have any ideas of what you’d like to give the bridal couple?”

Dusty frowns. “Abby has everything she needs and so does Greyson.”

“So, something for the apartment is out?”

“It should be something more personal, but for both of them.”

“Hmm…what things do they like to do together?”

“They like to go out to eat a lot and go to museums, plays, and concerts.”

Tamarind looks stumped. Then she asks, “And the honeymoon destination?”

“Tanzania. Unless Abby changes her mind again.”

“They’re planning to travel together often,” Autumn volunteers.

“Travel,” says Tamarind. “I have just the thing.” She hurries off to a corner of the store, stopping to compliment the duck and muskrat on their makeup choices. “You’re going to love that color, Audrey,” she calls to the muskrat.

In a moment, Tamarind returns holding a very large book. “I wasn’t sure how this would sell here, but it might be just what you’re looking for. It’s unique.” She sets the book on the counter.

The cover looks like it’s made of wood with the words “Our Travel Adventures” carved into it. There is a metal flap that swings up from the back cover to lock on the front keeping the book closed when not in use. Tamarind shows them the luxuriant heavy-stock pages with a tea-stained patina.

"It's a keepsake of travels. See, there are pages for photographs, ones with lines for writing, pockets to hold mementos," she says carefully turning the pages.

"It's beautiful," says Dusty. "I'm sure they would enjoy filling it up together. I knew you'd have the perfect thing, Tamarind. I'll take it."

"Now, what about you, Autumn?" Tamarind asks.

"I've no idea what to get, either."

"Let's see, they like to go out to eat, go to museums, plays –"

"And entertain," says Dusty interrupting Tamarind's out-loud thinking. "They will probably do a lot of entertaining at home."

Tamarind's face lights up. "Hang on."

In a few moments, she's back with three things.

"Would any of these work?" she asks.

First, she shows them a long wooden cheeseboard with insets holding three types of cheese knives. Then she displays a set of acacia wooden bowls in varying sizes, one nesting in the next. Finally, she pulls from a box a highly lacquered serving tray with handles. Etched into the tray is a map of the world.

"Oh!" Autumn exclaims. "That one combines entertaining with travel. I'll take it."

"Excellent choice," says Tamarind.

After dropping Dusty off at her apartment, Autumn heads for Oneness Park and Mama Cat's Kitchen. She's nervous about what type of mood Sukey will be in if Abigail has been here changing her mind about the groom's cake. But when she enters the kitchen, Sukey is rolling out dough and humming.

"I heard Abigail paid you a visit," says Autumn. "Did she change her mind again?"

"A change in the cake shape and a little surprise has been added."

"What is it?"

"She's sworn me to secrecy. You'll have to wait for the reception."

"Can you at least give me a hint?"

A wry smile plays around Sukey's mouth. "Let's just say Greyson will get a bang out of it."

Chapter 18
Is He The One?

"Didn't Winthrop know his own name?" Autumn asks. "Why didn't he tell the squirrels his name?" They are in the parking lot of Archer's office building waiting for Sasha and Marlon to arrive.

"I've told you a million times," says Smokey. "Of course, he knew his name. I have no idea why they call him Platelicker. Archer said he'll explain everything to us."

Sasha pulls into the parking lot with Marlon right behind her. Together the four of them climb the stairs to Archer's office. It's the first time Autumn has met Archer. When they enter, he's waiting for them in the lobby.

"Hi. Come on in," he says, holding the door. "Please, take a seat." He indicates a table in the center of the room. "You must be Autumn Amelia," he says, shaking her paw. "I'm sorry I wasn't here when you came in to sign the contract."

"Your secretary was a great help."

"I'm glad to hear it."

Archer's pronounced underbite gives his voice an odd quality, making it difficult to understand him at first, but before long she's caught on to the cadence of his speech.

At first his office looks slightly cluttered, but as Autumn settles into one of the chairs at the table and looks around she sees that it's not so much cluttered as it is full. There are several bulletin boards on the walls with photos and notes pinned to them. There are two other tables besides the one they're seated at, all of which have papers and file folders. Archer's desk sits in a corner with remnants of his breakfast on it. There's a laptop on the desk, and a PC on a stand across from their table. Above that, hanging on the wall is a huge screen.

Just as they are all settled, Archer's secretary, a gray and white poodle with such full, floppy ears that Autumn at first thinks they are pigtails, enters carrying a tray with a carafe of coffee, sugar, cream, five cups, napkins and stirrers on it. She sets the tray on the table.

"Thank you, Jean," says Archer. "Hold all my calls, please."

Once Jean has left the room and everyfur has a full coffee cup in front of them, Archer begins the meeting.

"Thank you all for coming. I think I have some very good news for you. I told you I had a lead on a cat I thought might be your brother. When my informant told me that the cat in question had just returned to Oakton, I took a ride out there to see him. I surveilled him for a while, got some photographs, and spoke with a few squirrels who seemed to know him well."

Archer turns to Marlon and Sasha. "You two told me that Winthrop got more of your mother's Maine Coon genes than your father's Russian Blue, but that he wasn't as fluffy as most Maine Coons. You also said he was orange with darker orange stripes and some white on his chin and paws. This cat fits that description."

"Don't a lot of cats?" asks Smokey.

"Sure. But there's more. He looked to be the correct age. With that information, I struck up a conversation with a squirrel who confirmed that this cat showed up when he was a kitten. Just wandered into their little band one day, looking dazed. He didn't seem to know where he was or where he came from, but he was young and lost, so they let him stay."

"Did a squirrel family take him in?" asks Sasha.

"Not exactly. This particular scurry of squirrels are...well, how do I put this? They're not a traditional family. I'm not even sure how many, if any, of them are actually related to each other. They're more like a nomadic commune."

"A cult?" asks Smokey, fear rising in her eyes.

"I wouldn't call them a cult. They don't seem to be following any particular ideology that they all have to subscribe to. Quite the opposite. They come and go as they please, do what they want, and generally have a good time."

Autumn frowns. "He was just a kitten then. He should have had some structure. Did he go to school?"

"I don't know, though he can read and write so somefur taught him."

"Is he...okay?" asks Marlon.

"Define okay."

"I mean, is he..." Marlon trails off, lost for words.

"Physically and mentally, he seems fine," says Archer.

A collective sigh of relief passes around the table.

"What makes you sure he's Winthrop?" Sasha asks.

"I interviewed him. I asked him how he came to live with the squirrels. He said when he was a kitten, he and his littermates were under a bush when a hawk crashed into it and everyfur took off in different directions. Sound familiar?"

"Oh, my!" says Smokey. "What else did he say?"

"When I asked him if he remembered the names of his littermates, he said Marlon, Sasha, and Smokerina."

"Oh, my catness! It is him," Sasha exclaims.

"He knew nothing of Autumn Amelia, of course, she not having been born yet when he disappeared."

"But Marlon told us this cat's name is Platelicker," says Autumn.

"Ah, yes. Well, when he first met up with the squirrels – seven of them in this scurry, by the way – he'd been wandering for a few days. He was hungry, scared, and disoriented. He didn't talk much at first so for a while they just called him Orange. It seems that every time they fed him, he would eat everything on the plate then lick it clean. So, they started calling him Platelicker and it stuck. He goes along with it, but he does remember that his real name is Winthrop. He volunteered that information. I didn't ask him. I'm very careful about not asking any leading questions."

Both Smokey and Sasha have tears streaming down their faces and Marlon looks close to joining them. Autumn is overjoyed for them as well as for herself.

"Take a look," says Archer. He clicks a remote in the direction of the huge flatscreen and a picture of an orange cat appears.

They all stare at it in silence for several seconds.

"Did you tell him about us?" asks Smokey.

"I did once I was certain he was Winthrop."

"What did he say? Does he want to meet us?" asks Sasha.

"He was grateful to learn that you were all alive and well. And pleased to learn that he has another sister." Archer nods towards Autumn Amelia. "I also broke the news to him about your parents. He was saddened by that. And, yes, he wants to meet you."

"When? Where?" asks Marlon, looking ready to fly out of his seat at a moment's notice.

"That's something for you and Winthrop to decide. I have his cell phone number. Frankly, I was surprised he had one, but I guess even a scurry of wacky squirrels want to be connected. Shall I call him now?"

"Yes!" They all say at once.

Archer dials the number, puts it on speaker, and lays the phone on the table.

"Hello."

"Hello, Platelicker? This is Detective Archer."

"Hey, detective dude! What's up?"

Autumn stifles a laugh.

"I'm here with Marlon, Sasha, Smokey, and Autumn Amelia. Would you like to say hello? You're on speakerphone."

"Hi, Winthrop. Is it really you?" asks Sasha, leaning close to the phone.

"It's me. Which one are you?"

"I'm Sasha. I can't believe we've found you. How are you? Are you okay?"

"I'm great, but my head is trippin' right now. I can hardly believe this is happening. I mean, it's like, totally acorns!"

"Hi, Winthrop. This is Smokey. I'm so excited to hear your voice."

"We all are," says Marlon. "We want to see you. When can we get together?"

"Where are you?" he asks.

"We're in Faunaburg right now," says Marlon. "Sasha and I live in West Lake and Smokey and Autumn Amelia live in Wild Whisker Ridge."

"Oh, yeah. Autumn Amelia. The little sister I didn't know I had."

"Hi Winthrop," says Autumn.

"Hi, little sis. I'm in Oakton. Let's meet somewhere. Hey, do you know The Screamin' Eagle? It's a café in Forest Junction on Market Street. We could meet there. You'll love it. The place is totally acorns."

"We'll find it," says Marlon. "When do you want to meet?"

"No time like the present. Let's meet at noon and have lunch."

When they finish the call, they are all hugging, holding paws, and wiping tears.

"Archer, how can we ever thank you?" says Sasha. "You've helped us reunite our family."

"Just doing my job," says Archer, though Autumn thinks she sees the hint of tears in his eyes. "Let me look up that café for you and get the directions," he says, quickly turning away to go to his computer.

Back in the parking lot, they leave calls of excuse. None will be at work today.

"Let's leave our cars at Oneness Park and all go together," Marlon suggests.

"Good idea," says Autumn.

"I can't believe this is happening," says Smokey as she and Autumn head towards the park. Autumn is driving Smokey's car because Smokey is too emotional to think straight.

"He sounds like a real character," says Autumn. "I can't wait to meet him. Just from what I know of Simon and Sam, I can only imagine what being brought up by a scurry of squirrels must have been like."

"I don't care," says Smokey. "I'm just so excited to have us all back together."

* * *

As they enter The Screamin' Eagle, Smokey only half takes in the dim lighting, brick walls hung with paintings, and sculptures set on carved wooden pedestals interspersed amongst the tables and chairs. She's looking for Winthrop, but she can't see a cat who looks anything like him.

"Welcome," says a deep voice from behind a counter. Smokey turns in its direction and is startled to see huge black bear grinning at them.

"Hi," says Marlon. "We're looking for an orange cat."

"Platey?" asks the bear.

"Um...maybe. He goes by Platelicker."

"Yeah, that's Platey. I'm Jasper. I co-own the Eagle."

"You do?" asks Sasha.

Jasper chuckles. "Yeah, I know. I don't look much like an eagle. I get that all the time. An eagle started this place, but he retired about ten years ago. My buddy, Wallace, and I bought it together, but it was already so well known as The Screamin' Eagle that we kept the name."

140

A door leading from what Smokey assumes must be a kitchen swings open. A long, broad nose followed by an enormous set of antlers emerges.

"Here's Wallace," says Jasper as a moose joins him behind the counter. "Hey, Wallace. These cats are here to see Platey. Where'd he go?"

"He's on the couch," says the moose.

Smokey glances around. No couch.

"It's around the corner," says Jasper. Go to the end of the counter and take a left. You'll see a section that looks kind of like a living room with chairs, couches, a coffee table and a fireplace."

"Platey's waiting for you," adds Wallace. "You must be some special cats. I've never seen him so excited and that's saying a lot."

They head in the direction indicated by Jasper and find an orange cat curled up on the couch sound asleep.

"He doesn't look excited," says Marlon.

Just as the words are out of his mouth, the cat uncoils and springs off the couch to land right in front of him.

"Is it you? Are you them?" he asks, hopping from one foot to the other.

"Winthrop?" asks Sasha.

"Yeah!" He peers at her intently then glances at Smokey. "You Sasha or Smokerina?" he asks.

"Sasha. This is Smokey."

Before Smokey knows what's hit her, Winthrop has them both in huge hug. Then he moves to Marlon and grabs him in a hug, too. Finally, he gives Autumn Amelia an almost reverent look. "So, you're my baby sister," he says.

"I am. Do I get a hug, too?"

He gently enfolds Autumn in his arms and pets her head. When he steps away, he says, "Hey, everyfur, sit down. Get comfy. I ordered some food for us. Lunch is on me. We're having a buffet so you can all take whatever you want."

"That sounds wonderful," says Smokey, settling onto one of the three couches forming a horseshoe before the fireplace.

"I'll set it up on the coffee table," says Winthrop.

He runs around the café retrieving trays of food from underneath the couches, chairs, and tables.

"Can I help you with that?" asks Marlon, though his voice holds a note of bewilderment.

"You won't know where I hid each platter. It will only take a minute."

When he's gathered everything onto the coffee table, they have a nice spread of sandwiches, salad, dinner rolls, and pastries.

He sticks his head around the corner and calls, "Hey Jasper, can you take our drink order?"

"Um...Winthrop, why did you hide all the food?" asks Sasha.

"The squirrels taught you to do that, didn't they?" asks Autumn.

"Yeah. You know about squirrels?"

"Oh my, yes. I've known Simon and Sam Squirrel for years. They're always hiding food all over the place. The only problem is, they often forget where they put it."

Winthrop lets out a belly laugh. "You got that right. My squirrel family designated me the Finder. I never forget."

Jasper appears with a pad and pencil. "What can I get you to drink?" asks the bear.

"They've got a hot chocolate here that's totally acorns," says Winthrop. "The hot mulled cider is really good, too."

"We've also got lattes, espresso, coffee, tea, milk, juice, soda," says Jasper.

They order, then turn their attention back to Winthrop.

"So, tell us what happened, Winthrop," says Marlon. "How did you end up with a scurry of squirrels."

"Oh, well it's like I told the detective. I ran when that hawk hit the bush. I didn't even know where I was going. I just ran and ran. I didn't know how to hunt so I got really hungry. I did happen by a stream, so at least I got a drink of water. A lot of that time is foggy in my memory. I just know I was in the woods most of the time."

Sasha and Marlon nod.

"At one point, I plopped down on the ground and couldn't move anymore. That's when I looked up and saw a whole bunch of faces staring down at me from the trees. We stared at each other for a moment, then they all scurried down the tree trunks. I was scared, but I was too weak to move.

"Squirrels?" asks Autumn.

"Yeah. They gathered around me and started asking questions. I was too scared and wiped out to talk. Then one of the girls ran off and came back with some fruit. I'd never had fruit before, but at that moment I didn't care what I ate. I chowed down.

"They took me to their den. They all lived in this one huge den inside a tree. It was about thirty feet up. They practically had to carry me there. Cool place, one gigantic room loaded with video games and pinball machines. They crashed on futons scattered around the room. They had a little kitchenette, and they made me something to eat then put me to bed on one of the futons. I think I probably would have died if they hadn't helped me."

"Do all squirrels live like that?" asks Smokey. She's never given the private lives of other furs and feathers much thought.

"No," says Autumn. "Simon and Sam live with their parents. It's in a den in a tree, but it has several rooms. The boys each have their own bedroom."

"How do you know?" asks Smokey.

"I've been there," says Autumn.

"You have?" Smokey never knew this.

"Autumn Amelia is right," says Winthrop. "Most squirrels live more or less like a lot of other furs and feathers. I just happened on a scurry who all live together and take care of each other. No pressure, no fur in charge, not much in the way of rules except be good to each other."

Jasper returns bearing a tray with their drinks. "You cats have enough of everything?" he asks. "Platey wasn't sure what you'd would want to eat, but he just couldn't stand the wait, so he kept himself busy ordering and hiding food."

"We're all set, I think. Thank you," says Marlon. The others nod.

"Okay. You need anything else just give me or Wallace a holler."

"Did you tell the squirrels what happened to you?" asks Sasha returning to their conversation. "Did you try to find your way back?"

"I guess I was pretty disoriented for a while. I couldn't seem to make myself talk. I sure was hungry, though. I'd lick my plate clean after every meal. That's why they started calling me Platelicker. Platey for short. Eventually, I did tell them my name was Winthrop and explained what happened, but it took a while. I couldn't tell them where I'd come from because I didn't even know where we'd been when the hawk attacked. They said I could stay with them, so I did."

"Did they send you to school?" asks Smokey, setting down her teacup for another bite of her sandwich.

Winthrop laughs. "Yeah. But that didn't go so well. They waited until I found my voice again. By then I was used to their laid-back lifestyle and no rules. I got in trouble in school a lot. I wasn't trying to misbehave. I just didn't understand. Anyway, they let me drop out and Angelina homeschooled me. She was great. I learned a lot from her."

"She's one of the squirrels?" asks Marlon.

"Yeah. Angelina is also called Mama sometimes because she's kind of like the mother of the group. She just likes looking after the others. She has a real motherly vibe."

"I'm glad to know that," says Autumn. "She must have been a comfort."

Smokey is not at all sure she approves of the situation, though she is definitely grateful that the squirrels saved her brother's life and took care of him.

"Angelina's the best. She's totally acorns. Better! More like peanut butter and corn on the cob."

"Do you have a job?" asks Marlon.

"I don't work in an office or pull a shift or anything. I could never do that. It would be like school all over again."

"So, what do you do?" asks Smokey.

"I'm an artist."

"Really?" asks Autumn.

"Yeah, little sister. I'm a woodworker. Reggie taught me. He's one of the scurry. He's just a little older than the others, like Angelina. Kind of fatherly. I started learning when I was still a kit. Took to it right away. Reggie's a woodworker, too. He makes the practical stuff – benches, tables, chairs, stuff like that. His quality is top notch. I do more artsy stuff. Did you see the pedestals here with the sculptures on them? I made them."

Smokey noticed them when she first came in. Even though she was focused on finding Winthrop, they did catch her eye.

"There's one over there," he says, pointing to an intricately carved pedestal in the corner.

"You made that?" asks Autumn astonishment evident in her voice.

"Sure did. I made all the pedestals here. Reggie made this coffee table," he says tapping the table with all their food on it.

"They're exquisite," says Marlon. "I hope you charge well for your work."

"Eh," says Winthrop, shrugging. "I love doing it. I give Jasper and Wallace a substantial discount. They're cool guys and I love this place. All the local artists hang out here. We're like a family. Jasper and Wallace watch out for us. I'd do anything for them."

"But how can you make a living?" asks Marlon.

"I do the craft fair circuit. The big fairs. There are some high rollers who come to those. The whole scurry goes. Megan makes jewelry. Angelina makes scented candles and soaps. Harley's a potter. Susan and Ralph are both painters. Leo's a sculptor. He did a few of the sculptures here. And of course, Reggie makes furniture. Some of us can charge a lot more than others. That's why we all stay together. We all contribute to a joint fund and keep some of our money for ourselves. If I sell a couple of my high-end pieces at one of these fairs, I'm set for quite a while. I'm happy to put the rest in the fund, so none of us have to worry. It's a great life."

"How do you get to these fairs and haul all your stuff?" asks Smokey.

"That's one of the things we used the fund for," he explains. "We bought an RV so we can all go together. It's totally seeds and berries! In fact, we just got back from a trip that went really well. We talked a bit about living in the RV full time and staying on the road, but I don't know. I'd miss my friends here at The Eagle."

"What a romantic sort of life," says Autumn, prompting a sideways glance from Smokey.

"Now that we've found you, we hope you'll stick around for a while," says Sasha. "We'd like to get to know you better and reunite our family."

"Sounds seeds and berries to me," he says. "So, what happened to you after you ran from the hawk?"

Sasha relates the story of how she and Marlon got lost and were taken in and raised by an owl.

"Really? An owl?" says Winthrop. "Hey, do you know Hoots Digny?"

"Who?" asks Sasha.

"No, Hoots. Oh. Sorry. Yeah, so Hoots is an owl. He's a friend of mine. Actually, his name is Edward, but we all call him Hoots. He plays the guitar. Cool guy."

"I'm afraid we've never met," says Marlon. "We stuck pretty close to West Lake."

"Yeah. I get it," says Winthrop. "Who was the owl that raised you?"

"Her name was Ophelia McGivney," says Sasha. "She passed away last year."

"Oh, I'm sorry," says Winthrop. "I'm glad she took you in."

"We are, too," says Sasha.

"What about you, Smokerina?" asks Winthrop. "Who raised you?"

Suddenly Smokey feels heat rise in her face. For the first time in her life, she feels embarrassed that she didn't lose her parents and wasn't raised by strangers. She lowers her eyes which are starting to fill with tears. "Mama and Papa Cat," she says. "I ran, but not that far. They found me."

"Pawsome!" says Winthrop. "At least they didn't lose you. You must have seemed like a humungous blessing to them," he says.

Was I a blessing? she wonders, thinking of her bratty behavior growing up.

"Oh, I don't know," she says. "They looked for all of you for a long, long time. Eventually, they had to assume the hawks – we...well...I, thought there was more than one – had gotten you all."

"Massive bummer," says Winthrop. A tear rolls down his face.

"But the four of us are together again," says Sasha. "And now we have Autumn Amelia, too. To me, it feels like a miracle."

"Yeah," says Winthrop. "It is totally acorns to the whiskers."

"We're having a Hunter's Moon Night party at our house," says Autumn. "We'd love it if you'd come. You can stay overnight. I know Wild Whisker Ridge is a bit of a drive.”

“I’d love to come, but…um…I don’t have a car. When we need to go somewhere, we just walk. To go far, we take the RV, but we always go together. I guess I could see if I could take it alone that one time. We have our den in the tree so it’s not like I’d leave them without a place to crash.”

“Bring them,” says Autumn. “They’re your family. We’d love to meet them, too.”

Smokey shoots Autumn a look that she completely ignores.

“Yeah? Okay! They love to party. Can we bring anything?”

“I think we’ve got everything covered. Lots of furs and feathers are coming so we’ll have a variety of foods and plenty of them.”

“No problem there. They’ll eat anything. Oh, *seeds*, this is going to be pawsome!”

Before their lunch ends, they get Jasper and Wallace to take group pictures of them on each cat’s cell phone.

Smokey says nothing to Autumn about inviting the squirrel scurry. They are, after all, responsible for Winthrop surviving his ordeal. She just wonders what condition the cottage will be in after they leave.

Chapter 19
The Hunter's Moon Night Party

The morning of the Hunter's Moon Night party dawns crisp and clear. Sasha slept over the night before. The three of them gave the cottage a thorough cleaning and put up all the decorations. Now, at the bottom of the staircase, Autumn surveys the living room festooned with maple leaf garlands. There are ceramic acorns in various sizes set about the room. Vases of mums, sunflowers, black-eyed Susans, and coneflowers are strategically placed throughout the living room and a large bouquet of them sits on the dining room table.

The main focus in the living room is the huge Hunter's Moon. It's a yellowish-orange full moon made of painted tin that sits in the corner. Though many furs and feathers today have high-tech moons projected onto their walls, Smokey and Autumn prefer their old-school moon. It reminds them of happy childhood memories. Sasha liked the retro aspect of it, so she didn't attempt to talk them out of it. "It will make a great conversation piece," she said last night after they set it up. "I'll bet it brings back memories for a lot of the guests."

Next, Autumn heads for the dining room. They put out all the plates, napkins, glasses, utensils, and food warmers last night. The two prep chefs she hired, a jackrabbit named Ronnie, and a red fox named Vicky, had prepared everything that could be done ahead of time yesterday and brought it over. They will be here later today to help with the rest of the cooking.

"Weren't there supposed to be pumpkins?" Autumn asks.

Smokey and Sasha stare at each other. Simultaneously, they each slap a paw to their foreheads.

"How could we have forgotten the pumpkins?" Sasha asks in disbelief.

"Don't worry," says Autumn. "Dusty will be here soon, and we'll make a run to the orchard."

"Dusty's coming over this morning?" Smokey asks.

"Mm-hmm. She needs to get away. Abigail is driving her furballs. What do you want for breakfast?"

After they eat and clean up, the doorbell rings. Autumn opens the door to Dusty and watches a groundhog drive off in the taxi.

"I really need to learn to drive and get my own car," says Dusty. "It's expensive to take a taxi everywhere."

"I'll teach you," says Autumn. "After the wedding."

"Pawsome!"

"Speaking of driving, we have to go to the orchard. Smokey and Sasha forgot the pumpkins."

"Okay."

"We're heading for the orchard," Autumn calls into the house. "Back in a bit.'

As they drive to the far end of Wild Whisker Ridge, they pass through the woods, a clearing with a large meadow, and finally come to the long dirt driveway that winds its way up a hill. At the top, they park and get out of the car.

"I love this weather," says Dusty.

"Me too. Smokey likes fall, but she's already dreading winter." Autumn notices the tendrils of vapor rising from her mouth as she speaks.

"I guess all this fur is good for something," says Dusty.

"Yeah. Go floof!"

They laugh as they head towards the pumpkin patch.

While they scour the patch for just the right pumpkins, Autumn glances across the field at the rows of apple trees, watching their reddish-brown leaves sway gently. Two apples drop to the ground one right after the other. Their tangy scent wafts across the crisp morning air. She takes a deep breath.

"That smells delicious," she says. "Let's get some apples while we're here. I used up all the ones I had for tonight's desserts."

"I love hot apple dumplings and ice cream," says Dusty. "What time does the snack bar open?"

"Not until noon. Smokey and Sasha will have hissy fits if we aren't back before then even though everything is under control."

"They're just excited," says Dusty.

"I know. I don't blame them. I can hardly wait for tonight."

"I can't wait to meet your boyfriend," says Dusty, giving her a wink.

"And I can't wait for you to meet him."

"Is it really serious?"

"Not yet. We haven't been dating that long."

"But it could be?"

Autumn feels something like a bubble well up in her chest that bursts across her face in a smile. "I think so."

Dusty practically squeals. "And what about Smokey's littermates? How are you getting along with them?"

"Great. I really like Sasha and Marlon. I've only met Winthrrop – or Platelicker – once, but I thought he was a hoot and half. I can't wait until he shows up with his squirrel friends tonight."

"I have a feeling this will be an unforgettable party."

They each carry three pumpkins of varying sizes to the orchard's store. While there, Autumn grabs a bag of apples. Dusty goes to the refrigerated section for a couple of dumplings. "I'm taking these home for later," she explains.

As they near home, Autumn notices a dog in a tweed jacket and newsboy cap walking down the street. "That looks like Professor Chewy," she says and slows the car.

"Professor!" she calls from the open window.

The dog turns in her direction.

"Professor Chewy," she says, now certain of his identity. She brings the car to a halt as he approaches.

"Yes? Oh, you're the cat from The Falling Leaf," he says.

"That's right. I'm Autumn Amelia and this is my friend, Dusty Fluffington. You're coming to my house for the Hunter's Moon Night party tonight."

"Oh dear," he says as though a thought has just surprised him.

"What is it?" Autumn asks.

"I meant to mention this earlier, but I forgot. My nephew, Bruce Lee, is staying with me for the holiday. He's a freshman at Verdant, you see, and I promised his parents I'd keep an eye on him."

"Bring him along," says Autumn.

"I should warn you, he's a Shih Tzu/Bichon Frisé mix. He can be a little rambunctious."

"That's okay," says Autumn. "There will be several squirrels at the party. He'll have a good time with them."

"Oh, my, yes, he will. Well, as long as you don't mind."

"He's more than welcome."

"Thank you. We shall see you this evening, then. Now, I shall finish my morning constitutional. Have a lovely day, ladies." With that, he tips his hat and strolls away.

"He's an interesting fellow," says Dusty.

They enter the house bearing their purchases. Smokey and Sasha rush to take the pumpkins from them and find the perfect location for them.

"We met Professor Chewy on the way home," Autumn tells them. "His nephew is staying with him for the holiday. He goes to Verdant. Anyway, I told him to bring his nephew to the party tonight."

"Okay," says Smokey, only half paying attention as she and Sasha try out various arrangements with the pumpkins.

Autumn shrugs and motions Dusty to follow her to the kitchen.

"What's up with Abigail now?" she asks as she starts putting together sandwiches for lunch. "I thought she was all set on the wedding dresses. What's she driving you up the curtains about now?"

Dusty heaves a heavy sigh. "It's about me getting my own apartment."

"She doesn't want you to?"

"She's worried about me finding a nice place that I can afford. She's given me lists of things to look out for, preferred neighborhoods, websites to check for rentals. At first, I was very appreciative, but she just never stops with the advice and the warnings."

"What warnings?"

"Mostly horror stories about unscrupulous landlords."

"You can check the reviews online, you know."

"I know, but she's relentless. She's so afraid I'll sign a lease that I can't get out of and be stuck with a landlord who won't take care of the place and keeps raising the rent. She doesn't want me to even start looking until she and Greyson get back from their honeymoon. I think she wants to pick out my apartment for me. I'm the one who's going to live there."

"I could help you look," says Autumn. "But I don't know anything about choosing an apartment. Hey, maybe there's one for rent in Jasmine's building."

"That would be great if I can afford it. The problem is that Abby thinks anything less than her apartment isn't good enough. On my own, I could never afford to live in our building."

"I'll ask Smokey to talk to Jasmine."

"Thanks, Autumn. Abby might even accept it if I could live in the same building as Jasmine."

"Actually, you could talk to Jasmine yourself. She'll be at the party tonight."

"Good idea. I need to get this taken into my own paws before I get so angry at Abby, I spit a furball at her."

* * *

As seven o'clock approaches, Smokey's heart starts to race. She's worried about the unknown variables. Professor Chewy's nephew who sounds like a pawful, the scurry of squirrels coming with Winthrop, and now, the last-minute addition of a flamingo. Only two hours ago, Jasmine called to say that an old friend of Louisa's had just flown in for a visit, a flamingo named Vivian. Louisa couldn't leave her friend, but she had been looking forward to the party and wondered if it would be okay to bring her along. Of course, Smokey said yes. What else could she say? She's never even met a flamingo before. She has no idea what they eat.

"It's fine," says Autumn when Smokey reveals her concern. "I had Dusty look it up online. We've got food she'll eat."

Smokey decides to leave that worry to Autumn who is busily arranging dishes and platters on the dining room table with the help of her two prep chefs. They've placed the last one when the doorbell rings.

Smokey takes a deep breath. Sasha squeals in delighted anticipation.

"Are either of you going to answer the door?" asks Autumn, heading back towards the kitchen.

154

"I will," says Smokey crossing the living room with a last glance around to make sure everything is in place. Her paws are shaking.

Relief floods her when she sees Greyson and Abigail on the doorstep, followed by Marlon.

"Come in, come in," says Smokey. "You're the first to arrive."

"Normally, I'm fashionably late," says Abigail, "but Greyson was afraid of losing out on any of the shrimp and insisted we arrive right on time."

"No need to worry about that," says Smokey. "We've got plenty of shrimp."

Greyson appears a bit sheepish as he hands her a beautiful centerpiece of fall flowers.

"Wow! Cool moon," says Marlon, stepping into the living room. "That will have the dogs howling." He laughs, but Smokey's eyes widen.

"You don't think they really will?" she asks.

"Does it matter? It is a Hunter's Moon Night party."

Hunter's Moon Night parties are known for getting a bit raucous so a little moon-howling shouldn't be considered out of line or even unexpected. Smokey knows this, but she's never attended a Hunter's Moon Night party with dogs before.

One after another in quick succession, guests arrive until the house begins to fill. Smokey has taken up a position by the door. So far, she has welcomed a tortoiseshell cat named Shirley who lives up the street, Miguel Gato, Rufus Tailwagger, Simon and Sam Squirrel, Tamarind from Tonk's Treasures, Tabby Furry, Mr. and Mrs. Mouse, Paulie Pomeranian, Sukey, Sally, Jerome J. Ratley, and Buster who Autumn whisked away before he was two steps inside the house.

Now the doorbell rings again, and this time she opens the door to find Professor Chewy accompanied by a small fluffy white dog with black ears, black nose, and a band of black fur extending back from each eye.

He's wearing jeans and a Verdant University sweatshirt while Professor Chewy is in his ever-present tweed.

"Welcome, Professor," she says. "And you must be Bruce Lee. Please come in."

"Thank you kindly for the invitation," says the Professor. "We are honored that you wished to have us at your party."

"Yeah, super pawsome of you," adds Bruce Lee.

"We're happy to have you join us. There's lots of food and—"

"Wow! Look at that!"

Smokey follows Bruce Lee's gaze to the huge metal moon.

"I've never seen anything like that before. Have you, Uncle Chewy?"

"Yes. When I was young, we all had those rather than the ones projected on the wall that everyfur has today."

"No way! So, it's retro. Cool!" He hurries over to examine the moon more closely.

"I must apologize for my nephew's outburst," says Professor Chewy, looking a bit embarrassed.

"Not at all," Smokey assures him. "I'm glad he likes it."

"Hello, Professor Chewy," says Autumn joining them at the door. Let me introduce you to everyfur and feather here and get you something to eat."

As the professor goes off with Autumn Amelia, the doorbell rings again. This time Smokey opens it to find Jasmine, Louisa, and the most vibrantly pink creature she's ever seen. *Wow!* She thinks and wonders, for a mortifying moment, if she's spoken it aloud.

"Hi Smokes!" says Jasmine, bounding inside to give Smokey a hug. "Happy Hunter's Moon Night!"

"Happy Hunter's Moon Night to you, too," she says. Then turning to Louisa, "Please, come in."

"Thank you for the invitation," Louisa says. "This is my friend, Vivian."

"Nice to meet you, Vivian," she says as the bird steps into the living room.

"Nice to meet you, too. Thanks for letting me come. I love parties."

"Vivian just flew up from Palm Ray," says Louisa.

"Really? That's where my cousin, Greyson, is from. He's here. You'll have to meet him."

"I'd love to. I dropped in on Louisa unexpectedly. I'm on my way to the Canary Islands to meet up with my dance troupe. As I was flying over, I looked down and saw her apartment building and thought, why not stop for a visit. I've got time. The dance competition isn't for another two weeks."

"I'm so glad she did," says Louisa. "We haven't seen each other since college. That's where we met." The two birds glance at each other and giggle.

"We had some wild times in those days," Vivian explains to Smokey.

Smokey has a hard time picturing the staid Louisa being anything remotely resembling wild.

"I'm dying to hear some of those stories," says Jasmine. "Give me something blackmail-worthy, would you Vivian," she jokes.

"Oh, sweetie, that's all I've got."

The three of them burst out laughing.

"Um...There's lots of food in the dining room. Please, help yourselves," says Smokey, totally befuddled.

"There's shrimp, right?" asks Jasmine.

"Yes."

Vivian claps. "I adore shrimp."

"It's why she's so flamboyantly pink," says Louisa as they head towards the dining room.

Smokey catches sight of Greyson across the room holding a plate of shrimp. As Jasmine and the two wading birds make their way towards the food, she smiles at the worried expression crossing his face.

Smokey hears the crunch of a large vehicle on the crushed stone of the driveway and faint music. She opens the door to see a van with a massive oak tree painted on its side. The limbs of the tree reach out in all directions. Giant acorns in psychedelic colors dangle and drop from it. Painted beneath the tree are reclining squirrels, some on plush cushions, others in huge piles of leaves, all with beatific smiles. In the middle is an orange and white cat leaning against the trunk of the tree. Beneath the mural, painted in white script, are the words *Life is Totally Acorns!*

"Oh. My. Catness." Smokey stares at the van, not sure what to make of it. Glancing at the windshield, she sees Winthrop driving. As soon as he brings the vehicle to a stop, a door slides open, and a scurry of squirrels tumbles out.

"Wow!"

"Cool!"

"Totally pawsome!"

Smokey turns to the voices behind her to find Simon and Sam Squirrel and Bruce Lee staring out the window at the van.

"Who are they, Miss Smokey?" asks Simon.

"They're friends of my littermate, Winthrop. He's the one driving," she explains.

"Oh, yeah," says Sam. "Miss Autumn told us about finding your littermates."

"I thought his name was Platelicker," says Simon.

"That's what the squirrels call him."

"We can't wait to meet them," says Sam.

By now every guest at the party has congregated near the open door or the living room windows.

"They'll be a lot of fun," she hears Vivian exclaim. "This party is going to be a blast!"

A glance in her direction shows Smokey that Vivian's plate is piled even higher with shrimp than Greyson's.

Winthrop and his squirrel friends scamper towards them.

"Hi Winthrop," she calls, waving to him.

"Let's go," says Sasha, nudging Smokey out the door.

She runs with Sasha and Marlon, Autumn right behind them. The five of them fall into a group hug. It takes a moment before Smokey realizes that the squirrels from the scurry are dancing around them, jumping over each other, and hooting and hollering with delight.

Once the group hug breaks up, Winthrop introduces them to the squirrels. As each squirrel steps forward, they present Smokey, Autumn Amelia, Sasha, and Marlon with gifts, all paw-made.

Angelina, or Mama, as the others call her, places her homemade catnip-scented soaps into Smokey's paws. Smokey inhales the aroma with delight.

When Angelina finishes handing out her soaps, she steps away and Megan, the jewelry maker, takes her place. Megan dangles a beautiful necklace with a heart-shaped pendant in front of Smokey. "Would you like me to put it on you?" she asks.

"Yes, please," says Smokey. "It's gorgeous."

"Thank you," says Megan clasping the emerald necklace around her neck. She does the same for Sasha whose heart pendant is a striking ruby color, and Autumn for whom she has made one in brilliant topaz.

"Mind necklaces?" she asks as she approaches Marlon, holding out a black cord from which dangles a small acorn pendant.

"That's pawsome," he says as she places the cord over his head.

While Megan is distributing her gifts, Smokey notices the other squirrels run back to the van. Now they emerge with larger items.

From Reggie, Winthrop's woodworking mentor, they each receive a paw-carved scratching post.

Harley, the potter, gives each of them a ceramic bowl in the shape of a large acorn.

Leo then hands each cat a small sculpture of an ancient Egyptian cat.

"Smokey, look!" says Sasha, turning her sculpture towards Smokey to show that it has her face. Smokey looks at the sculpture she was given and sees her own face staring back at her. Autumn's and Marlon's are sculpted with their faces as well.

"This is amazing," says Autumn. "You are incredibly talented," she tells Leo.

"Thanks," he says, backing away. "But wait until you see what Susan and Ralph have for you."

Smokey remembers that Susan and Ralph are the painters. Wondering what they've created, she glances around for them. All their guests have come out to meet the squirrels and have been oohing and aahing over the gifts. Now all of them, along with Smokey and her siblings, are looking for Susan and Ralph who are nowhere to be seen.

"Bring them out now," Winthrop calls in the direction of the van.

Two squirrels emerge from the van, each carrying a large canvas under an arm.

Sasha whispers in Smokey's ear, "These squirrels are amazing artists."

As Susan and Ralph approach, Harley and Leo scamper up behind them, each carrying two easels that they quickly set up on the ground before the cats.

Susan and Ralph place the paintings on the easels then step away.

Smokey's gasp of astonishment is lost amongst those of every fur and feather present. She knows her mouth is hanging open, but the thought to close it doesn't occur to her for several seconds. She is staring at four pictures identical to those Jasper snapped with Winthrop's cell phone at the Screamin' Eagle. Not only do the cats in the paintings look exactly like them, but the images appear so lifelike that she half expects them to step right out of the canvases.

"Wow!" says Marlon, the first to recover. "They're blowing my whiskers off!"

Winthrop laughs, jumping up and down on the lawn, capering just like a squirrel. "Told you," he calls, "They're all totally, acorns like I said."

Smokey steps closer to the canvases. She reaches out a paw then pulls it back, afraid to touch it. Sasha and Autumn move to either side of her. It's not until a tear drops onto her whisker that she realizes she's so overcome with emotion she's crying.

"These are incredible," she whispers.

"They are," Autumn agrees. "I can hardly believe what I'm seeing."

Smokey glances around at the scurry lined up in front of her. "I don't know how to thank you all for such beautiful gifts," she says.

"You don't need to say anything," says Reggie. "We're all so happy that Platey has his family back."

"You should have seen him when he came home from the Screamin' Eagle," says Megan. "We've never seen him so deliriously happy. And he's a naturally happy cat so that's saying something."

"You're his family," Autumn tells the squirrels. "And now you're ours as well."

"It was simply the right thing to do," says Reggie. "And we've always been glad to have him in our lives."

"Yeah, he remembers where we hide all our acorns," says Harley with a laugh.

"Let's get all these wonderful gifts safely inside," says Marlon. "We have a celebration to get underway."

"Woo-whoo!" yells Winthrop. "Let's pa-a-a-r-tay!"

* * *

"Have I told you how radiant you look tonight?" Buster whispers in Autumn's ear as she replaces the empty shrimp platter with a fresh one.

"Four times," she says, turning towards him. "But you can keep it up."

They are the only two in the dining room. Buster takes the opportunity to give her a kiss. A moment later they are distracted by a howl from the living room that quickly grows into a cacophony.

"It's the dogs," says Autumn.

Returning to the living room, they find every dog at the party arranged in a semi-circle before the metal full moon and every squirrel sitting on the head or back of a dog. The rest of the guests have formed a more compact semi-circle behind them, watching in fascination as the dogs howl, first in unison, then taking turns, then creating harmony as some howl at different times and in different keys while others howl together.

Autumn marvels at how unexpectedly lovely it sounds. "Too bad the coyotes couldn't make it."

"Why didn't they come?" asks Buster.

"The coyote colony has a long-standing tradition of their own for Hunter's Moon Night. Celia Wooders explained to me that it's very sacred to them. They were grateful for the invitation, but they needed to be there."

"I had no idea."

"Neither did I. Her husband is a minister, and he leads it."

"I'll bet it's beautiful."

The room breaks into applause as the dogs' howling comes to an end. Then Marlon announces, "Is everyfur and feather ready for the Hunter's Moon Night games?"

Whoops and shouts of assent greet his question.

"Let's head outside. Everything's set up."

As they all troop out to the backyard, Smokey grabs Autumn's arm and holds her back.

"Did you invite Rivet?" she asks.

"Yes," says Autumn. "Is there a problem?"

"No, I was just surprised. Actually, I was surprised when Professors Bob and Gromit showed up, but at least I remembered that you invited them. I assumed you did it because they were sitting in the same booth as Professor Chewy at the restaurant, but why the waitress? She wasn't there when you spoke with the professors."

"Professor Chewy was bringing his nephew, and I remembered that our waitress at the Falling Leaf was a student at Verdant, too. I figured it would be nice for Bruce Lee."

"But you didn't tell me. I didn't even recognize her. It was awkward for both of us."

"I'm sorry, Smokey. We all got so busy preparing for the party that I forgot.

Outside, Marlon is separating guests into two teams in front of four gigantic piles of leaves. It had taken Autumn, Smokey, Sasha, and Dusty forever this afternoon to rake them into equal piles, first placing a single pumpkin seed under two of them. The four of them won't be playing this game since they all know where the pumpkin seeds are, so they stand off to the side to watch the fun.

"When I blow my whistle the first one for each team dives onto a leaf pile. Notice I said onto, not into. You have to start at the top of the pile and work your way down. After thirty seconds," he holds up his stopwatch, "I'll blow the whistle again and whoever is in the pile has to get out and the next competitor takes his or her place. You keep going until someone finds the seed. The winning team is the one who finds the seed first. Remember, only one of your leaf piles has a seed. You can go through the piles one at a time or back and forth. You can remove leaves or just dig through. The strategy is up to you. Pick team captains and devise your game plan."

Autumn listens as the teams come up with their plans. Greyson has been chosen as one of the team captains and Sally the other. As Autumn strolls behind the teams, she hears whispers of "We'll go back and forth between the piles," "Toss the leaves out as you go so the piles keep getting smaller," "Let's rip through one pile first, then, if it doesn't have the seed, hit the other one," "One of you squirrels go first. Run up a tree and drop into the pile."

Autumn giggles at that. The piles are taller than any of them, even Louisa and Vivian.

"Alright," Marlon calls. "Let's get started. Re-form your lines."

Once the lines are straight, all of them practically hopping from one paw to another, with excitement, Marlon says, "Ready? One. Two. Three. Go." A loud blast on the whistle sends Simon from one line and Bruce Lee from the other. Simon scampers up the closest tree, runs out on a branch overhanging the nearest pile and jumps, bellyflopping on top of the pile. Bruce Lee clambers up Rufus Tailwagger's back and onto his head, then jumps, sailing through the air to land nose-first in one of his team's leaf piles.

Both teams laugh and shout encouragement as leaves fly through the night air. The whistle blows again. Simon and Bruce Lee emerge from the piles and run to the end of their lines. The piles, though a little lower, are still too high so both teams send a squirrel up the trees for the second time.

Once the piles become more accessible, other cats and dogs take their turns. Greyson's team abandons their strategy of going from one pile to the other. Now that the pile they've been working on exclusively is low enough, Greyson sends Louisa in.

She launches herself into the air and as she lands in the pile, leaves scatter in all directions covering even the cats standing on the sidelines. Once in the pile, Louisa spreads her wings, her huge wingspan sending what's left of the pile flying.

"Watch out, Louisa!" Greyson calls. "You're making our other pile bigger."

"If the seed is in this pile, it won't matter," she calls back. She cocks her head, trying to get a good look at the now leafless ground beneath her feet. The whistle blows and she has to leave. "It's not under that pile," she says returning to her line. "Better concentrate on the other one."

As the contest continues and the leaf piles dwindle, each line only has three team members left. Mr. and Mrs. Mouse and Vivian are still to go on Sally's team and Sukey, Tamarind, and Abigail on Greyson's team.

"You're up, Abby," says Greyson.

"Me? Why me? Sukey and Tamarind are younger. And they're athletes. That pile is even bigger than it started out now that Louisa has flapped so many of the other pile's leaves onto it. Send one of them to knock it back first."

Greyson laughs. "Abby, if the other team finds their seed first, you might not get a chance at all. Wouldn't that be a shame?"

"Indeed! I'm staging a coup. I am now captain. Sukey, you're up."

Not needing to be told twice, Sukey leaps onto Rufus' back and springs off the Husky's head into the pile. She claws fast and furious at the leaves working her way down as quickly as she can.

"Your team better get in there fast," says Marlon to Sally. "What's the hold up?"

"I'm next," says Mr. Mouse, but I can't figure out how to get to the top of the pile."

"I'll help you," says Vivian. She leans down and opens her hooked bill. Mr. Mouse climbs in, hanging on to her tongue. Lifting her head she gently flings him to the top of the pile where he promptly disappears.

"Why didn't you send Vivian in?" Marlon asks Sally. "She could clear that pile fast just like Louisa did."

"Tell him, Mrs. Mouse," says Sally.

"Rodney can slip down from the top of that pile to the bottom in no time. He's probably already there now."

Marlon checks his stopwatch and blows the whistle.

Sukey climbs out of her pile and Tamarind takes her place. They wait a few seconds, but there's no sign of Mr. Mouse.

"Mr. Mouse, did you hear the whistle?" Marlon calls into the pile of leaves. There's no answer.

Mrs. Mouse runs up to the base of the leaf pile and yells into it. "Rodney, the whistle blew. Your turn is over. Come out."

Marlon crouches down beside the pile of leaves. "I think I hear him," he says.

"He may be stuck," says Mrs. Mouse. That's a heavy pile of leaves."

"I'll get him," says Vivian who launches herself into the air landing on the pile. Half the leaves fall away at once. Kicking her legs and flapping her wings rids the pile of more leaves. Then she points her bill down and dives like she's going for a fish in the water.

Pink feathers peek from under the leaf pile which begins to move like a living thing as she roots around for the mouse. Marlon blows his whistle again and Tamarind exits her pile. But before Abigail can jump in, the other team's wiggling pile of leaves bursts upwards like a spewing volcano and Vivian rises like a phoenix from the ashes, bill half open, Mr. Mouse sitting inside it, clutching a pumpkin seed in his paws.

"We have a winner!" Marlon proclaims.

All the animals applaud amid shouts and laughter.

"Well, done, Mr. Mouse," says Autumn running over to congratulate him as Mrs. Mouse helps him out of Vivian's bill.

"That will be story for our grandmice," says Mrs. Mouse, giving him a kiss on the whiskers.

"Thanks for the help," he says to Vivian.

"My pleasure. What are we playing next?"

* * *

It's after midnight when every fur and feather return to the cottage. They've played more games, including an impromptu brusselball game and danced in the moonlight to the music from the speakers Marlon set in the window, Vivian shaking loose so many tail feathers that the leaves are now covered in a layer of pink. When the dogs gathered to howl at the real moon all the others joined in as best as they could. The howls, mixed with the noises the others attempted, made such a discordant racket that they all wound up in a laughing heap on the ground.

Now back inside, they help themselves to dessert. Vivian plops a spoonful of fresh whipped cream onto her plate then swirls a shrimp in it. "Delicious!"

"Really?" asks Greyson. "I wouldn't have thought of that."

"Try it," says Vivian, holding the plate out to him.

Greyson picks up a shrimp and dips it into the whipped cream with a wary expression that changes to delight once he pops the shrimp into his mouth. "Wow!" he exclaims and grabs a plate, piles the whipped cream on it, and loads another plate with shrimp.

"Leave some for the rest of us," admonishes Louisa, snatching a shrimp from his plate.

"There's plenty," says Autumn.

Smokey thought Autumn had bought too much shrimp even for a party that included Greyson. Now she's glad they have so much, though she is decidedly not inclined to swirl any in the whipped cream.

They all retire to the living room with their dessert plates where the music is now playing softly in the background. Smokey watches, intrigued, as their guests gravitate into pairs, trios, and small groups. Autumn, Sasha, and Marlon make the rounds trying to spend some time with each group. Smokey knows she should be doing the same, but she's so interested in watching how they've divided themselves up that she doesn't want to interrupt.

Not surprisingly, Bruce Lee and Rivet have found a cozy corner all to themselves. The cute little French bulldog had eyes for Bruce Lee from the moment she entered the house. Smokey wonders if she'd seen him on campus. After tonight, she's sure they'll be seeing a lot more of each other.

Greyson and Abigail are mingling with Jerome J. Ratley and Sasha. Miguel Gato is chatting with Tabby Furry. Mr. and Mrs. Mouse are deep in conversation with Professor Chewy and Sally. Rufus is having a lively chat with Professor Gromit in the center of the room, a wide swath around them keeping all the others clear of Rufus' wildly wagging tail. Winthrop is showing Buster and Marlon how to juggle acorns. Dusty and Sukey are in a tête-á-téte Smokey hopes isn't about the wedding from which they both need a break. And Autumn has gone off to the dining room, presumably to see the fox and jackrabbit prep chefs about starting the clean-up.

Smokey is especially surprised that Professor Bob, who she found out teaches physical science with a specialty in plate tectonics, has thoroughly captured the attention of her neighbor, Shirley, a loan officer at the Faunaburg National Bank. The two cats are seated in chairs they've pulled close together. They lean towards each other, Bob talking and Shirley listening with rapt attention. What on earth could he be telling the tortoiseshell that she'd find so interesting? Smokey likes Shirley, but occasionally thinks her tortitude a bit much. Bob, however, seems enamored of her.

Smokey is about to wander over when raucous laughter erupts from the other side of the room. She turns to find Jasmine at one end of the couch with Paulie Pomeranian next to her. On the other end is Louisa with Tamarind seated beside her. In the middle, holding court, is Vivian. Simon, Sam, and every squirrel in the scurry are lined up on the back of the couch.

"You did that, Louisa?" exclaims Jasmine.

"And that's the tamest story I have to tell," says Vivian.

"Oh, stop!" says Louisa, flapping the tip of her wing in Vivian's direction.

Everyfur in the room has turned towards them.

"What did I miss?" asks Autumn returning from the dining room.

"Vivian was just telling us about the time when they were college roommates and Louisa moved everything in her professor's classroom so that it was all in the opposite place like a mirror image then got all the students to pretend that's the way it had always been," Tamarind explains.

Smokey stares at Louisa in disbelief.

"Don't you two get any ideas," Professor Chewy calls to Bruce Lee and Rivet.

Paying no attention, the two dogs make their way to the couch and sit on the floor in front of Vivian. "What did the prof say?" Rivet asks.

"She thought she was losing her mind," says Vivian, laughing at the memory.

"It took her several minutes to remember it was Prank Day," says Louisa. "Then she started laughing."

"What's Prank Day?" Bruce Lee asks.

"It was a tradition that one day a year the students could play elaborate pranks with complete immunity as long as there were no injuries or damage to property," Louisa explains. "It was a different day each year. The day would be chosen near the start of the school year and announced in the school paper only once. Professors who had been there for a while made note of the date, but the new ones didn't know any better. That teacher was new – first year. The poor thing was a prime target," says Louisa sounding anything but remorseful. "She was a good sport, though."

"Does Verdant have anything like Prank Day?" Bruce Lee asks, turning to his Uncle Chewy.

"No!" all three professors say in unison. "And don't even think of starting it," Chewy adds.

"If that's the tamest story you have about Louisa, what are some of the others?" asks Simon.

"Well, there was the time that she had a huge test she was not ready for. A little too much partying. So, on the morning of the test, instead of studying, she made a huge banner with the words 'All classes canceled this afternoon' and flew over the campus with it tied to her tailfeathers, hoping no one would show up for class and the test would have to be rescheduled."

"Did it work?" asks Rivet.

Vivian snorts and Louisa groans.

"No," says Vivian. "But she did get out of the test after she flew straight into tree and spent the rest of the day in the infirmary."

"Louisa!" Jasmine exclaims.

"Don't remind me," says Louisa, covering her face with her wing. "That was the worst headache of my entire life," she tells Vivian. "You were at that party, too."

"But I did not have a test the next day."

"Oh, yes, the model student. But what about the time we went to the Bahamas?"

Vivian sits taller. "We had a lovely time."

"Sure, until the last night. Remember the beach party?"

"Oh. That," says Vivian trying to stifle a giggle by wrapping a wing around her bill.

"What happened?" asks Sam.

"We'd been invited to a party by some iguanas we'd met at the hotel," says Louisa. "It was great fun. We had a cookout and, once the sun went down, a bonfire on the beach. Besides the iguanas there were parrots, turtles, and bats."

"All of them quite pleasant," says Vivian.

Louisa snorts with laughter. "Pleasant," she says in a mocking tone. "One of the iguanas...what was his name?"

"Ramon," Vivian answers, rolling her eyes.

"Well, Ramon asked Vivian to dance and, as you've seen tonight, dancing is something she can't resist. So, the two of them started dancing and before long, poor Ramon was besotted. One of Viv's favorite songs, "The Tailfeather Shuffle," played."

"It's a popular dance among flamingos," Vivian explains. "We'll be doing a version of it in next week's competition."

"Ramon thought it was a mating dance." Louisa doubles over with laughter.

Vivian groans and slaps both wings over her face.

"They were both feeling the effects of the tropical cocktails that Iggy had been stirring up all night. Halfway through the song, Ramon launched himself into the air just as Vivian fully unfolded her wings..." Louisa stands and unfurls her own wings in demonstration... "and he landed on her with his little green arms around her neck, and shouted, 'yes, my love, I will marry you.'"

"What!" exclaims Tamarind. "What did you do?" she asks, pulling Vivian's wings away from her face.

"You tell them," Vivian demands of Louisa.

"She stood there with Ramon hanging from her like some kind of weird necklace.

Before she could say anything, Iggy yells, 'there's going to be a wedding! Drinks all around!'"

"Now, Louisa," says Vivian. "Tell them what you did then."

"Whatever do you mean, Viv? I did what any good friend would do."

"Uh-huh. She accepted Iggy's drink," Vivian takes over, "lifted it in the air and asked if she could be my maid of honor. A very drunk iguana headed for his jeep saying he was going for the minister. Fortunately, he drove straight into a sand dune. While the others were helping him out, I managed to disentangle myself from Ramon, grabbed Louisa and we made a wobbly flight back to the hotel."

"It was a memorable night," says Louisa. "We flew home the next morning."

"Did you ever hear from Ramon again?" asks Paulie Pomeranian.

"No, thank goodness."

"Are you still engaged?" Winthrop asks, looking impish.

"I was never engaged!"

"Except for when that goofy pelican who wanted to date you," says Louisa. "She got out of that by telling him she was engaged."

"We could have left it at that, but you had to tell him my fiancé was a jealous iguana."

"You should have seen the look on that pelican's face," Louisa laughs.

After they say goodbye to their last guest and Autumn Amelia pays and thanks the prep chefs for their help, Smokey and Autumn collapse on the couch.

"Phew!" says Autumn. "That was a great party!"

"Yes, it was."

"I'll hire Ronnie and Vicky again. The kitchen is spotless."

"That's good," says Smokey surveying the living room. There are quite a few leaves and feathers to be picked up. "I guess we can clean the rest in the morning."

Smokey replays the events of the evening in her head, especially the side of Louisa she hadn't known. She would never have dreamed Louisa would have done all those things with Vivian. Maybe that's why Jasmine enjoys working with her so much.

"Autumn?" Smokey asks. "Do you think I'm boring?"

Chapter 20
The Fitting

"Smokey, you look beautiful," Autumn marvels as Smokey emerges from behind a screen in Dusty's sewing room.

"Now, let me see if I need to make any adjustments. Please walk to the center of the room and turn around."

While Dusty is sticking pins in the dress here and there, Autumn gets a closer look. "I love this. It's like scrollwork," she says indicating the lacy embroidered pattern shot through with sparkling beads over the fitted bodice. The forest green chiffon dress features a boatneck and three-quarter length sheer sleeves. The lacework finishes at the waist where the dress drops to the floor in an A-line.

Stepping back, Autumn claps her paws to her face. "Smokey, the color of that dress makes your eyes look like sparkling emeralds."

"Bring that mirror over," suggests Dusty, nodding towards a cheval mirror in the corner as she squats to adjust the hem length.

Autumn sets the mirror before Smokey and says, "See?"

Smokey gasps. "Dusty, you really have outdone yourself."

"It's not bad if I do say so myself," Dusty admits. Now, I just have to do the fitting for my cousin, Pearl. She won't get here until a week before the wedding. I hope I won't have to do too much adjusting. Now go back and take it off but try not to jostle any of the pins."

Once Smokey's fitting is over and she's left for Fluffington's, Dusty says, "I have a surprise for you,

Autumn." She rolls out a rack from the back of the room. Dusty holds out tea-length, V neck dress with a wrap-around bodice and a pleated skirt.

"I made it for you."

"When did you find the time? You've been so busy with the dresses for the wedding party."

"I can always find time for my best friend. Do you want to try it on?"

"I sure do," says Autumn, taking the dress and scooting behind the screen.

Emerging, she heads straight for the mirror. "I love the color," she says, twisting this way and that to watch the full skirt flair. "It reminds me of caramel."

Dusty laughs. "You do think of everything in terms of food, don't you?"

"Occupational hazard."

"It looks lovely. I think some minor adjustments to the waist are all it needs."

"Dusty, thank you so much. Being a calico, it's hard for me to find something that goes with my fur. This is perfect."

"I thought a rich brown would go well with your burnt orange. That's the only issue you have with your fur color. The rest being white and varying shades of gray work with anything."

"Yes, the orange is what throws everything off."

"But it's a beautiful shade. You need to find the colors that work with it. Warm beige, charcoal, and black should do nicely as well as the deep browns and maybe even teal. And, of course, white goes with everything. Now, what to wear for jewelry? Do you have a chunky gold necklace?"

"No, I don't."

"Well, that's a good excuse for a trip to Tonk's Treasures."

"It is," Autumn agrees, ducking back behind the screen to change.

"Have you finished Abigail's wedding gown?" Autum asks, handing the dress back to Dusty.

"Final fitting yesterday. She has exactly one month to go before the wedding. I warned her not to gain or lose a single pound before then."

Autumn laughs. "My weight fluctuates by the day."

"When you and Buster get married, I'll have to do your final fitting on the morning of your wedding," says Dusty. "How are things going with him?"

"Great!" says Autumn. "We have lots in common and we have the best time together. I've enrolled in an online boating course. We're both very excited about that."

"Do you love him?"

"I've never been in love before. How will I know?"

"You're asking me? I was stuck in this apartment for years until you finally broke me out. Not even a chance to date. You'll have to ask someone who's been in love." Dusty sits bolt upright. "Let's ask Darlene."

"Do you think she'll mind? It might be kind of personal."

"She's pretty good at giving advice. Let's try."

They cross the hall into Dusty's bedroom and lay down on the floor near the little door leading to the Mouse home. Dusty knocks gently on the door. "Darlene, are you home?" she calls.

"Yes, Dusty," Mrs. Mouse says, opening the door. "Oh, hello, Autumn Amelia."

"Hello. I hope we're not disturbing you."

"Not at all. Rodney is at work and the kids are off to school. I'm just cleaning."

"We have an important question to ask you," Dusty explains.

"But only if you don't mind answering," says Autumn. "It might be none of our business. You can tell us so. We won't be upset."

"Sounds interesting."

"How can Autumn tell if she's in love?" asks Dusty.

Autumn's embarrassment grows as she sees Mrs. Mouse trying to suppress a laugh.

Clearing her throat, Mrs. Mouse asks, "that friendly young mancat I met at your party? Buster?"

"Yes," says Autumn. "We've been dating for a few months, but I've never been in love before, so I don't know how to tell if I am."

"We thought we should ask someone who's been in love," Dusty explains. "So, we came to you."

"I see. Well, first of all, I'm still in love, so please don't put it in the past tense. Now," she says, turning her attention to Autumn. "A few months isn't very long. It's great that you enjoy doing things together, but you could say that about Dusty, too, or any other friend, right?"

"Right."

"True love takes time. It's something beyond friendship, though that's still a part of it."

"How did you know you were in love with Rodney?" Dusty asks.

Mrs. Mouse leans against the doorframe, a dreamy look coming over her face. "We'd been dating seriously for over a year. One evening as we were strolling through a meadow, Rodney said he had a surprise for me and reached into his pocket. Then he handed me a wedge of cheese." Mrs. Mouse gazes off in the distance. She puts her paws on either side of her mouth. "It was the most perfect wedge of cheese I'd ever seen. And the aroma..." she draws in a deep breath. "Intoxicating.

"He said he'd searched for a cheese wedge worthy of me, but there wasn't one. This was the best he could do. I had a momentary twinge of doubt, thinking he was just trying to flatter me. It was gone, though, when I looked in his eyes. He has the most expressive eyes, you know. That's when I knew for sure I loved him. I told him so, too. I think it surprised both of us."

"Did he say he loved you too?" Dusty asks.

"He did." She chuckles a little. "After he regained his composure."

"How romantic," says Autumn, imagining the scene, especially the cheese.

"Is that when he asked you to marry him?" Dusty asks.

"No. That was still a while in coming. But I'm glad we didn't rush. It's important to take your time and be as sure as you can be about something as important as that."

"So, when did you decide to get married?" asks Autumn.

"When we each knew how the other responded in the good times and the bad. I realized that he was always there for me and supported me and I knew I'd always do the same for him."

Mrs. Mouse turns to Autumn Amelia, looking her in the eye.

"You have to feel in your heart that you want to make a life with Buster. That living with him day in and day out would not drive you crazy." She stops for a moment, contemplating something. "Or if it did, that it would be a kind of crazy you could live with and sometimes even like. You need to believe that you would want him to be the father of your kittens. You have to feel sure that the two of you can become like one cat while still being yourselves. You must feel at ease sharing intimate things with him and letting him do the same with you. You have to know that you both want the best for each other and are willing to sacrifice for each other when necessary. Finally, you must both be willing and committed to seeing each other through building a home, family, and life together. You know the wedding vows, right?"

"Yes," says Autumn. "The bride and groom promise to love and cherish each other, to always share the catnip and treats, and to be faithful to each other forever."

"Those vows aren't just words," says Mrs. Mouse. "Don't go into a marriage if you can't live them." Then her face breaks into a huge smile. "But if you both believe you can live them, then get married. A good marriage is true blessing."

"Thanks, Mrs. Mouse," says Autumn.

"I wish you all the best," says Mrs. Mouse. "Buster seems like a very nice cat. Now, maybe the two of you can help me with something."

"What is it?"

"Now that the kids are in school, I'd like to find a part-time job. Do you know of anything?"

"What skills do you have?" asks Autumn Amelia.

"I used to work as a cashier at the grocery store on Rodent Way before I had the babies. I helped stock the shelves sometimes, too. It wasn't the most challenging job in the world, but I didn't mind."

"We will certainly let you know if we hear of anything," says Dusty.

As they leave the apartment headed for Tonk's Treasures, Autumn's mind is reeling from all Mrs. Mouse has told her.

When they arrive at the boutique, they first think the store is empty. It's devoid of customers, and its owner is nowhere to be seen.

"Tamarind?" calls Dusty.

"Back here." Tamarind's voice comes from deep within the store.

They follow the voice to find Tamarind on all fours, her hind quarters sticking out of a closet.

"What are you doing?" Autumn asks.

"Trying to...unpack...boxes." She pulls free to sit on the floor, arms loaded with clothing, more spilling out of a huge container laying on its side, her fur disheveled.

A bell rings at the front of the store.

"Oh, no," says Tamarind, letting go of the clothes and trying to smooth her fur. She scrambles to her feet. "Do I look okay?"

"You're fine. Go on. We'll pick this up," says Dusty.

"You're pawsome," she says, then hurries towards the front to help her customer.

Dusty and Autumn fold the clothes and pile them neatly on a nearby chair, then go to look at the jewelry selection.

"Autumn, this one's perfect," says Dusty, holding up a gold necklace with three large, irregularly shaped disks.

"Oh, I like that." Autumn tries it on then heads for a mirror. "You're right, Dusty. This will look great with that dress."

Tamarind is just checking out the bunny who had come in. "You're going to love those carrot-scented candles, Harriet," she says. "They're very romantic."

"That's what I'm hoping," says the bunny with a little giggle before hopping out the door.

"Did you ladies find what you were looking for?" Tamarind asks.

Autumn places the necklace on the counter. "Dusty made a gorgeous chocolate brown dress for me to wear to the wedding. I'll wear this with it."

"Isn't that a cool piece?" asks Tamarind as she rings it up. "I love it."

"Me too," Autumn agrees.

"We folded up the clothes and put them on a chair in the other room," says Dusty. "What happened back there?"

"Thank you. I ordered loads of new clothes that came in last week. I've been so busy I haven't had a chance to unbox them until today. It's the first time it's been quiet enough in here to do it."

"Business must be good," says Autumn.

"I'm not complaining. But I have to unpack the boxes, steam the wrinkles out of all the clothes from being folded, get them priced and listed in my inventory, and put them on the racks. I've stayed late every night this week."

"Is anyone helping you?" asks Dusty.

"No, and, you know I may need to find someone."

Autumn and Dusty look at each other then back at Tamarind. "We can help with that," says Dusty.

"You two? Aren't you busy enough?"

"Not us," says Autumn. "Mrs. Mouse. She wants to get a part-time job."

"She has experience working in a store," Dusty adds. "She's stocked and cashiered at the grocery store on Rodent Way. What do you think?"

Tamarind grabs a business card from beside the cash register, and hands it to Dusty. "Tell her to call me right away."

As they head out of the store, Dusty starts giggling.

"What's so funny?" Autumn asks.

"Before Oneness Park opened, Mr. and Mrs. Mouse were terrified of cats. It's amazing how much has changed.

Chapter 21
An Unexpected Visitor

It's Sunday. Smokey's assignment is due for tomorrow night's class. She'll be working during the day, so this is her last chance to finish it. Ever since lunch she's had one interruption after another, mostly phone calls, but now the doorbell. Autumn has left for the restaurant, so Smokey's on her own.

Shirley, the tortoiseshell cat from up the street is on her porch. Oddly, Shirley's car is parked in their driveway. Why did she drive here? She's only a few houses away.

"Hi," says Shirley. "I don't suppose Autumn is here, is she?"

"She won't be home until tonight."

"Did she tell you I was going to drop off a few things today?"

"What things?"

"At the Hunter's Moon Night party, she told me all about the garden you two are planning in the back yard — the kitchen garden idea with the vintage furniture and appliances. I told her I have a few items that would work. You can have them."

"That's very generous, but we won't be setting that up until spring."

"I'm cleaning out my basement. If I don't give them to you now, I'll have to take them to the dump. Autumn sounded very interested, so I'll bring them in now."

"Now?"

"I had to fold the back seats down to get them in. I could use your help."

"Um...okay," says Smokey, grabbing a jacket from the closet. She follows Shirley to the car, hoping that there won't be too much and that they're not monstrosities.

Laying in the back of Shirley's car is a white porcelain pedestal sink with the hot and cold faucets on either end, two pie safes, one of walnut with pierced tin plates in the doors, the other white with screened doors, and a large box, the contents of which rattle loudly when Smokey moves it aside to grab hold of one end of the sink.

"How did you get this stuff into your car by yourself?"

"Where there's a will there's a way. And I have a very strong will. It is much easier with someone helping, though."

"I guess we should put this stuff in the basement," says Smokey. "There's nowhere else for it and we won't be using it for several months."

After lugging the sink and the two pie safes downstairs, Shirley says, "I'll grab that box and that's it."

"The box, too?" Smokey had hoped that wasn't part of the donation.

"Yes, Autumn said she'd take it."

Shirley returns a moment later and places the box on the floor. "I understand you're the one designing the garden, so why don't you look through the box now. If there's anything you don't think you'll use, I'll take it back for the recycling bin."

"I don't have time right now," says Smokey.

"Then you'll have to dispose of whatever you don't want yourself. Once I'm rid of a thing, I can't bear to lay eyes on it again."

"Oh," says Smokey. "I guess I can take a quick look."

She opens the box to find it packed with vintage kitchen implements – canisters, flour sifters, an egg beater, potato mashers, whisks, slotted spoons, cookie cutters, a colander, measuring cups and spoons, a glass jar with an odd handle stuck in its lid with a four-pronged blade halfway into the jar that was some sort of chopper, and handfuls of silverware. Her mind is already conjuring garden uses for several of the items.

Finally, she says, "Leave the box here. I'll put it in the basement for now. Whatever we don't use, we'll dispose of. Thank you for sharing this with us."

"My pleasure. I'm going to have my basement finished."

"That will be nice. Autumn and I should do that someday. Well, again, thank you. She inches towards the door. She needs to get back to her homework.

"Before I go," says Shirley, "Thank you again for inviting me to your Hunter's Moon Night party."

"We're glad you could come."

"I had a wonderful time."

"I'm happy to hear that." The tortoiseshell isn't budging.

"I was especially delighted to meet Professor Bob."

"You two hit it off."

"He's asked me out to dinner next Saturday."

"How wonderful."

"Might we sit down?"

Confused, Smokey stops halfway to the front door. "You want to talk to *me* about him?"

"Please?" she says, gesturing towards the couch.

"Okay," says Smokey.

"I don't date any cat without knowing a bit about him first. It just seems the prudent thing to do."

"Sure," says Smokey, baffled.

"I told him I would check my calendar and get back to him. So, what can you tell me about him?"

"I hardly know him."

"How did he end up at your party?"

"Oh, that was Autumn. He and Professor Gromit were there when she invited Professor Chewy so she felt it wouldn't be polite if she didn't invite them too."

"Then I should be asking Autumn?"

"She doesn't know any more about him than I do. Professor Chewy is the one to ask."

Shirley's eyebrow whiskers shoot up. "I can't do that. I don't know him any better than I know Bob. How well does Autumn know Professor Chewy?"

"Not much better than you. We invited him and Buster to the party because they're new in the neighborhood and we wanted them to meet other neighbors and friends. But you spent a lot of time talking to Bob at the party."

"Yes. He told me he's a professor of Physical Science at Verdant University, he likes to travel, go out to eat, and enjoys art museums. But I want to hear what someone else thinks of him. His character. Is he trustworthy? He seemed kind, but was he just on his best behavior? Things like that."

"I can't tell you that. You already know more about him than I do. Do you like to do the things he likes?"

"Yes, very much. Though I have to admit that I know very little about physical science, especially that plate tectonics stuff he's so enamored of. He did make it sound interesting though. He's probably a wonderful teacher. I'd like to go out with him."

"Then go. It's just dinner."

"But it's not my policy."

"So, update your policy. Isn't the dating process the way you find out more about each other?"

"Well, yes, but there needs to be a starting point first."

Smokey worries that Shirley's had a horrible dating experience in the past and is frightened. She puts her paw on Shirley's and in a gentle tone asks, "Are you afraid? I'm sure Autumn and Buster would be happy to double date with you and Bob at first if that would help."

Shirley laughs. "Oh, dear, Smokey," she says. "No, I'm not afraid. My policy is in place simply to avoid wasting my time. But thank you for your concern. Well, since you aren't able to enlighten me any further, I'll be going."

"Um...okay," says Smokey getting up to walk Shirley to the door. "So, will you go to dinner with him?"

"You know, I think I will."

"I hope you have a wonderful time. Thanks again for the donations for the garden."

"Think nothing of it." With that, Shirley steps out the door, heading for her car.

As Smokey watches her go, she thinks, *Oh, Professor Bob, I sure hope you like tortitude.*

Chapter 22
The Pirate Museum

"Why are you going to Niptucket in the middle of November?" Smokey asks Autumn. "Won't it be cold?"

"Not with my fur. Besides, I didn't even know there was a pirate museum on Niptucket. Did you?"

"No. Is it new?"

"Buster says it opened a few years ago." She's excited about experiencing it for the first time with Buster.

Autumn stands at the counter, buttering a piece of toast. She turns to look at Smokey who is eating a bowl of cereal while scrolling on her phone. It's Tuesday. Smokey will be leaving shortly for work. Buster has taken the day off, leaving the print shop in the paws of his assistant so that he can take Autumn Amelia to the Pirate Museum on Niptucket.

Once Smokey has left the house, Autumn heads to her bedroom. Opening her closet door, she takes a box from the shelf, sits in the middle of the closet floor and opens it, gently unwrapping the layers of tissue paper. Removing the multi-colored glass pirate ship from the box, she sets it on the floor. As always, the pirate ship reminds her of her mother who purchased it for her when she was a kitten.

"Mama Cat," she whispers towards the ship. "I have a mancat friend. His name is Buster. You'd like him. Today he's taking me to the new pirate museum on Niptucket Island."

Autumn gazes at the ship, gliding a paw over the surface. She thinks of what Mrs. Mouse told her about how she'll know if Buster is the right mancat for her.

Mrs. Mouse said that she and Buster would need to feel comfortable sharing intimate things with each other.

Could I tell him about my pirate ship? she wonders. He'd think it was a pretty trinket, a keepsake gift from her mother. The real test would be if she could tell him about how she takes it out and sits in the closet with it when she's very upset and that it allows her to fantasize about captaining her own pirate ship. And that makes her feel better. She knows it's odd. That's why no one, not even Smokey, knows about it. Telling him would be a huge risk. He might think it's too weird and not want to date her anymore.

I'm not ready for that yet. She gets a queasy feeling wondering if she has to ever tell him. Would it be okay if she has one thing she keeps all to herself?

Hugging the ship to her chest, she wishes Mama Cat was here. She'd know the right answer.

As if the ship is a conduit, she hears Mama Cat's voice in her head telling her that she needn't worry about it. They haven't been dating for very long. If and when the time comes, she'll know it.

Smiling and feeling relieved, Autumn wraps the ship in its layers of tissue paper and returns it to its box just as the doorbell rings.

* * *

Autumn hardly knows which way to look. On the walls are large paintings of famous pirate captains. She recognizes some of the names. Black Jack the Jackal, a zebra named Ziggy the Striped Bandit, and the most infamous of all, a crocodile known as the Green Menace. But the museum's main focus is on the replica of the pirate ship Sea Raider that was wrecked off the coast of Niptucket 245 years ago.

Reading the wall plaque, Autumn learns that the wreck was discovered after a grouper who had been living inside it decided to vacation closer to the surface where he met a seagull and told her about the wreck. In turn, she conveyed the information to her friend Tom Glourp, a bullfrog, who happened to be an underwater archaeologist. His team found the wreck. Not wanting to disturb the home of several schools of fish, they made no attempts to raise the ship, but instead took measurements and hundreds of photographs. The fish were happy to donate some of the items found on the ship to Glourp for study and eventual use in this museum.

A shiver of anticipation runs through Autumn as they walk the carpeted hallway leading to the main room. As they round the corner, she nearly loses her breath. A life-size replica of the Sea Raider stands in the center of the room.

The ship, a 100 foot, square-rigged, three-masted galley towers over her. Its massive sails almost scrape the ceiling. In the dim lighting – spotlights hanging from the ceiling provide the only illumination – she feels as though she's stepped into another world. Beneath her paws, the floor is painted an ocean blue with what appear to be dark green fronds just below the surface. A mild strobe effect gives it the feeling of undulation.

"Shall we go aboard?" Buster asks.

"Can we?"

"Of course. But first, let's meet the captain." He extends a paw towards the wax figure of a honey badger standing at the end of the gangway. In one paw, the figure holds a cutlass, in the other a rifle, a knife is tucked into its boot, and six pistols are strapped across its chest. Next to it is an interpretive sign. Autumn reads:

Zena, also known as the Terror of the Waves, was a honey badger from southern Morrocco. She captained the Sea Raider with an iron paw. Along with her crew, she captured 200 ships. Her pirating career was cut short when a violent storm sent the Sea

Admiration rises so powerfully in Autumn that she can't help but clap her paws over her mouth and spin in a giddy circle like a kitten.

"You approve?" asks Buster.

"I didn't know there were any female pirates. She was pawsome!"

Buster chuckles. "Fearsome, too. Shall we tour her ship?"

"Yes!"

They walk up the gangway and step onto the deck. Twenty canons stud the ship's side.

"Where is the ship's wheel?" Autumn asks.

"You mean the helm? It should be on the quarter deck. Over here," Buster says, leading her towards the stern.

"Give it try," says Buster as they reach the top of the quarter deck's stairs. "The sign says you can."

Sure enough, a sign posted near the replica wheel encourages visitors to take a turn at the helm. Autumn steps into place. At first, she finds the wheel heavy and hard to turn, but soon gets the hang of it. The museum falls away around her and she's mentally transported to the sea. She imagines herself dressed like the wax figure of Zena, ruler of the waves. She can almost feel the wind ruffling her fur, the sea mist landing on her whiskers.

"Autumn? Autumn Amelia?"

A tap on her shoulder brings her back to reality. "Oh." She sees a line has formed behind her of puppies, cubs, kits, and one fawn all waiting their turns for a try at the wheel. "Sorry," she says. "I got carried away."

Embarrassed, she hurries down the quarter deck's stairs.

After touring the upper decks, Autumn and Buster head for the ladder to the lower decks.

"This is the captain's quarters," says Buster as they enter an area at the furthest end of the stern. Three large windows line the far wall. In the center is a small table on top of which lay sheets of parchment, pen, and ink. Another wax figure of Zena sits at the table appearing to write on the parchment. An hourglass holds down one corner of the paper. There are trunks on the floor and a large shelf beneath the windows that holds books, ledgers, more parchment, and a decanter of brandy. On one side is a bunk with a pillow and blanket. On the other side, large maps are tacked to the wall.

Autumn has the urge to sit at the table, write on the parchment, and climb into the bunk, but of course, she doesn't.

"Cozy," says Buster. "But I guess the captain gets the best accommodations."

"I could live here and captain this ship."

"You could?" Buster asks.

She glances at him, embarrassed at his amused expression. She hadn't meant to say that out loud.

"Shall we see where the crew slept?" he asks. "It won't be as nice as this."

"I want to see it all." She does, but she wishes she could stay in the captain's quarters. Buster was right when he said it was cozy. That's just how it makes her feel.

Hammocks line large areas belowdecks, some of which are occupied by wax figures of sleeping honey badger crew members.

"Not much privacy," says Autumn. "I'd rather be in the captain's cabin."

"Who wouldn't?"

Next, they step into the galley. "Surely, this would be your favorite place on a ship," Buster says, ushering her in. It's larger than she expects with lots of barrels, pots, pans, and cauldrons. Dry fish hang from ropes held up by hooks on the walls. Wheels of cheese and large loaves of bread sit on the counters. A large iron stove sits in one corner with huge piles of wood nearby. The stove is on a stone hearth which, in turn, stands on tin and sand. An interpretive sign explains that it was to protect the deck.

"Well?" asks Buster. "Would you try your paw at cooking here?"

"I've never used a wood-burning stove before and I doubt there was much variety in the food, but I might have come up with a few interesting meals."

Buster lets out a hearty laugh. "With you as ship's cook, the pirates would be so busy eating they'd forget all about raiding. Once word spread, everyone would want to be captured just to get some of your cooking."

"Oh, Buster," says Autumn, playfully shoving his arm. "That's silly but thank you." She's feeling torn now between wanting to be the captain and wanting to cook for the crew. She doesn't suppose those two jobs went together. But, she thinks, if it was her ship she could do as she liked. What would be the point of being the captain if she couldn't make the rules?

They finish the tour of the ship with the hold where they find barrels full of rum and whisky and trunks overflowing with imitation emeralds, diamonds, pearls, and gold.

After disembarking, they head for an adjoining room where they find pieces of the real Sea Raider, a display of weapons used by pirates, a full-size replica anchor, and small pieces of treasure secured under glass with signs explaining each one.

"Autumn, you must try this," says Buster leading her to an alcove in the center of which is a small platform and a replica of a ship's wheel.

Autumn climbs onto the platform and takes hold of the wheel. She's facing a screen that shows a video of the ocean making it look and feel as though she's really on the sea.

"Can I push the button?" asks Buster.

"Go ahead."

The platform begins to gently move. Now Autumn has the wheel in her paws, the rolling deck underneath, and the wide ocean ahead of her. All she needs are pirate clothes and she'd be in paradise. She doesn't even notice when Buster pulls out his cell phone. It's not until they get in his car to head home that he hands her the phone. She gazes at the images of herself standing tall, proud, and fearless.

"Did you enjoy the museum?" Buster asks as they pull out of the parking lot.

"Couldn't you tell?"

He smiles. "Yeah, I could tell."

"What about you? Did you like it?"

"It made me want to go back in time and captain my own pirate ship with you as ship's cook. What do you think?"

"I think I'd like to be the captain and the cook."

"You'd be busy."

"I could do it."

Bringing the car to a halt at a red light, Buster looks Autumn in the eye. "Yes, Autumn Amelia, I believe you could."

Chapter 23
The Perfect Gift

"I still haven't bought their wedding gift yet. I hope Tamarind can help." Smokey watches the November evening wind ruffle Autumn's fur. She hugs her fall jacket tightly around herself. Sometimes she wishes she'd gotten Mama Cat's Maine Coon genes. Autumn only needs to wear a coat on the coldest days.

"Hey, ladies," Tamarind calls as they enter the boutique. "I'll bet you're here to buy something for the shower on Saturday."

"And I need to get a wedding gift, too," says Smokey.

"How did you know?" asks Autumn.

"You're not the first. Besides, Darlene is going, too."

Just then Smokey catches sight of Mrs. Mouse behind the counter ringing up a sparrow's order.

"Anything in mind?" Tamarind asks.

"Nope," says Smokey.

"Let me show you a few things."

They wait near the counter while Tamarind goes off.

"How do you like your new job?" Autumn asks Mrs. Mouse.

"I love it. Thank you so much for recommending me. Tamarind is a dream to work for. Plus, I get a discount."

"Is Mr. Mouse going to Greyson's bachelor party?" Smokey asks.

"Yes. And since both parties are on the same night, I'm glad the shower is being held at the apartment, so we don't need to get a sitter. I'll be able to keep an eye on the kids."

"Here we go," says Tamarind, returning with her paws full. "Start looking at these while I go grab some more." She goes off in another direction.

There is a crystal trinket box with lilies of the valley in relief on the lid, a set of stone coasters with 'Mr. & Mrs.' etched into them bordered by pretty, red roses, and a bride-to-be box filled with scented soaps, candles, a mani-pedi set, fur conditioner, and two pairs of fuzzy paw socks.

"These," says Autumn, picking up a coaster. "They look like her wedding roses."

"Nice," says Smokey. "But I'm not sure."

Tamarind brings over another armful.

"What are you giving her?" Autumn asks Mrs. Mouse.

"I heard Abigail and Greyson talking about picnics together next summer, so I got them one of these," she says, pulling up a picnic basket from behind the counter. It's a wicker box with an insulated interior and straps on the inside of the lid to hold plates and two sets of utensils. There's a small compartment on the outside to hold a blanket.

"That's adorable," says Smokey.

"I hope they like it."

"They will," Autumn assures her.

Smokey continues to examine the items Tamarind has placed on the counter. They're all great, but she's now Abigail's partner and their families will be joining together. She wants something special.

"I'm going with the stone coasters," says Autumn. "Whenever she uses them, she'll think of her wedding because of the roses."

"Good choice," says Tamarind. "Do you want Darlene to ring you up now?"

"Yes, please."

"Smokey, see anything you like?" Tamarind asks.

"I can't decide. Abigail is responsible for giving me my big break in architecture by making me her partner. I want to give her something very special."

"Hmm...let me look around some more." Tamarind wanders off.

"I think I've got it!" Tamarind calls. She hurries over carrying a wooden box. Mrs. Mouse makes room on the counter.

"Check this out," says Tamarind, setting down the box.

"It's beautiful," says Smokey, admiring the rose border carved around it. "But what is it?"

Tamarind opens the latch and lifts the lid. Inside are two wine glasses nestled in black velvet. One glass is etched with the words 'I do' and the other with 'me too'.

"Buy a bottle of their favorite wine and put it in here," Tamarind says indicating the space between the glasses. "But here's the really cool part." She pulls back the pouch set into the box's lid. Sewn into the fabric are the words, 'Our Wishes For You'.

"You write a note saying what you wish for them and get some of their other guests to write them, too. Then put them in here."

"Perfect!" says Smokey.

"And so romantic," says Mrs. Mouse. "They can read them while they drink their wine together. Too bad there's no fireplace in their apartment. Can't you just see them snuggled up together before the fire?"

"Darlene, you are a true romantic," says Tamarind.

Mrs. Mouse's whiskers twitch as she giggles softly.

"Smokey still needs to get a wedding gift," says Autumn. "I told her about the travel book Dusty is going to give them. Do you have any other travel stuff?"

"Something came in last week. Let me go get it."

Before Tamarind can hurry off, the bell over the door rings and an opossum enters followed by a raccoon.

"Good evening, ladies," Tamarind calls. "I'll be with you in a moment."

"I can help them," says Mrs. Mouse, scooting out from behind the counter.

"Thanks, Darlene." Turning to Autumn, Tamarind says, "Darlene's amazing. I don't know what I ever did without her. She can do everything, and she gets along great with Collette."

"Collette?" asks Autumn.

"She's the Canada goose who's helping out on weekends and two evenings. That's when the two of them work together. She would have been here tonight, but she has a cold. Be careful. There's a lot going around. Now, let me go get that travel item."

Smokey glances across the store. Mrs. Mouse stands on the raccoon's shoulders to get something off a shelf for the opossum all the while talking about how wonderful the fur cream is and how much she will love it.

"She does seem to be in her element," says Smokey. "That's really nice to see."

Tamarind returns with a globe. She sets it on the counter. "This is made from cotton canvas," she explains. She opens a little door in the globe's base exposing a package of blue and red pushpins. "They use one color for the places they've been and the other color for the places they want to go."

"Cool," says Smokey.

"And," says Tamarind, "it also comes with these." She reaches into the box that holds the globe and takes out a metal case. Inside is a stack of papers. "There's a paper for every country in the world. Each one tells what the country is known for, information about the climate, languages spoken, exchange rates, major cities, don't-miss sites, and any other important information about that country."

"Fantastic!" says Smokey. "Autumn, don't you think they'd love it?"

"I do," says Autumn. "You should get it."

"I'll take it," says Smokey.

Peeking over Smokey's shoulder, Tamarind says, "Darlene's busy. I'll ring you up."

"Will you write your note for wine box tonight?" Smokey asks as she and Autumn get into her car.

"Sure. I'll call Dusty for a list so you can get notes from others."

"There are so many coming, I doubt I could get them all. I wish there was more time."

"At least try to get a note from everyone who will be at the shower," Autumn says.

"There sure is a lot that goes into a wedding. It's not even just the day itself, but everything leading up to it," says Smokey, thinking about how much she'll need to do if Autumn and Buster decide to get married. "Are you making the food for the shower?"

"Yes, but it's only appetizers. It'll be a snap."

Autumn is quiet for a while. Smokey wonders if she's thinking about marrying Buster.

"Smokey, do you think you'll ever get married?"

This is not the question she expected. "Um...maybe. Someday, I guess."

"I hope you do. If you want to, I mean."

"Yeah. If I find the right cat, I will. What about you and Buster?"

"It's too soon."

"But you like him?"

"Very much."

"Do you love him?"

Autumn is quiet for a moment. Then she says, "I think maybe. I'm taking everyfurs' advice and not rushing."

"That's good."

For the rest of the drive home, Smokey ruminates on what Abigail told her about how she was so hyper-focused on building her business that she never had time for romance. She hoped Smokey wouldn't make the same mistake. But Abigail built her business and a stellar reputation. She's found love now with Greyson. She's getting married. If you ask Smokey, Abigail has it all. Of course, she didn't have kittens, but maybe she didn't want to.

What about her? There's no guarantee her life will turn out the same way. Smokey has always been career-oriented, but now she wonders if she will end up lonely. She's always pictured herself living with Autumn forever, but in a luxury apartment like Abigail's. That's not very likely – the living with Autumn forever part, not the apartment. She is going to get that apartment. But Autumn will have her own life with her own family.

"Autumn," she asks, "If you and Buster do get married, will you still run Mama Cat's Kitchen?"

"Of course."

"Do you want to have kittens?"

"Absolutely!"

"How will you do both?"

"Lots of furs and feathers have babies and still work."

"How, though? Who will watch the kittens?"

"That's something Buster and I will have to figure out. There's day care or we could get a nanny. If we decide to get married, we'll talk about it first and make sure we're in agreement."

Smokey tries to picture herself as a mama cat and can't quite do it. If she had kittens, she'd love them, but does she want to have them? Well, she'll need a husband first. Better decide if she wants one of those.

Chapter 24
Abigail Fluffington's Bridal Shower

"Do you think we'll have enough?" Autumn asks. She looks over the massive cheese board with its assortment of gourmet cheeses, grapes, figs, and crackers along with the serving plates of lobster pasta salad, basil, tomatoes, and feta on skewers, the basket of gourmet nuts and berries, the deviled eggs, baked brie with cranberries, baked oysters with bacon and parmesan, roasted cherry tomato bruschetta, and the row of niptini glasses each filled with a bed of lettuce and topped with shrimp.

"There's plenty," says Dusty.

Autumn giggles. "Does Abigail suspect?"

"I don't think so. I'm glad our cousin, Pearl, came early. I had her take Abby out shopping so we could set up. I told her not to come back until I text her. The two of them have likely wiped out every store in Faunaburg by now."

"I'm looking forward to meeting Pearl," says Autumn. "What's she like?"

Dusty stands, paws on hips and says, "She's a couple of years older than Abby, a gorgeous silver Persian, retired bank CEO, twice widowed, very wealthy, well-traveled, and, in my opinion, a total snob."

"Oh," says Autumn. "Do she and Abigail get along well?"

"Abigail has lots of practice hobnobbing with the hoity toity."

"Excuse me." They both turn to see Mrs. Mouse coming down the hallway.

"Yes, Darlene?" says Dusty. "What do you need?"

"A small favor."

"Of course."

"It's the kids. They know there's going to be a party here this evening. Would it be alright if they came for a few minutes? Once they realize it's for grownups, they'll get bored," she says, her tiny hands wringing her apron. "I wouldn't ask except they are driving me crazy."

"Of course," says Dusty. "And they can stay as long as they like."

"Oh, thank you," says Mrs. Mouse. "They'll come in their pajamas and be ready to fall asleep long before the party is over. Honestly, I was a little nervous about leaving them even though I'd be in the same house. They've never been alone before."

"I understand," says Dusty. "They might like some of the appetizers, especially the berries, and we have desserts."

"Thank you. They've had supper, but I'm sure they'd love some dessert if you have enough."

"Autumn made plenty."

"Thank you so much. I'm going to get them washed up and ready for bed. See you soon."

"Hmm..." says Autumn. "Do you think Pearl will mind?"

"If she can't tolerate a few mice babies, too bad for her."

"You don't like her much, do you?"

"Sometimes she can really rub my fur backwards."

There's a buzz from the intercom. It's Jasmine and Smokey, the first to arrive. They are soon followed by Sasha, Louisa, Sukey, and Sally. Mrs. Mouse returns with all eight of her children – the mousekins as Autumn calls them. Just as the little ones run into the living room, the buzzer sounds again. This time it's Claudette, the receptionist at Fluffington ArCATechture, followed by Nadine, a border collie and

Adele, a Turkish Angora, both architects from Fluffington's.

In between greeting guests and taking coats, Dusty sends a text to Pearl letting her know it's time to bring Abigail back.

"They're only a few blocks away," Dusty tells Autumn.

Autumn goes to the huge window to keep an eye out. In the light of the streetlamp, she catches sight of Abigail striding down the sidewalk with a silver Persian cat by her side. She's slightly taller than Abigail, equally fluffy, and wearing a deep blue sweater set with matching ankle-length skirt, silver shoes and a matching silver clutch purse. She's every inch as stylish as Abigail.

Autumn hurries over to Dusty.

"Attention, please!" calls Dusty over the chattering.

When she has their attention, she continues. "Abigail and our cousin, Pearl, are about to enter the building."

"This will be fun!" Exclaims one of the mousekins.

"Hush," says Mrs. Mouse. "Not a peep."

All the guests gather in the center of the room. Their whispering quickly dies away. When the drone of the elevator tells them that Abigail is seconds from entering the apartment, even the stifled giggles of the mousekins stop. The room is bursting with so much contained excitement that Autumn's fur is standing on end. She watches intently as the key rattles in the lock and the doorknob turns.

Abigail Fluffington steps into the apartment calling, "Dusty, we're —"

"SURPRISE!" They all shout. The mousekins race from one end of the living room to the other.

"Oh, my," says Abigail, a paw to her chest. Pearl stands regal and unfazed beside her.

Abigail remains motionless for a moment, taking it all in.

"Well, come in and join the party," says Dusty.

Pearl nudges Abigail forward. She quickly gets lost amongst the hugs and kisses.

Once the initial greetings have subsided and Pearl introduced, Dusty encourages them to help themselves to the food. After filling their plates and grabbing glasses of wine (juice for the mousekins) they all settle on the sofa or into the many chairs that have been drawn up around the guest of honor.

"You must be excited, Abigail," says Sasha.

"I'll admit when I think about the wedding I feel like a young kit."

"That's wonderful," says Louisa.

"I suppose. I just hope I don't get too flummoxed during the ceremony."

"You'll be fine," says Smokey.

Autumn notices Pearl's look of disdain. Does she not approve of Abigail admitting to being less than a cold block of steel?

"I thought you two went shopping," says Dusty. "You've come home with nothing. That's unlike you."

Pearl looks down her whiskers. "We wouldn't be so gauche as to carry bags home. We're having everything delivered."

"But of course. How boorish of me," Dusty retorts.

Autumn can't help but think of how much Dusty has changed since they first met. The old Dusty would be hiding in her sewing room.

"What does boorish mean?" asks one of the mousekins. The question is met with a hush from Mrs. Mouse.

"Is everything ready?" asks Adele. "I remember rushing around right up to the last minute before my wedding."

"Greyson ensures that all is running smoothly."

"Greyson?" asks Collette. "The groom? That must be a first."

"He didn't have a paw in much of the planning other than the DJ and the bartender, but he did manage to get all the vendors together at once so we could sort everything out." She launches into how Greyson gathered all the vendors at Miguel's.

"He's quite a catch," says Nadine.

Autumn Amelia has been watching the border collie trying hard to ignore the mousekins while they tear around the room, her urge to herd them barely subdued. And Nadine's food is lined up on her plate in order of size and color. *I'll bet her blueprints are perfect.*

"Don't forget to save room for dessert," Dusty reminds the guests.

"Dessert?" asks Herbie, one of the mousekins.

"Yes. Miss Autumn made lots of delicious goodies for us."

Autumn removes the empty serving plates and replaces them with desserts. There are plates of petit fours, chocolate eclairs, macrons in several colors, cupcakes with rose-shaped frosting, and frosted sugar cookies in the shapes of wedding gowns and gold rings.

"I want one of everything," shouts one of the mousekins who is riding on Louisa's sleeve.

"Silas!" warns Mrs. Mouse just as he prepares to dive onto the table.

"Okay," he says sounding dejected.

"Don't worry," says Louisa. "I'll fix a plate for you of whatever your mom says you can have."

Silas looks hopefully at Mrs. Mouse.

"One," she says. "Not one of everything."

Louisa and Silas are the last to leave the dessert table as he finally decides on a cupcake.

Conversation resumes over desserts.

"Where are you going on your honeymoon?" Sally asks.

"Tanzania," says Abigail.

"Sounds exotic," says Sukey.

"I think when I get married, I'll honeymoon in the Canary Islands," says Louisa. "Vivian and her dance troupe are having a magnificent time there."

"How did they do in the competition?" asks Abigail.

"They've made it to the finals. It finishes in two days. I hope they win."

"Will she stop by again? I so enjoy her stories."

"She didn't say. She may go straight home. With Vivian you never know."

"I'd love to see her troupe dance," says Dusty. "Have you ever seen them, Louisa?"

"A couple of times. They've won lots of competitions. They're amazing."

"Even in all my travels, I've never seen a flamingo dance troupe," says Abigail. "They must be a sight to see. Have you, Pearl?"

"Certainly not, though I did witness a lovely performance by a flock of macaws once while I was in the Amazon Rain Forest."

"What's a macaw?" asks one of the mousekins, jumping up onto the arm of Pearl's chair and taking a bite of her cookie at the same time, crumbs sprinkling onto Pearl's skirt.

"It's a...very...colorful...bird," says Pearl, brushing crumbs from her lap and scooting as far as possible to the far side of her chair.

The mousekin, taking this action as an invitation to join her, hops from the arm of the chair to the seat.

"Mindy!" exclaims Mrs. Mouse. She hurries over to remove Mindy from the chair. "I am so sorry," she tells Pearl.

Pearl tilts her head at a haughty angle. "You must be the mother of the *mouse* family that I understand lives in the *wall* of Dusty's bedroom.

"Yes, I'm Darlene Mouse."

Autumn notices Mrs. Mouse's whiskers quiver, but she's not certain if it's from fear or anger.

"And we are delighted to be sharing a home with you," says Abigail, her voice serene, her glance at Pearl frosty.

"Come, children," says Mrs. Mouse. "It's past your bedtime." She rounds them up. They say goodnight before she leads them down the hallway.

An awkward silence fills the living room. Dusty clears her throat. "Time for presents," she announces. "Autumn, would you help me bring them out?"

Dusty has piled all the presents in her bedroom. When they enter, Dusty heads straight for the door to the Mouse's house.

"Darlene," she calls, tapping on the door. When it opens, she says, "Pearl can be such a pain in the paws. I hope you're not too hurt by what she said. It's not you. She's a snob to everyfur."

"Mindy should not have jumped up on her chair like that. I apologize."

"Mousekins are curious. There's nothing wrong with that."

"Still, it was impolite. We will work on better manners."

"You are coming back to the party, aren't you?" asks Dusty.

"I need to get the children into bed."

Autumn lies beside the tiny door. "What if we give her your gift last?" she suggests. "I'll come get you when it's time."

"I doubt my gift will meet with Pearl's approval."

"Will anyfur's?" asks Dusty.

"I'm sorry. I shouldn't be speaking badly of a member of your family."

Dusty giggles. "I certainly do."

Mrs. Mouse tries not to grin. "Alright. You come get me later and, if they're all asleep, I'll return."

"That will make Abigail happy," Dusty assures her.

They return to the living room, arms filled with wrapped gifts.

"Isn't Darlene coming back?" asks Abigail. "I hate to start without her."

With an eye roll, Pearl says, "she has other priorities. You needn't wait."

Autumn can't help but think that for a cat who prides herself on being sophisticated, Pearl certainly has some rather uncouth behaviors.

"Darlene knows you're going to start without her," Dusty explains. "It's fine. It may take her a while to get them all to sleep."

"Well, if you're sure," Abigail concedes. "Pearl, why don't you be useful and keep a list of who each gift is from?"

Though Pearl looks as if she's been asked to clean every litterbox in the building, she does not refuse, so Dusty gives her a pen and pad of paper.

Abigail is delighted with all her gifts. She's especially enamored of Smokey's. In the days leading up to this party, Smokey had gathered notes from each guest to tuck into the pouch of the box with the wine and glasses.

"I'm going to save them to read with Greyson on our honeymoon," she says, tears welling in her eyes. "Thank you so very much, Smokerina. What a thoughtful gift."

"I'm so glad you like it," says Smokey.

"There are only two gifts left," says Dusty. "Autumn, would you go see if Darlene can rejoin us?"

Autumn heads down the hallway to Dusty's bedroom wondering how she'll manage to knock loud enough on the door for Mrs. Mouse to hear without waking the mousekins. She needn't have worried. Mrs. Mouse is standing outside the door. She holds a finger to her lips. "I'm leaving the door open so I can hear them if they wake up."

Autumn nods and together they return to the living room. Abigail has just finished opening the last gift before Mrs. Mouse's.

"You're back," says Abigail as Darlene takes a seat next to Autumn. "Are the little ones asleep?"

"Yes. I'm sorry if they caused any trouble."

"They are delightful and always welcome, as are you and Rodney."

"Thank you," says Mrs. Mouse.

"Shall we get on with it?" asks Pearl.

"Here," says Dusty, giving the final present to Abigail. This is from Darlene."

The box is prettily wrapped in paper with red roses on a cream background and tied up with a green ribbon.

"I just love how you've all managed to tie in the wedding theme even down to the wrapping paper," says Abigail as she slides a claw beneath the tape, unwrapping the gift without making a single tear in the paper. "This shower couldn't have been more perfect. Thank you so much, Dusty. And you, too, Autumn. I know you did all the cooking and helped Dusty get ready."

Pearl's paw flies to Abigail's arm.

"What is it?" asks Abigail, alarmed.

"Autumn made the food we had this evening?"

"Why yes. Autumn Amelia is an amazing chef."

Autumn braces herself for whatever complaint Pearl is about to make.

"Not *that* Autumn Amelia?

"What on earth are you –?"

Staring straight at Autumn, Pearl asks, "She's not the same Autumn Amelia who improved Chef Gustave's sauce, is she?"

"She certainly is. And she'll be overseeing all the cooking for the reception as well."

Pearl finally tears her gaze away from Autumn and rests it on Abigail. "It's the best food I've ever tasted."

"Well, perhaps you should tell her so," says Abigail.

Pearl turns back to Autumn. "Your talent is outstanding."

"Thank you. How did you know about me and Chef Gustav?"

"Everyfur and feather knows about it. Gustav is one of the world's greatest chefs. Word has spread throughout the culinary circles, which includes those of us who have sophisticated palates and appreciate the finest dining as well as those who cook. I would like to offer you a position as my personal chef."

A group gasp resounds throughout the room.

"Thank you, but I love being in charge of Mama Cat's Kitchen."

"But I would take you everywhere with me. I travel the world, you know. The very best hotels. Private luxury suites, of course. I'll make sure you have your own little quarters. That way you could be nearby whenever I wanted you to cook something. Oh, how jealous my friends will be!"

Autumn stiffens. Is there no end to this cat's self-importance?

"I like my cottage in Wild Whisker Ridge."

"Oh, you'd forget all about that once you started traveling." She waves a dismissive paw. "You'd see the most exotic sites and cook for furs and feathers of the highest quality."

Autumn has the unfamiliar desire to scratch the smug look off Pearl's face. Instead, she says, "I prefer to cook for my family, friends, and customers. I also prefer *to eat with them*." She turns to Abigail. "May we see your gift from Mrs. Mouse?"

"Oh, yes." Abigail removes the last of the wrapping paper. The wicker picnic basket sits on her lap. She opens the lid to find that Mrs. Mouse has added the plates and utensils. Rolled up inside is a red and white gingham blanket.

"The blanket is to be carried by the straps on the outside," explains Mrs. Mouse. "But it was easier to put it inside to wrap it."

"I see," says Abigail. "Darlene, this is perfect. How did you know I wanted one?"

"I heard you and Greyson mention wanting to go on picnics in the summer."

"Nothing worse than an eavesdropping mouse," mutters Pearl.

"I wasn't eavesdropping," says Mrs. Mouse. "I was simply nearby and overheard them."

"Really?"

"That's right," says Abigail. "I remember the conversation. Greyson and I were in the kitchen, and you had come in looking for Dusty. Of course, you weren't eavesdropping. Honestly, Pearl," she says turning to her cousin. "I wish you wouldn't jump to conclusions."

Pearl shrugs.

"Thank you, Darlene. It's perfect," says Abigail.

When the party breaks up and most of the guests go home, Autumn and Smokey stay behind to clean up. Pearl heads for the guest room.

"About Pearl's offer," says Smokey. "She probably can't believe you said no."

"She's not finished with you," says Dusty. "When Pearl wants something, she doesn't give up easily."

"My answer will always be no." Autumn shudders at the thought of working for Pearl.

"My apologies, Darlene," Abigail says to Mrs. Mouse who is cleaning up crumbs from the floor. "Sometimes, I don't know what gets into Pearl."

"I don't take it personally," Mrs. Mouse assures them. "Dusty tells me she's like that with everyfur."

"It's rude and unacceptable. I will speak with her tomorrow."

Mrs. Mouse grins. "I'm planning a lesson on proper manners for my mousekins tomorrow. By all means, send her in. She can audit the course."

Chapter 25
The Rehearsal Dinner

"I'm glad Greyson decided on The Red Dot for the rehearsal dinner," says Smokey, pulling out of the lot at Oneness Park. The wedding rehearsal at the park's chapel has just finished.

"Me too," says Autumn. "I could have done it, but now Miguel has told me to make the reception dinner for ten more."

"Ten more? Who?"

"No idea. Oh, don't say anything."

"I wonder what he's up to," says Smokey. "Pearl can't complain about him. He's wealthier and even more worldly than she is. A lot nicer, too. I hope she takes note of how he treats other furs and feathers."

"She gave Dusty a hard time about her bridesmaid's dress."

"Are you fluffing me?" asks Smokey. "Those dresses are gorgeous. That forest green will be perfect with her silver fur."

"She says three quarter inch sleeves annoy her. She wanted Dusty to change hers, but Dusty refused because the bridesmaids' dresses are supposed to match. Pearl told her to change them all then, but Dusty said there isn't enough time. She wasn't about to give in to Pearl's tyranny."

"Good for Dusty! Pearl's such a pain in the paws. I can't wait for her to go home."

"Imagine how poor Dusty feels. She's stuck in the same apartment with her."

"Dusty will soon have the place to herself. I'm sure that will be a relief."

"She's going to use that time to find a place of her own. Oh, that reminds me, Jasmine was supposed to investigate any units available in her building. Has she mentioned anything to you?"

"No. Take my phone and call her now. It's in my bag."

Autumn makes the call.

"Not in Jasmine's building," she reports, "but two units have just opened in Louisa's building, one next door to her."

"Oh," says Smokey. Her attitude towards Louisa has been in flux lately. After the Hunter's Moon Night party, she realized that Louisa wasn't as stand-offish as she'd thought. At least not with others. She's still reserved around her, though. It's possible Louisa just doesn't like her. But why? Perhaps, she'd picked up on Smokey's attitude towards her. She'd always been polite around Louisa, but nothing more. Well, she did agree to invite her to the party and even bring her friend, Vivian, at the last minute. That should count for something. She hopes Jasmine hasn't said anything to Louisa about Smokey not liking her. For Jasmine's sake, Smokey has been trying, but Louisa is still keeping her distance.

"What's wrong? Asks Autumn. "Isn't Louisa's building alright?"

"Never seen it. I don't even know where it is."

"It's on Parkview Street."

"That's a nice area," Smokey concedes.

"I said I'd help her look," says Autumn. "It will be fun to go apartment hunting. What about you, Smokey? I know you want a luxury apartment like Abigail's. Are you planning to move?"

"I'll wait until I can afford it. Why? Do you want me to leave?"

"Of course not! I just know an apartment like Abigail's is your dream home. I want you to have it."

"Oh. Sorry. I thought you might be looking forward to having our home to yourself."

Autumn shrugs. "I might be lonely in the cottage by myself."

Smokey grins. "Not if there's a mancat in it with you."

"Smokey!"

"As a husband, of course. If you married Buster, would you two live there?"

"I'd like to live in the cottage. I have such wonderful memories of my kittenhood growing up there. I'd like for my kits to make their own memories there, too. But if Buster really didn't want to, I'd be alright with starting somewhere new."

Smokey brings the car to a stop in the parking lot of The Red Dot. Then she gives Autumn a good, long look. For her sister to even consider living somewhere besides the cottage would have been beyond unthinkable before she met Buster. *Well, if this isn't an interesting development.*

"How do I look?" she asks as Autumn comes around from her side of the car.

"Exactly the same as you did at the rehearsal. Perfect."

"Thanks. Shall we go in or wait for the others?"

"Let's wait for Grayson and Abigail," says Autumn. They can't be far behind.

Smokey huddles in her coat. The late November evening has the feel of the coming winter. She wishes she hadn't voiced an option. Autumn isn't even wearing a coat.

Fortunately, they don't have to wait long. Greyson and Abigail arrive followed by the others from the rehearsal – Reverend Alistair Wooders who will perform the ceremony and his wife, Celia, Dusty and Pearl who along with Smokey make up the Maid of Honor and bridesmaids, Miguel as best man, and the two groomsmen, Rufus Tailwagger and Jerome J. Ratley. Smokey was surprised that Greyson had asked Ratley to be part of the wedding. "Ever since he changed his mind and decided to back Oneness Park, he's kept his word and thrown himself into it whole-heartedly," Greyson explained. "I've worked paw-in-paw with him on several PR projects for the park and we've become friends. I wanted him to know how much I value his integrity."

They enter The Red Dot to find that Greyson has reserved the same alcove spot as when he brought Smokey, Autumn, Dusty, and Abigail here. Open towards the main dining room, it is set off to one side to afford some distance and privacy. It had proved perfect for allowing Autumn to enjoy the meal without absent-mindedly scooping up food that belonged to other diners.

"I'm afraid it won't be a nine-course tasting dinner this time, Miss Autumn," Greyson teases, "but I think you'll enjoy it just the same."

"I know I will," she says. "The food here is scrumptious."

"Although nothing is as good as yours," says Miguel.

Smokey sees that Pearl has maneuvered herself next to Miguel. He pulls out her chair for her.

"Thank you," says Pearl, giving Miguel a wide smile.

Pearl looks stunning in an A-line burgundy dress with matching lace jacket. Smokey's glad she didn't wear her burgundy dress, but at the last minute opted for her sapphire blue.

The waitress, a fox who introduces herself as Natalie, sets three appetizers on their table – filet mignon bites, cheesy mushroom puff pastries, and smoked salmon.

"I hope no one minds that I pre-ordered the appetizers. I figured we'd want something right away."

"Wonderful, Greyson," says Abigail. "Excellent choices."

After taking their drink orders, Natalie leaves them to peruse their menus. Smokey is finding it difficult to make a choice. Everything at The Red Dot is superb.

She sneaks a peek at Autumn. If she's having this much difficulty, she can only imagine Autumn's dilemma. Autumn, however, is busy enjoying the appetizers. She's not even looking at her menu. Smokey nudges Autumn and whispers, "aren't you going to decide what you're having?"

"I already have," Autumn says. "I went online, looked at the menu, and made my decision this morning."

Smokey is impressed. Autumn really has been working hard at trying to overcome her food problems.

"Good idea," says Smokey. "What are you getting?"

"Lemon chicken soup, bouillabaisse, bread, and braised carrots."

Smokey turns back to her menu, still indecisive.

"The lobster thermidor here is excellent," says Greyson. "I highly recommend it."

"That's what I'll have," says Abigail.

"I think the bluefin tuna is speaking to me," says Miguel.

"That sounds delightful," says Pearl. "I'll try that myself."

Rufus Tailwagger declares that he will order the beef bourguignon, Dusty the red king crab, and Jerome Ratley, the grilled brie with blackberry salsa on flatbread while the two coyotes, Alistair and Celia Wooders opt for the steak tartare. Smokey finally settles on the lobster.

Orders taken, conversation resumes.

"Jerome, why don't you ask the others what they think of your idea for future employment?" says Greyson.

"I didn't know you were thinking of changing jobs," says Abigail.

"I'm not," he says. "I'm considering something new."

"What would that be?" asks Miguel.

He clears his throat. Smokey notices his whiskers twitch.

"Well," he says, "Running for Mayor of Faunaburg."

There are gasps of surprise then words of encouragement.

"You would make a wonderful mayor," says Autumn. "I'd vote for you."

"Me, too," Dusty agrees.

"You'll have my backing," says Miguel.

"Thank you," says Ratley, letting out a relieved breath. "I need the opinion of furs and feathers I esteem before committing. So, you think I stand a chance?"

"An excellent chance," says Smokey. "Every fur and feather knows how much you've done to promote Oneness Park as well as your work with the Rodent Placement Agency and all your activist work."

"But they also know that I tried to prevent the park from being built."

"It seems to me," says Alistair Wooders, that the park exists specifically because of you. If you remember, it was originally supposed to be a cat park, not a park for all furs and feathers."

"That's right," says Celia. "If you hadn't created the Rodent Action Taskforce and staged a protest, the park would never have become what it is, a place for all furs and feathers to gather."

"And a place to show that we can all live together peacefully," adds Rufus. "That's thanks to you."

"But my original intention was just to shut down plans for the park completely. I'm afraid my opponent will use that against me."

"Do you have any sense of who that might be? I understand that Quillbert is planning to retire when his current term is up. He and his wife are hoping to retire to a prickle of porcupines in the rainforest."

"I've heard a few names bandied about, but at this point it's all rumor and conjecture."

"You'll outshine them all, Jerome," says Abigail.

"Thank you for your confidence in me," says Ratley.

"You have our full confidence," says Autumn. "And when the time comes, you'll have our votes, too."

Smokey can't help but think back to the days when Ratley was fighting them tooth and claw over the park. How things can change!

"Enough about me. This is your evening," says Ratley to Abigail and Greyson. "You must be excited for tomorrow."

Abigail and Greyson give each other a dreamy-eyed look.

"It is all very romantic, don't you agree?" Pearl asks Miguel.

"Indeed," he agrees.

Smokey watches as Pearl inches closer to him and wonders if she's thinking of making him husband number three. When Pearl's paw *accidentally* touches Miguel's, Smokey wants to reach across the table and swipe at her nose. How dare she try to lure Miguel? But Miguel is a worldly cat. Surely, he won't be fooled by Pearl.

Their food arrives and there's a lull in the conversation while they all relish their meals.

"I hope you don't mind," Greyson announces, "but I took the liberty of ordering dessert ahead of time, too. I wanted something special."

Natalie returns with a tray of pavlovas. Smokey has never had one before. The cool white mound topped with fresh whipped cream beneath a layer of blueberries and sliced strawberries, dripping in strawberry juice is almost too pretty to eat. The others have started eating theirs, though, and by their looks of rapture it must taste even better than it appears. She cracks the meringue with her spoon. Crunchy on the outside and soft as marshmallow fluff on the inside, the flavor explodes in her mouth as she encounters the berries and whipped cream and finally the lemon curd at the center.

She turns to ask Autumn if she can make pavlovas. Autumn is swooning. She'll ask later.

Before they leave the restaurant, Abigail reminds all the ladies present that they are to meet her at The Sharper Claw the next morning where they are to have a full spa treatment in preparation for the wedding that evening. "I've invited Sukey and Sally as well," she says. "They're going to be working so hard on the food that I want them to have this special morning, too."

"You've invited the help?" asks Pearl, her eyes going wide. "Wasn't it enough to have them at your shower?"

"They're not *the help*," says Abigail. "They are friends. Sukey and Sally are Autumn's pastry and sous chefs. They will make our wedding a perfect day. I want to do something special for them in return."

"Then give them a generous tip. If they do well enough to earn it, that is. Honestly, Abigail." She turns to Miguel, places a paw on his arm. With a coquettish look she purrs, "Can't you talk some sense into her?"

"I don't see the need," Miguel states, deftly extracting his arm. "Sukey and Sally used to work for me at my private club and I consider them friends as well."

Take that, Pearl! thinks Smokey.

Pearl lifts her nose higher in the air. "I see," she says, drumming her claws on the table.

"One misses much by not associating with a wide variety of furs and feathers," says Greyson. Friends are one of the greatest gifts we have. It is truly a blessing that they can come from every walk of life."

"Indeed," drawls Pearl, rolling her eyes.

Smokey wishes Abigail could send Pearl packing. She hopes Pearl will at least keep her thoughts to herself while they're at The Sharper Claw.

"We should be going," says Abigail. "We've a big day tomorrow."

As they rise, Pearl moves away from Miguel, apparently no longer interested in him. A wave of relief washes over Smokey. She wonders why. Certainly, he can take care of himself. Yet she becomes aware of a deeper feeling. Jealousy.

Oh dear, she thinks as an unwelcome question arises bringing her to a halt in the middle of the parking lot. *Do I have a crush on Miguel?*

Chapter 26
The Sharper Claw

"Welcome, ladies. Come right in," says the lovely cockatiel at the reception desk of The Sharper Claw. Her name is Bella, and Autumn thinks she's well named as she is truly beautiful with her soft yellow feathers, cream-colored wings, and perfect circles of reddish pink on her cheeks.

"Here are your itineraries," she says, indicating a set of papers on the counter.

Abigail picks up the papers, each of which has a name at the top, and hands them out.

"Are we all doing different things?" asks Sukey. "We're not together?"

Autumn notices Sukey's pace increasing as she speaks. She must be getting nervous about the wedding. Autumn's not sure why. She's seen the wedding cake Sukey made. It's amazing. She has not seen the groom's cake. Sukey's not letting anyone see it until it's presented at the reception. Maybe it has something to do with that. Sukey, being Siamese, has a tendency to talk a lot and when she's stressed or had too much catnip her speech get faster and she runs her words together until Autumn gets dizzy listening to her.

"Most things are together. Your itinerary tells you where to be and when," Bella explains.

"Okay, great, no problem," says Sukey.

"Please take a locker key from the pegboard," says Bella. "Lockers are around the corner. We ask that you kindly leave your cell phones in your lockers. Changing rooms are just beyond, though I suppose most of you know your way around.”

With The Sharper Claw being the spa in Oneness Park, Smokey knows it like the back of her paw. She designed it. As for the others, most of them have been at least a few times. Pearl, of course, has never been and neither has Celia.

“As you can see from your itineraries, you all begin the day with yoga. It will be perfect for getting you totally relaxed. Our new yoga instructor will lead you. Her name is Serena. She recently moved up here from Columbia. You will love her. Have a wonderful spa day, ladies. You’ll be feeling fantastic by the time of the wedding.” Bella’s crest feathers rise as she speaks.

“Thank you, Bella,” says Abigail. Turning to the others, she says, “Ladies, shall we?”

Smokey, Autumn, Dusty, Pearl, Sukey, Sally, and Celia follow Abigail down the hall.

“Have any of you met the new yoga instructor yet?” asks Sukey. “I haven’t. I liked the one that was here before. I hope I like this one, do any of you know her, what did Bella say her name was?” Her words come out in a rapid-fire stream.

“Serena,” says Autumn.

“Oh yeah right Serena that’s a good name for a yoga instructor don’t you think it sounds very calming?”

“Uh-huh,” says Autumn thinking, *I sure hope she can calm you down.*

“Siamese chatterbox,” she hears Pearl mutter under her breath then stifles a giggle when Abigail pulls Pearl’s tail.

They all change then head down another hallway towards the studio. It is a large, open room with a wooden floor and teal painted walls. Large oval windows along one wall let in the sunlight and offer a view of the woods. Yoga mats in the same color as the walls are arranged on the floor. Autumn feels herself start to relax just by stepping into the room.

"Namaste." They hear the word uttered in a soft Spanish accent.

"Namaste," they all say, looking around for the instructor. An aerial sling floats gently down from the ceiling. Slowly the instructor descends. When she finally reaches the floor, she turns to them. Autumn has never seen an animal like her in real life, but she has seen pictures. It nearly takes her breath away to realize she's looking into the smiling face of a sloth.

"I am Serena," says the sloth. Her speech is as slow and fluid as her movements. "Please take your places on the mats. And observe silence."

Once they are settled, Serena tells them they will begin with centering, focusing on their breathing.

"Close your eyes and take deep, slow breaths."

After a few minutes, Autumn hears an odd sound. She opens her eyes to see Serena dragging herself along the floor towards Sukey. "Too fast," she tells the Siamese. "Inhale as I count to three." It's the slowest count to three Autumn has ever heard, but Sukey finally manages to match her breathing to it.

For the rest of the class, Autumn feels as though she's moving in a dream. Her body relaxes more and more. She credits Serena's voice as much as the stretches and poses. By the time they reach the Savasana pose that ends the class, she's not sure if she ever wants to get up. Lying on her back, eyes closed, breathing deeply, she's never felt so relaxed. Serena intones instructions to bring them out of the Savasana pose. As she feels herself come back to awareness of her surroundings, Autumn notices a light rumbling coming from the mat next to her. Dusty is snoring.

After yoga it's on to the baths. Autumn loves the baths, just like she loves swimming. Sally and Celia head there just as eagerly. Dusty, Abigail, and Pearl, all being Persians don't mind too much. Smokey and Sukey, however, detest baths. So, the two of them go off in a different direction for a waterless bath, especially for them.

Autumn enters a room filled with in-ground tubs. The air is warm and humid. She and the others step behind their own curtained areas to undress, then each slips into her own bath. The warm water is redolent with the scent of bath salts. Ember, the bobcat who monitors the baths, strolls through the room making sure everyfur is safe and has all they need. She turns on some relaxing music then disappears so that she's just out of sight but there if needed.

Once Autumn is finished, she rings the bell next to her bath. Ember arrives with fur shampoo and conditioner on a serving platter. She leads Autumn to an adjacent room with a smaller tub and a shower. Autumn lathers herself with fur shampoo then immerses herself in the tub. Stepping out, she does the same with the conditioner, then washes it all off in the shower. Ember hands her a large fluffy towel. She leads her to the next room filled with mirrors, sinks, and all sorts of fur-care implements.

"Welcome, Autumn. I'm Daisy," says a labradoodle, one of several fur stylists in the room. "I'll be doing your fur today. Would you like anything special?"

"I just need to look good for the wedding."

"Hmm..." says Daisy. "Does your dress have an opening in the back for your tail?"

"Of course."

"Would you like me to fluff out your tail fur?"

"That sounds nice."

As Autumn takes a spot before Daisy's mirror, she notices Smokey and Sukey at the other end of the room. Their stylists are finishing. Their fur is so clean and smooth it's practically glowing.

"What time is the wedding?" asks Daisy.

"Four o'clock."

"Is the reception at your restaurant?"

"Yes, in the function room."

"Are you in the wedding party?"

"No, but my sister is."

The conversation carries on while Daisy blow-dries and brushes Autumn's fur. The others stroll in one by one from the baths and are met by their own stylists. Autumn can't believe her tail when Daisy finishes. Normally fluffy, it looks twice as thick as usual and luxuriously fanned out.

"Wow!" she says. "I hope it stays this way until the wedding."

"I'll give it lots of fur spray. It will hold as long as you don't sit on it."

Once they are finished getting their fur styled and have dressed, they gather in the dining area. Lunch is brought over from Mama Cat's Kitchen consisting of poached salmon, salad, and lemon chicken, cucumber and tomato sandwiches on fresh whole grain bread, and to drink, orange and rosemary infused water. Dessert is a fruit salad.

"What's after lunch?" asks Sally.

"Ear cleaning," says Smokey. "Then a mani-pedi with a toe bean exfoliation."

"I'm going to ask for a floof trim," says Dusty. "I don't want to slip during the wedding."

"Good idea," Autumn agrees. "I will, too."

"I think that's an excellent idea for all of us who have floof," says Abigail. "We don't need any falls today."

"This has been such an amazing experience," says Celia. "I've never been to a spa before."

"Never?" asks Pearl.

"No, never."

"How unusual. But I suppose there are many things the common furs don't experience that Abigail and I take for granted. It's sad, really."

"I take nothing for granted, Pearl," says Abigail. "You grew up in luxury. I was a *common fur*. I only experienced luxury when we visited your family. I have what I have now because I worked very hard for many years to build Fluffington's into a highly successful company. I *earned* everything I have."

"Of course, dear. You rose above others."

"May I ask, Pearl," says Celia leaning towards her with a look of genuine interest, "what is it that makes you believe money and position places any fur or feather above all the others? We are equally beloved by the Great Creator, after all."

"I suppose all furs and feathers, scales and fins, and what have you will be gathered into the Oneness at some point. But here in this life there is a hierarchy. It's simply the natural way of things. I didn't create it so don't blame me."

"I wasn't. I was just curious about how you see things because it's very different from my world view. Forgive me, but I'm having trouble understanding yours. Perhaps it's because my husband is a minister, but I do believe that the Great Creator wants us to start living the Oneness as much as possible in this life."

"That's what Oneness Park is all about," adds Autumn.

"Yes, yes," says Pearl. "Lovely sentiment, but hardly realistic."

"Is that so?" asks Dusty. "You haven't spent time in Oneness Park since you've been here, but if you had you'd see it for yourself. All types of furs and feathers enjoy everything the park has to offer together."

"But what about outside the park? What do they do in the real world?"

"I can't say that everything's perfect," says Abigail. "But it has made a noticeable difference. The way creatures treat each other has improved."

"That's true," says Dusty. "Before the park, rodents never shopped at Tonk's Treasures because it's owned by a cat and cats and dogs made up most of its clientele. Now loads of rodents and birds of all kinds go there."

"The same is true for other places in Faunaburg. Things are changing for the better," says Sally.

"I've no problem with all furs and feathers getting along," says Pearl. "I have many bird and canine friends."

"All of them rich," says Abigail.

"I can't help that. They're who I know."

"Now you know us," says Celia, sweeping her paw around the table. "Except for Abigail, we are not wealthy. We're average furs and feathers. Are we so bad?"

"I didn't say any of you were bad."

"Yet you've been looking down your whiskers at all of us since you got here," says Sukey.

"My apologies. I didn't mean to give offense."

"'Siamese chatterbox?' How could I take offense at that?"

"Ladies, please," says Abigail. "This is supposed to be a happy day."

Pearl puts up a paw. "Sukey is right. That comment was uncalled for. I'm sorry, Sukey."

"Thank you," says Sukey, though Autumn's not sure she's truly mollified.

When lunch is finished, they move on to having their ears cleaned, then each takes a seat in an adjacent room where a team of parrots and macaws clip and shape their claws, exfoliate their toe beans with pink Himalayan salt scrub, and do a floof trim for those who need it.

When the spa experience is over, Autumn, Sukey, and Sally hurry to Mama Cat's Kitchen. Autumn heads for the function room. The florist is just putting the finishing touches on the tables.

"Elaine, everything looks beautiful," Autumn tells the snowy egret.

"Thank you. Have you seen the chapel? I think Abigail will be very pleased."

"I'm certain she will be. This wedding is going to be perfect."

Sally rushes into the function room and grabs Autumn's arm. "Autumn, come quick. The groom's cake exploded!"

Chapter 27
The Wedding

Smokey stands in the vestibule of Oneness Park's chapel waiting for Paco, a pug-chihuahua mix, to begin the music.

"Excuse us." She turns to see Autumn Amelia and Sukey trying to slip past the line of bridesmaids.

"Where have you been?" Smokey asks.

"There was a little mishap with the groom's cake," Autumn explains.

Smokey steps aside so the two cats can enter the chapel, but she continues to watch them. Sukey looks nervous. Autumn keeps whispering to her as if she's trying to calm her down. She notices that Autumn's tail, though still lovely through the opening in her dress, isn't quite as perfectly fanned out as it had been. And, if she's not mistaken, Sukey has smudges of moth flour and whitefish frosting on her dress.

Once Autumn and Sukey are seated, Smokey's attention returns to the end of the aisle where Greyson takes his place at the altar with his best man, Miguel Gato, and his groomsmen, Rufus Tailwagger and Jerome J. Ratley, lined up next to him. They all appear suave in their tuxedoes, especially Miguel. That cat looks like he was born to wear a tux.

"Go, Smokerina," Pearl whispers while nudging Smokey's back. She starts down the aisle with a few quick steps to catch up to the music. So much for making a stately entrance.

Once she reaches her place at the altar with Pearl and Dusty beside her, she turns to watch Abigail make her way down the aisle. She is stunning. Dusty outdid herself with Abigail's gown. Smokey sneaks a peak at Greyson. He's wide-eyed and grinning. Abigail, being an older cat, her parents gone, had asked their coyote friend, Leo Birch, to escort her down the aisle. He looks dapper in his tux, head held high, expression serious. Smokey thinks how just a year and a half ago she was terrified of coyotes and now here she is in a wedding party with two of them, both of whom she likes and trusts along with their families. Oneness Park really has worked miracles.

When they reach the altar, Leo bows to Abigail before taking his seat with his wife Ivy, and their pup Rusty. Then all eyes turn towards the minister.

"My fellow furs and feathers," begins Reverend Wooders. "We come together this afternoon in the presence of the Great Creator to join these two cats, Greyson and Abigail in holy matrimony. It is indeed a joy for me to preside at the nuptials of two cats who I have come to admire and consider dear friends."

As he speaks, Smokey takes a moment to admire Elaine's floral arrangements. The end of each pew has a white tulle bow holding a single red rose backed by two deep green leaves. Set on pedestals on either side of the altar are a total of four arrangements of red roses, baby's breath, and dark greenery all of which pop next to the white altar. The dark green of the bridesmaid's dresses matches perfectly. As maid of honor, Dusty's gown is set off with sprigs of white reminiscent of the baby's breath among the roses.

Smokey catches a movement out of the corner of her eye. Turning her head, she spies Phil. The ferret is peeking out from behind one of the floral arrangements, his camera pointing at the wedding party. After a few clicks, he scurries down the pedestal in search of another angle. He took pictures at the rehearsal dinner last night and was with Abigail from the moment she left the spa this morning. Smokey can't wait to see them later. Phil can get into the most unusual spaces. He's sure to get some spectacular shots.

Sensing a shift in the wedding party, Smokey brings her attention back to the ceremony. Abigail and Greyson are holding paws.

Reverend Wooders asks, "Greyson, do you take Abigail to be your wife?"

"I do," says Greyson.

"Do you promise to love and cherish her, to always share the catnip and treats equally with her, to give up the best nap spot in a sunbeam to her, and to always be faithful to her?"

"I do."

Then Reverend Wooders turns to Abigail.

"Abigail, do you take Greyson to be your husband?"

"I do."

"Do you promise to love and cherish him, to always share the catnip and treats equally with him, to give up the best nap spot in a sunbeam to him, and to always be faithful to him."

"I do," says Abigail. "And I also promise to give him extra shrimp."

"Then by the power vested in me, I now pronounce you husband and wife. You may exchange eye kisses."

Gazing deeply at each other, Greyson and Abigail each close their eyelids halfway three times. Then the entire chapel erupts in applause. Smokey stifles a scream when Jerome J. Ratley goes careening across the floor and into the organ. Paco jumps from the organ bench and Reverend Wooders hurries over to help. Together, they get Ratley up and set him on his feet.

"What happened?" asks Miguel as they rejoin the group at the altar.

Ratley shakes his head, straightens his whiskers, and says, "I was watching the bride and groom when I was suddenly swept up by a murderous feather duster."

"Oops," says Rufus. "That must have been my tail. Sorry."

"No harm done," says Ratley, adjusting his bow tie that's been knocked askew.

With the wedding party reassembled, Paco starts the recessional, the Kitty Cat March. They fall into line behind the bride and groom, Smokey paired with Ratley right behind Pearl and Rufus. She fights a case of the giggles watching Rufus's tail swing wildly back and forth all the way down the aisle, coming within a fur's width of smacking Pearl on the rump. Phil scampers in and out among them and hops onto pew backs, and finally onto the chapel door's handle all the while clicking away on his camera.

The wedding party remains in formation all the way to the copse of trees on the way to Mama Cat's Kitchen. They stop in front of the trees where formal pictures of the newly married couple and the wedding party will be taken while all the guests continue to the restaurant's function room.

"That was a beautiful ceremony," Smokey tells Abigail. "Nice touch about giving Greyson extra shrimp."

Abigail glances at Greyson who is posing for pictures with his best man and groomsmen.

"Don't say anything," says Abigail, "but I have a big surprise for Greyson during the reception."

"Oh? What is it?"

"I'll just say it's something I cooked up with Sukey for the groom's cake."

* * *

"I can't believe I let her talk me into this." Autumn has lost count of how many times Sukey has said that to her since she raced back to the kitchen to find a deflated cake covered in cocktail sauce and shrimp all over the floor and counter.

"It's all set now. Don't worry, Sukey."

They are in the kitchen at Mama Cat's staring at the groom's cake.

"I'm not sure I've done it right," says Sukey. "What if the same thing happens to this one?"

"It won't. It will bubble like a fountain. We'll use less dry ice."

Sukey stares at the groom's cake covered in a base of blue fondant with tiny candy starfish, mollusks, and sea turtles weaving in and out of a multitude of strands of rock candy coral. There is a hole in the top of the cake in which sits a large glass jar for holding dry ice, cocktail sauce, and shrimp. The idea is for the coral reef cake to gently erupt with the shrimp and sauce. Earlier she'd used a dummy cake to test it out. It had sent the shrimp and cocktail sauce spewing all over the counter.

"I wish we'd stuck with a simple shrimp-shaped cake. I thought this was a fun idea when Abigail first suggested it," says Sukey. "Now, I think it's awful. Volcanoes erupt but coral reefs don't."

"That doesn't matter," says Autumn. "It's for Greyson so it's all about the shrimp."

"Either nothing will happen or the whole thing will explode."

"It will be fine. It's beautiful. Even if nothing happens, Greyson will be delighted to find all the shrimp when he cuts into it. He won't know it was supposed to erupt."

"But Abigail will. She'll be disappointed."

"She'll get over it. Besides, I think it will work."

"I wish we could test it on the real cake, but there's no time to make another. It took forever to make this one."

"Not to mention, we'd run out of shrimp," says Autumn. "We'll have to hope for the best. Take your mind off it and help me with the soup. Cocktail hour will be over soon, and the wedding party will be here."

"Sally comes into the kitchen. "You're missing all those great appetizers."

"I want to start heating up the soup."

"Come on, Autumn," Sally coaxes. "Vicky and Ronnie will take care of that."

"Take care of what?" asks Vicky, entering the kitchen with an empty tray.

"The rest of the food for the reception."

"We've got it all under control, Chef Autumn. You and Sukey should go out and enjoy yourselves."

Everything that could be prepared ahead of time is done, and Vicky and Ronnie have detailed instructions. The fox and jackrabbit did a fantastic job at the Hunter's Moon Night party so Autumn knows they can handle it. Still, despite her calming words to Sukey, she is anxious.

"Let's go, you two," says Sally, taking one of Sukey's and Autumn's paws in each of her own and tugging them out of the kitchen.

The party in the function room is in full swing. Appetizers disappear quickly from the silver trays carried by servers as do the ones on the long tables. All the guests are mingling, talking, and laughing. Autumn scans the crowd while downing a stuffed mushroom. She's glad her function room is big considering all the additional guests Abigail kept inviting. Then she remembers Miguel saying there would be ten more. She wanders through the crowd, stopping to chat with several furs and feathers, but she doesn't see any she's not sure were on the invitation list. Every fur and feather from the Hunter's Moon Night party is here, except for Vivian, along with all the staff of Fluffington's. Several of Greyson's friends from PAWS UNITED have flown up for the wedding. She doesn't know them, but she's pretty sure she can pick them out. She turns when she feels a tap on her shoulder.

"I was beginning to think I wouldn't see you," says Buster, grinning at her. "I thought you'd be holed up in the kitchen all evening."

"Vicky and Ronnie have it all under control. I'm free to enjoy myself."

"Well, your appetizers are divine. I can hardly wait for the dinner."

"Thanks."

Just then the DJ, a Great Dane named Hazzard, announces that the bridal party has arrived. The talking ceases and all heads turn in the direction of the door.

"It is my pleasure to introduce flower girl and ring bearer, Mindy and Herbie Mouse," Hazzard announces.

The two mousekins skitter nervously across the room where a space has been cleared for a dancefloor, then take their seats at the head table to the accompaniment of applause.

"Now, please welcome bridesmaids and groomsmen, Smokerina Koshkyn and Jerome J. Ratley and Pearl Flooferson and Rufus Tailwagger." The two couples cross the room to the head table, more applause accompanying them.

"Please, give a warm welcome to the maid of honor and best man, Dusty Fluffington and Miguel Gato," Hazzard continues.

Hazzard pauses for dramatic effect after Dusty and Miguel reach the head table. Then, with her voice starting out low and growing louder and stronger as she speaks, she says, "And now, please give a warm welcome to..." Here, she stops, hits a button on her console that plays a drum roll, then continues, "Mr. and Mrs. Greyson and Abigail Kazzie!"

Wild applause erupts as Greyson and Abigail step through the doorway. Paw in paw they stride to the center of the dance floor where they stop. Still holding paws, they raise their arms in a triumphant salute and wave to their guests before continuing to their seats of honor.

Once the head table is full, all the guests take their seats at their own tables. Autumn is seated with Sasha, Marlon, Winthrop, Sukey, and Sally. The squirrel scurry is seated at the table next to them, an extra chair pulled up to make room for all seven.

Hazzard announces that a toast is about to be made by the best man.

Miguel Gato stands, holding his glass of nip-paign. "I have had the pleasure of knowing Abigail for many years. Fluffington ArCATechture had just moved to the Faunaburg Office Tower when we met. I was working for my father at the time. He was close to retiring and I was to take over the business. He suggested I meet an up-and-coming cat whose architecture firm was really taking off. He knew her because being the enterprising businesscat that she is, she'd sought him out as a mentor. He'd met with her off and on over the previous year or two. His advice and contacts helped her build her business. My dad thought very highly of Abigail and sensed that she was headed for great success. One day he invited me to join him and Abigail for lunch. We hit it off immediately and have been good friends ever since. I will always be grateful to my father for introducing us.

"As for Greyson, we met when he came up from Palm Ray to visit his cousins, Smokerina and Autumn Amelia, a couple of years ago. What a fortunate visit that was. As retired CEO of PAWS UNITED, he has tremendous diplomatic skills and great aplomb. When he became spokescat for Oneness Park, I knew beyond doubt that it would become a reality. And now, here we are enjoying it together.

"When I first realized that Greyson and Abigail had fallen for each other I was only a little surprised, mainly because I've always been convinced that Abigail was a confirmed bachelorette. I assumed that having reached retirement without ever marrying, the same was true for Greyson. As I watched their budding romance progress, I realized that the Great Creator must have been saving them for each other and for the right time in each of their lives for them to be together. Frankly, as they fell more deeply in love, this conviction grew.

When they announced their engagement, I could not have been more delighted.

"Individually Greyson and Abigail have given so much to their families, their communities, and their work. As a couple, I can only imagine what joy they will bring to one another and to us all.

"So, I ask you all to raise your glasses and join me in toasting Greyson and Abigail and wishing them great happiness together for the rest of their lives."

As Miguel raises his nip-paign glass towards the beaming couple, so do all the guests with shouts of "here, here!"

After Miguel takes his seat, Dusty rises, her own nip-paign glass in paw. She swallows hard a few times. She and Autumn have practiced her speech over and over again. Though she has it down pat, she is terribly nervous. Public speaking is not Dusty's forte. Despite how much she's come out of her shell since meeting Autumn, she's still shy at heart.

Autumn sits up straighter to catch her eye, giving her a nod of encouragement.

Dusty clears her throat. "I'm not much at making speeches," she says. "In fact, this is my first one ever." She turns towards Abigail and Greyson.

"Abby is not only my big sister, but after we lost our parents, she became like a mother to me. She has always looked out for me, protected me, and watched over me. She's the one who noticed my love for designing and sewing clothes and encouraged me in that pursuit. She bought me my first sewing machine.

"I've always looked up to Abby. The success of Fluffington's has always astounded me though really it shouldn't have been any surprise at all. Abby's always been able to accomplish anything.

"I've always wondered why she didn't marry. She did go on dates, you know. And some of those cats were really dreamy."

A few giggles erupt from the crowd.

"But she never got serious. I know it was partly because of her business, but I think, though she won't admit it, that it was partly because of me. She didn't want me to be on my own. You see, I used to have a problem that made me very afraid to leave the apartment, so Abby let me stay there. If she'd married, her husband might not have wanted me to live with them and I don't think she would ever have allowed that."

Autumn notices Abigail wipe a tear from her eye.

"But," Dusty continues, "thanks to the help of a very dear friend, I can leave the apartment whenever I want. I now love going places and I have started selling my clothes and miniature textiles at Tonk's Treasures. I'm getting a business degree and I'm going to have my own business one day. So, I think Miguel is right. The Great Creator *was* waiting for everything to fall into place before he let Abby and Greyson meet. I know it because my first foray out of the apartment happened on the day Greyson, Smokey, and Autumn came to visit. That was also when the first sparks between Abby and Greyson started to light up. Seriously, you could almost see them."

More giggles.

"So, here's to Abby, Greyson, and the perfect timing of the Great Creator who I know will bless their marriage with abundant happiness!" She raises her glass, and the guests follow suit.

As soon as the toasts are finished, several of Autumn's waitstaff appear with bowls of steaming cream of mushroom soup. Conversation ceases throughout the room once they all start eating. Only, murmurs of "mmm..." and "yummy" can be heard.

After clearing away the soup bowls, the waitstaff brings in plates of salad followed by huge platters filled with dinner plates. Autumn had had a difficult time deciding which of the three options to choose. Buster had come up with the idea of each of them requesting a different dinner and sharing each other's. At least that had narrowed Autumn's choice to two. Still difficult. In the end, she'd chosen the seared sea bass with garlic lemon sauce while Buster had picked the sliced tenderloin of beef with a wine glaze and sauteed onions and mushrooms. She notices that Sasha has gone for the butternut squash ravioli in white wine sauce as has the entire squirrel scurry. She sincerely hopes there will be some left over in the kitchen for afterwards.

"Chef Autumn, you've outdone yourself," says Sally, licking the wine glaze from her lips.

"Thanks, Sally. I wanted Greyson and Abigail's reception dinner to be perfect, so I gave everything extra attention and very detailed instructions to Vicky and Ronnie. I must tell them what an excellent job they've done."

"I agree," says Marlon. "This is the best sea bass I've ever tasted."

"I'm loving the beef," says Winthrop. "He turns in his chair to call over to the table of squirrels. "How's your dinner?"

"Totally acorns!" Reggie calls back, he being the only one whose mouth isn't completely stuffed with ravioli.

"Everyfing's dewishioush," Autumn hears from another direction. She turns to see Simon and Sam Squirrel at the next table.

"Thank you, boys, but please don't talk with your mouths full," she says.

Autumn glances at Sukey who seems fidgety. "Is your dinner alright?" she asks.

"Excellent," says Sukey. "I love sea bass." She tosses a quick smile in Autumn's direction then returns her focus to her plate. *Still worrying about the groom's cake, no doubt*, Autumn thinks.

Once the dinner plates have been cleared away, Hazzard announces the arrival of the wedding cake. Gasps of delight resound throughout the room as the cake is wheeled in on a cart covered with a pristine white cloth.

"Oh, my!" exclaims Sasha. "Sukey, that's gorgeous,"

"What? Oh, thanks." Sukey keeps glancing towards the kitchen, paying little attention to the wedding cake and the crowd's delighted response to it.

Autumn can't help staring at the cake. It is breathtakingly beautiful with its cascade of roses down the tiers, perfectly mimicking Abigail's bouquet.

"I'd like to paint that cake," Autumn hears Susan, one of the squirrels in the scurry, say.

"I'd like to eat it," says Winthrop.

"Well, one of you will get your wish," Autumn answers with a laugh.

"Can I get a copy of the picture?" Susan asks. Phil has snapped several shots of it. "I really want to paint it."

"What's the frosting?" Marlon asks Sukey.

"Ocean whitefish," she says, her voice a monotone.

Autumn glances at Sukey who is biting her claws. She's about to suggest they go check on the groom's cake when Hazzard announces that the bride and groom are about to cut the wedding cake.

Greyson and Abigail take their places. "Sukey, where are you?" Abigail glances around the room."

"She's over here!" calls Sasha.

"Please stand, Sukey," says Abigail. "I want every fur and feather to see who made this gorgeous cake."

"Oh, no," Autumn hears Sukey mumble as she stands amidst thunderous applause and shouts of "bravo!"

"And while we're at it," Abigail continues, "let's hear it for Chef Autumn Amelia. Wasn't her food spectacular?"

Autumn stands to another round of applause. Then Greyson picks up the knife, and Abigail places her paw over his. Together they cut the first slice from the lowest tier. Once the slice of cake is on a plate, Abigail puts a piece on a fork and raises it to Greyson's mouth. Then he does the same for her.

"It tastes as good as it looks," says Greyson.

As the waitstaff takes over cutting and plating slices of cake for all the guests, Abigail calls out to the room, "I know the groom's cake is usually just set out but we're keeping it for later. It's very, very special so be sure you all save some room."

"I can hardly wait," Greyson says.

"Autumn!" Sukey calls across the table in an exaggerated whisper, her voice desperate.

"I wish Abigail hadn't told the whole room," Sukey laments as they enter the kitchen. "What if it doesn't work right?"

"Don't worry," Autumn says. "The looks alone will astonish them."

"But what if it erupts too much like the dummy cake?"

"They'll be astonished by that, too." Autumn is not completely successful in her attempt to stifle a giggle.

"I wish I was certain of how much dry ice to use."

An idea springs to Autumn's mind. "Come with me," she says.

The two cats go to Autumn's office.

"What are you doing?" asks Sukey.

"Looking up how to make a cake erupt."

"I know how. I just don't know how to keep it from over-erupting."

"We should be able to find that, too."

They scour the Internet, but all they can find is how to make a volcano cake that spews chocolate lava.

"You see," says Sukey. "And there's a big difference between marshmallow and chocolate sauce and a pound of shrimp with cocktail sauce. Either it will do nothing but send up a few puffs or it will over-erupt and destroy the cake."

Autumn sighs. "You're right. Maybe you should tell Abigail what happened and ask her if it's okay if it doesn't erupt. When Greyson cuts it all the shrimp and cocktail sauce will pour out. That ought to be good enough.”

“Do you think she’ll go for it?”

“You won’t know unless you ask.”

“I have no choice.”

They return to the kitchen as the fox enters with an empty tray.

“Vicky please, ask Abigail to come in here,” says Autumn.

A few moments later, Abigail breezes into the kitchen. She gasps when she sees the groom’s cake, her paw over her mouth.

“Oh, my. Oh, my!” she exclaims. Abigail admires the cake from every angle. “It looks so real. You are a genius.”

“I’m glad you like it, but I need to talk to you about the eruption.”

Abigail tears her gaze away from the cake with a broad grin. “I can’t wait for that,” she says. “Just imagine the look on Greyson’s face when shrimp pop out of the top, then cascade down, the cocktail sauce slipping in and out of the coral. Oh, Sukey, I could just kiss you.” She plants a peck right on Sukey’s whiskers. “Thank you. Now, I must get back to the reception. You two missed our first dance. And now Miguel promises a surprise. Come back out for that. Ta-ta!” She sails out of the kitchen, waving her paw.

“Cascading gently down the cake,” says Sukey, her voice flat.

“Let’s check the dry ice, then go back out so we don’t miss Miguel’s surprise,” says Autumn.

Back in the function room, the dance floor is filled. Autumn and Sukey stand at the edge watching them twirl past. Her neighbor, Shirley, is dancing with Professor Bob. Mr. and Mrs. Mouse whirl by, followed by all the mousekins paired up and trying to copy their parents. Bruce Lee and Rivet are doing some new style of dance Autumn has never seen before but looks like fun. Every squirrel in the scurry is bopping around with or without a partner. Marlon and Louisa breeze along, then Sally on the arm of Professor Chewy. And is that Smokey dancing with Miguel?

The song ends and another begins. Buster reaches Autumn's side and asks her to dance just as Ratley invites Sukey onto the dance floor. It's a fast-paced number that has them all twisting and spinning. When it ends, they hear Miguel's voice instead of the DJ.

"May I have your attention, please," he says. All eyes turn towards him at Hazzard's microphone.

"Please clear the dance floor. We have a treat for you, but we'll need the entire floor."

Curious murmurs fill the room as they all make their way to the tables. Miguel continues.

"Ladies and gentlemen, I am delighted to present to you the winners of the International Flamingo Dance Championships. Here to perform their first-place routine in honor of Abigail and Greyson Kazzie, please welcome the Flying Feathers Dance Troupe."

The back door of the function room opens and in stride ten beautiful flamingoes in sparkling red, blue, and gold sequined outfits with Vivian leading the flock. Taking their places in the center of the dance floor they await their music.

"Autumn, did you know about this?" Buster asks.

She shakes her head. "I don't even know where Miguel has them hiding all this time."

The music begins with a blare of trumpets, and all ten flamingoes strike a pose in unison, then begin to move with perfect precision in time to the music. The guests are mesmerized by their performance, clapping along with the tune and whooping when each flamingo, in quick succession, lifts into the air, executes a back flip and lands in the splits to end the routine. Wild applause follows.

"Now you know why they're the champions," Miguel announces. "Would we like an encore?"

His question is met with thunderous applause and whistles. Hazzard cues up the music and the flamingoes begin a number that has them leaping, high kicking, spinning, and finally, rocketing nearly to the ceiling. The wedding guests jump up and down by the end.

"I sure hope we've left enough food," says Miguel when the routine ends, "because these ladies are probably hungry."

"So those are the ten extra meals," says Autumn, hurrying off to find Vicky and Ronnie. She needn't have worried. They are already carrying plates to a table where the flamingoes take their seats.

The dancing resumes. Then Abigial takes the microphone to make her own announcement, Greyson by her side.

"Thank you for sharing this joyful day with us," she says. "Miguel, what a fabulous surprise. Flying Feathers Dance Troupe, your gold medal was more than well deserved. Don't you all agree?"

A long round of applause follows.

"Now, I have a surprise of my own." She turns to Greyson but continues to speak into the microphone. "Greyson, as you know the groom's cake is usually set out during the reception to be enjoyed at leisure. However, our wonderful pastry chef, Sukey, has created an unforgettable cake for you. It's so unique, I wanted it to be showcased in a special way."

Sukey has dragged Autumn near the kitchen door.

Autumn feels claws dig into her shoulder. "Ouch!"

"Sorry," says Sukey. "I didn't mean to do that. I'm so nervous."

Ronnie and Vicky wheel out the groom's cake on a cart. All the guests are on their feet, oohing and aahing over the depiction of a coral reef with all its accompanying starfish, shells, seahorses, clams, small fish, and sea turtles.

Greyson looks stunned. "Wow!" he says. "Abigail, what a gorgeous cake." He searches the guests until his gaze lands on Sukey. "Sukey, this is fantastic!"

Agreement in the form of applause thunders through the room.

"But Greyson, wait until you see what it does," says Abigail looking as though she can barely contain herself.

Vicky whispers in Abigail's ear, then she and Ronnie go to stand near Sukey who is chewing on her claws.

"Don't worry, Sukey," says Vicky. "Ronnie and I noticed that you didn't add the baking soda and lemon juice, so we did."

"What?" Sukey screeches.

"Didn't you want it to explode?" asks Ronnie.

"No! It just erupts enough to get the shrimp and cocktail sauce to ooze out of it and slide down the sides.

"Your small amount of dry ice won't do the trick. Shrimp and cocktail sauce are too heavy," says Vicky. "Trust me. This is better. I made an exploding cake for my niece's birthday last year. The kids thought it was hilarious."

"Abigail and Greyson aren't kids. This is not what Abigail wanted." Grabbing Autumn's paw she says, "We have to stop them."

They reach the newlywed couple and the cake just as Abigail says, "Okay, Greyson, remove the lid from the center of the cake."

"Wait!" yells Sukey.

Too late. Greyson has pulled off the plastic lid. Shrimp, cocktail sauce, and hunks of cake and frosting shoot into the air, spraying the entire function room.

Autumn looks upwards, watching the shrimp zoom in all directions. The entire Flying Feathers Dance Troupe stands, heads tilted upwards, bills open catching all the shrimp falling in their direction.

"Wow! Totally acorns!" yells Winthrop.

Pandemonium breaks out. Some furs and feathers take cover under the tables. Others try to catch the flying shrimp. The squirrels and mousekins squeal with delight as they slip and slide through the cocktail sauce.

Abigail stares dumbfounded at what's left of the cake that is now obscured and slowly deflating beneath a pile of lightly bubbling sauce.

"That wasn't supposed to happen," says Sukey. Her voice pitches higher. Her words speed up until they blur into each other. "There was too much dry ice in the dummy cake I used to test it. It exploded but not like this I made another one and used less dry ice that's what I thought was being wheeled out here I wasn't even sure it would erupt at all that's what I wanted to tell you in the kitchen but there was a mix up and lemon juice and baking soda got added, but I promise it wasn't on purpose just a misunderstanding, and..."

Sukey stops, inhales sharply as she takes in Abigail's cocktail sauce-covered wedding gown and a lone shrimp perched on her shoulder. She bursts into tears. "I'm so sorry."

Autumn enfolds Sukey in her arms. Vicky and Ronnie hurry over. They begin explaining how and why the lemon juice and baking soda got added to the cake.

Autumn glances at Greyson who is eating shrimp with one paw and using another to shove more into his pockets.

Several shrimp, stuck to the ceiling in the explosion, fall all around them, landing with light plops on the table and floor. One lands on Greyson's head. He gives Abigail a huge grin. "I've just married the cat of my dreams and now it's raining shrimp. This is the best day of my life!"

Chapter 28
What's Next?

"Abigail! Greyson! I'm glad I caught you."

Breathless, Miguel Gato arrives at the gate just as they are about to board the plane. A butterfly flits around in Smokey's heart. She danced three times with Miguel at the reception last night. *Stop, it! You're being ridiculous*, she admonishes herself.

"Miguel, what are you doing here?" asks Abigail.

"I meant to tell you last night but forgot in all the excitement with the shrimp."

"Tell us what?" asks Greyson.

"About a surprise."

"Another?" asks Abigail. "You're full of surprises, Miguel."

"This is part of my wedding gift. When you get to the airport in Tanzania there will be a zebra named Theodore waiting for you. He's a good friend of mine. He's going to take you to the Zanzibar Luxury Resort."

"But we have reservations at the Serengeti," says Greyson.

"I, um...canceled them."

They all stare at him, perplexed.

"I hope you'll forgive my taking such liberties. I got in touch with Theodore and set everything up with him. He's going to have his limo driver take you to the hotel where you will be given the royal suite. It should be dinnertime when you arrive. A feast will be brought. A few other goodies await in your suite. Theodore has arranged transportation for you for anywhere you want to go throughout your stay."

The last call for boarding is announced.

"That is so generous of you," says Greyson.

"The two of you were instrumental in making Oneness Park happen. It could have been a disaster and, since I blundered in purchasing that parcel of land right next to Rodent Way, it would have been on me."

"Nonsense," says Abigail. "It was fortuitous that you bought that parcel. If you hadn't things would never have worked out as splendidly as they did. Besides, many furs and feathers made Oneness Park happen."

"Including you, Miguel" adds Greyson.

Miguel shakes his head. "I am indebted to you all. You saved my whiskers. Now, get on that plane."

Hugs and kisses exchanged all around, Abigail and Greyson gather their carry-ons and board the plane. The others stand before the large plate glass windows.

"What other surprises are in store for Abby and Greyson when they get there?" asks Dusty.

"Nip-paign on ice and chocolates awaiting them in the room to go with their dinner. And a private tour guide, a giraffe named Olive who Theodore says is the best in the business. Olive will help them decide where to go, organize all their excursions, and show them around Tanzania."

Smokey sighs. *What must a life like that be like?* "You are amazing, Miguel," she says.

"I want everything to be perfect for my dear friends."

"And there they go," says Autumn as their plane taxis down the runway and lifts smoothly into the air.

"I can hardly wait until they get back to hear all about their trip," says Smokey.

Once in the parking lot, Miguel says goodbye and heads off in another direction.

"Wow! What Miguel did," says Smokey as the trio of cats walk towards their cars.

"I just hope Abby and Greyson don't mind too much," says Dusty.

"Mind?" asks Smokey. "That's a dream come true."

"Maybe at first. But if they have to go wherever that giraffe says it could get old."

"Olive is in their service. She'll make suggestions, but take them where they want to go," says Smokey.

"You're probably right," says Dusty. "What are you two doing for the rest of the day?"

"I'm going into the office," says Smokey.

"On a Sunday?"

"With Abigail gone for the next three weeks, I'm in charge of Fluffington's. I want to be sure everything is in order for the coming work week."

"You sure are dedicated," says Dusty.

Smokey shrugs. She's excited. Fluffington ArCATechture is all hers for the next three weeks. There isn't much she has to prepare before Monday, but she can't stay away. Besides, she's pretty sure she's going to be overcome by the urge to do zoomies all over the office. She wants it out of her system before she faces the staff. Jasmine has promised to meet her for lunch. Louisa has the entire flamingo dance troupe staying at her apartment, though Smokey can't imagine how they can all fit, so she won't be spending time with Jasmine.

"What's your day look like?" Dusty asks Autumn.

"I don't have to be to the restaurant until this afternoon so I'm going to get started on my online boat safety course. Buster promised to come over and help me."

Smokey notices how Autumn's eyes light up when she mentions Buster's name. She's not so worried anymore. She's decided she likes Buster, and she thinks he and Autumn make a good couple. She'll keep an eye on them, she just can't help it, but she's more at ease now.

"What about you, Dusty?" asks Autumn. "You've got that whole apartment to yourself."

"Are you forgetting the Mouse family? Anyway, I'm going to start searching for an apartment of my own. With all the preparations for the wedding on top of schoolwork, I haven't had much time for that. I'll be checking out available apartments online and making lists of the ones I want to look at. You're still coming with me to see them, aren't you?"

"Of course," says Autumn.

"I'm having lunch with Jasmine," says Smokey. "I'll ask if those two units in Louisa's building are still available."

"Thanks," says Dusty. "Can you believe it, Autumn? When you met me, I wouldn't even leave the apartment. Now I'm looking for one of my own. And I'm going to school, selling my clothing line, and getting my license. Look." She pulls a paper from her purse and gives it to Autumn.

"Dusty! Your learner's permit!" Autumn exclaims. "That's wonderful!"

"Congratulations, Dusty," says Smokey.

It's all because of Autumn," says Dusty. She's the best friend I've ever had."

"You did the real work to overcome your fear."

They reach Smokey's car. Thoughts tumble one after the other in Smokey's mind as she drives. So much has happened in the past few months. Finding out that her littermates are alive and well, becoming partners with Abigail and poised to take over Fluffington's, Greyson and Abigail getting married, Autumn dating, and, if she's really being honest, discovering that she has feelings for Miguel Gato.

"What?" asks Autumn from the passenger seat. "You look dreamy and you're smiling. What are you thinking about?"

Smokey feels a blush rising under her fur.

"I was thinking about how much all of our lives have changed. It's astounding."

"I'll say," says Autumn. "I can hardly wait to find out what will happen next."

The End

About the Author

Eileen O'Finlan lives in Central Massachusetts with her adorable calico Maine Coon cat, Autumn Amelia. She writes historical fiction and fantasy. Visit her website at eileenofinlan.com to learn more and sign up for her free monthly author newsletter containing the award-winning column, The Cat's Corner.